SIN AND SWOON

BOOKS BY TARA BROWN ALSO WRITING AS T. L. BROWN, A. E. WATSON, ERIN LEIGH, AND SOPHIE STARR

Blood and Bone
Blood and Bone

The Devil's Roses
Cursed
Bane
Witch
Hyde
Death
Blackwater
Midnight Coven
Redeemers

The Born Trilogy
Born
Born to Fight
Reborn

Imaginations
Imaginations
Duplicities

The Blood Trail Chronicles
Vengeance
Vanquished

The Light Series
The Light of the World
The Four Horsemen
The End of Days

The Single Lady Spy Series
The End of Me
The End of Games
The End of You—a Novella

The Lonely
The Lonely
Lost Boy

The Seventh Day
My Side
The Long Way Home
First Kiss
Sunder
In the Fading Light
For Love or Money
The Club
Sinderella

Tara Brown

SIN AND SWOON

BOOK 2 IN THE
BLOOD AND BONE SERIES

Text copyright © 2015 Tara Brown
All rights reserved.

Published by Montlake Romance, Seattle
www.apub.com

Amazon, the Amazon logo, and Montlake Romance are trademarks of Amazon.com, Inc., or its affiliates.

ISBN-13: 9781503945456
ISBN-10: 1503945456

Cover design by Kerrie Robertson

Printed in the United States of America

This book is dedicated to the readers who like it better when I take things all the way the wrong way.

Thank you for letting me be me.

1. THE IRON BUTTERFLY

The mist swirls, attempting to blind me, but I don't dare back down. I push through, sucking in air so heavy I can barely inhale all the way. Something in my back stings—my lungs maybe, from the thick, heady air of the sea. But that doesn't seem like the answer. It doesn't feel like sea air at all. It's something else altogether.

And as if the air isn't bad enough, the dense forest looks like a trap set just for me. My bare feet push for it, running toward the chaos of fallen trees, rocks, and holes. Branches stab, but I don't feel them the way I should. Even my feet ignore the pain. My mind reels at that, and my fingers reach for the branches as I enter the silent woods.

My panicked breath and heaving chest are like percussion instruments in my ears, where blood is racing through at a rapid rate. The crunching of the sticks and branches seems to scream my trail. Even the rocks and dirt try to betray me by announcing where I'm running.

Light filters in through the green canopy as I slide over logs and branches to get deeper into the woods.

"Ashley! I know you think you can get away, but it's a hundred miles in every direction! Princess, we can talk about this!"

I duck, hearing the shouted words, hiding behind a log and

some ferns. I know my dark hair and filthy skin have to be shielding me from his eyes, but the shaking in my aching body and groggy mind seems to be making the woods move in an unnatural way. The trees vibrate with me, and the leaves crinkle and crunch even though nothing is moving, nothing but my beating heart.

"Ash, Princess, I'm not mad, I swear! Just come out and let me tend to your wounds! Come on, Princess, come back!"

His voice grates on my skin. It doesn't matter if he whispers or shouts, the sound is the same. It nauseates me and haunts my mind. My memories are all groggy, as if they're leftovers from a drug-laden haze. But his whispering breath on my rocking body is as clear in my mind as it is there in the woods. He fills me up, holding me down, and as much as I beg my brain to turn off, it catalogues every moment. I don't know to what end.

I hold my breath as he enters the woods. "You're bleeding! Let me make it better! The animals will track you!"

I tremble but I don't move. I don't dare run for it. I wait. He can't see me, and I might have run in any direction for all he knows.

His breath and heavy steps fill the forest with echoing noises. It's then I see the clouds rolling in behind us, over the mountain peaks. I realize the air is colder than I thought it was, and I am not on the coast at all. When I take a breath I realize the air isn't heavy. I'm high in the mountains. The air is thin, and the ache in my chest and lungs is from the elevation. I'm not used to it. I'm usually at sea level when I am forced to exert myself.

I hold my breath, straining my lungs and making the pounding in my head worsen, but it isn't worth it to let him find me. I force the image of him pinning me down, whispering his love for me. It stops the pain and pushes it away with intense amounts of fear.

"Ash!" His voice sounds farther away, but I don't lift my head to look. I wait, because there is no way to be sure. My ears are still thick with the thin air and elevation.

A hot shiver breaks out, making me breathe again. The feeling of a fever and possibly a sickness of sorts starts to surface. I don't know how long I've been here. I don't know how long I will last here in the woods, bleeding and cold. I do know I will die here, surrounded by trees and freezing, before I will let him find me.

His footsteps crunch, leading away from me, but his bellow is still audible: "When I find you, you'll be punished for every day you hide! Make no mistake, Princess, I'll find you!"

The name *Princess* makes me want to vomit. Not violently and noisily, but the retching is difficult at this elevation, regardless of not getting sick or making a sound. It makes me dizzier.

I sit, wondering if he's messing with me, waiting for me to make the mistake of standing. But I'm not that dumb. Not to mention, my legs are not that strong. They've sort of failed me, in either paralyzing fear or crippling weakness. When I needed them to run they worked, but now they're heavy like they're soaked in concrete or caked in mud.

My brain whispers something about adrenaline and lactic acid, but I don't care for the medical knowledge I have locked away from the three months of nursing courses I've taken.

I care about getting off this hill and finding help.

When I don't hear him again I start to breathe normally. I don't move until I hear the Jeep. He skids away, driving like a maniac. The maniac I didn't know he was, in the beginning. Now I am painfully aware.

The adrenaline hits again.

I force myself to stand, emerging from the forest in a ragged run toward the barn. I turn as I leave the woods, pushing my feet and legs as I make my way to the road. The drive up here to the cabin revealed several other cabins along the way. If I can get to one before he finds me, I might make it.

I run into the ditch, splashing the frigid water up my legs as I make my way to the closest driveway. I'm out of breath and light-headed,

3

but clear-minded enough to realize the closest cabin is a mistake. He'll go there once he realizes I haven't made it to the bottom of the hill.

I run past the second driveway, scrambling from the ditch and crossing it carefully. When I get to the third driveway I almost run up it, but my twin brother's voice rings through my head. *Three times lucky.* I don't know why; perhaps because I'm dehydrated and exhausted and my mental state is a mess.

The fourth driveway is a ways down the hill. The corners frighten me. I struggle to get past the ditches and rocks. My feet have stopped hurting, with the cold water making them numb.

Breathlessly and staggering with a limp from my muscles freezing up, I turn and back up the driveway, forcing myself to watch the road and woods, in case he's there somehow. He's smarter than I am. He's a fucking professor, for God's sake.

My legs buckle, dropping me like a sack of rocks to the gravel. I wince, feeling the jarring in my neck, but I grip the cold rocks and scramble back up.

A shrill noise rips through the air. I think it's an animal dying, but I don't know what kind it is. It sounds terrifying and close by. I hurry, limping brutally because the lower part of my left leg has gone totally numb.

The cabin is nicer than his, but has no barn for the ATVs and snowmobiles. I hurry to the back, trying every window and door until I run out. None are left open or unlocked. Defeated and exhausted, I slide down the back of the door, desperate to rest a minute and listen for him.

Every sound becomes louder as my breath softens in hesitation. I expect him to run from the woods any moment, leash and collar in hand. I expect him to make me beg and make me tell him I love him and he's the man for me. I expect to die, crying and begging for it—not his love but death itself.

My eyes long to close, my body whispers *Let's give up* as my heart aches from the memories that are filtering back in. Memories I will never be rid of or solve. I won't ever know what it all meant to him, what I am to him. What I am representing or curing. What void I am filling.

A sound catches my cold ears. I glance up into the darkening sky as snowflakes begin to fall. A tear drips from my eye as I realize it's the first snow of the season.

The sound gets louder as a vehicle makes its way up the hill.

For a moment, I ignore the sound of the tires skidding around the gravel corners, and stare up into the sky. The flakes swirl, taking my care and depth perception away. I tilt my head even more, letting the fat flakes fall in my mouth and land on my lashes.

I don't close my eyes. I don't try to block out the sound again as it gets closer. I stare up into the snow and force a memory, one of a time when I was happy. It was a moment, fleeting and precious. Her face makes me happy. She brings me joy as she becomes all I see in the swirling snow.

I close my eyes, waiting for the separation of Ashley's mind from mine, or rather mine from hers. The forced abandonment of her leaves me feeling hollow and detached from the real world I live in. I feel even more so from the dream world inside of Ashley's mind, as the forest becomes a room in a lovely house with floral and pastels and a French flair for decorating.

In the distance I can see Ashley still standing, waiting to tell me the rest of the story, shivering and cold. She looks confused and lost in the forest, as I become me, escaping the horrors that lie within her tale.

I blink three times as the wallpaper and pastels eat up the forest and all that exists around me is the country home in France. I lean forward in the armchair, taking a deep breath before lifting the lid of a jewelry box with four-leaf clovers on it, and peek inside, whispering, "Tell me about the swans, the way the swans circle the stars and shoot across the sky." They are the words that send me all the way home. The key to escaping the dream world.

I sit back, letting the ceiling melt away and revealing the sky. Clouds move rapidly, fast-forwarding the time as I get lost in the stars and the blackness of the sky. Everything twirls in a circle, like a girl in a tutu spinning and dancing. My eyes lose focus, as a sickening wave of heat washes over me.

I am not her; she is not me. I am Jane. I am free of Ashley.

A slow and yet noisy breath leaves my parted lips as the coolness of the mountain vanishes and the warmth of the room I am in surrounds me. Still I shake and shiver because my body is in shock from detaching from the mind of the girl lying next to me. The girl who is sleeping as I roam about in her brain.

When I open my eyes, my mouth is still shivering from the cold of the mountaintop. I glance at Angie's expectant face. "What in the bloody hell was the point of that? Ya just got in there, Jane."

After a few moments my body starts to feel like it's mine again, and I can use my mouth. "I need to know what the map looks like, Angie. Don't be a pain in the ass," I snap, and continue to take deep breaths. "I went in blind. We have nothing on this girl. All I knew going in was that she was missing and found on a riverbank. Now I know our guy might be a professor and he owns a Jeep and a family cabin."

My heart rate lowers enough that I'm not just sweating for no reason, and I sigh. "She escaped, ran for her life. Hid behind a cabin until she thought it was safe. Then she ran through the woods to the lower cabins and found an old truck. She stole it and drove as far as she could before she crashed. His face is a blur in her mind. She never let me see it. He somehow brought her back to the cabin. I didn't see much, but I know what I have to do." I cough a little, certain I've crashed in the truck with her. "Don't tell Dash I needed to go in twice, promise?"

She rolls her eyes. "Lucky number nine then, eh?"

I lift my thumb and close my eyes again.

2. THE LENGTHS I WOULD GO AND THE DISTANCE HE WOULD WALK

Angie takes a deep breath over me and counts backward, sending me back in.

5

4

3

2

1

She becomes me and I become her in swirling motion, similar to water falling into a drain. It goes in a circle until you're so dizzy you can't tell up from down.

"Who's a pretty girl? Where do you live?" I pet the ginger tabby, glancing around the small room. The odd little room is still hard for me to wrap my head around. I keep waiting for my bedroom back home to appear before my eyes.

The kitty rubs her face and whiskers on me, purring and mesmerizing me. Her eyes move to the mirror behind me. I glance over my shoulder, following her gaze. When our eyes meet in the mirror, my deep-brown stare narrows. She hisses and scratches my hand, turning and running from the dorm.

In the mirror the trickle of crimson blood seems brighter somehow than any single thing I can see. Everything fades as the blood catches my eyes, making my heart beat a little harder, a little faster. I could swear for a second I saw blue eyes, and one was dark and one was light.

"Ash?"

I lift my gaze in the mirror, smiling, half at myself and half at the girl looking perplexed. Her name is Michelle, and she's my new roommate. She's the angst-ridden, annoying type of girl I always avoid. They love drama and complaining and making everything a fucking mission. She is exactly the sort of girl who has a Facebook page to save the world, whereas the rest of us want to see puppies and recipes and selfies.

"Hey."

She scowls. "What's with the cut? You need a bandage?" She sounds moodier than normal.

"No." Slowly and purposely I lift the hand to my lips, closing my mouth around the wound. The cat that has run away reminds me that mine is still missing. My mom called yesterday to let me know Binx ran off when I left home. "You haven't seen my cat, have you?" I nod at the photo of the black-and-white fluff ball in the frame on my desk.

She cocks a thin eyebrow, maybe too thin for her round face. "Dude, I already told you he couldn't come here. You can't have cats in the dorm. People have allergies and shit."

Did she not just see the orange cat?

The conversation floats around in my foggy head. "Right, but I think he tried to follow me when I left. He isn't at home. My mom called and said he ran away the day I left."

She winces. "Cats are assholes; he probably hasn't even noticed you're gone. He probably left because he was finally free of the hugs and kisses. They're selfish. They can't even help themselves. You need to get a dog. Did you know that a dog would starve for days next to your dead body if it were trapped in the house with you when you die? Cats will start eating you before you're even fully dead."

Sadness creeps in, and I start wondering if she's right. Did he run away, or did he escape? I shake my head, pushing the idea away. "Binx loves me. He's had plenty of opportunities to kill me and he hasn't."

She nods, widening her eyes like she's already tired of me, even though it's only been a week as roomies. She mutters something under her breath, something about bullshit. A strange anger fills me up.

I get up, still sucking my wound, and grab my cell. When I lift it to text, I catch a glimpse of my face—my eyes. They're cold, so very cold. I never noticed it before this moment, but they actually look broken. Dark eyes surrounded by thick black lashes, and worry. So much worry you'd have thought I smeared it on in the morning like black eyeliner on a metal rocker.

The image on the screen of the phone makes me stop to reflect on the idea of what I am truly about to do.

But his little face with his whiskers and unconditional love fills my mind. He loved me, absolutely loves me. He wouldn't eat my dying body. I know that, and I hate her for saying it.

The question is, do I hate her enough to do the thing I am thinking of doing?

A meow fills the air behind me. I glance back to see the ginger tabby. She rubs against the door frame, sliding upon the wood and purring. She's a temptress; she isn't like Binxy. She meows again and turns, running out the door.

I lower the phone and follow her down the long corridor with the blinking lights, old fluorescents that could cause a seizure for an epileptic. She runs down the stairs, rubbing against the door.

I scowl. "You'll die out there. Wild animals or cars or other terrible things."

She purrs, rubbing the door persistently. So I follow, assuming she must know what she's doing. When I open the door she bolts, pausing when she's halfway across the grass in the commons. Something else moves out there with her.

I walk into the dimly lit field, a little scared of the commons at night. But when I see what she's rubbing against now, I break into a run.

His little black-and-white face is a miracle. He followed me, like I knew he would. I drop to my knees when I get close enough, squishing into the damp grass. I put a hand out for him to smell. He tiptoes along, not even making a sound as he walks. His whiskers have fog on them, mist from the thick ocean air that's making the lights glow.

He creeps closer—close enough for me to pick up when his cold nose touches my fingertip. I nestle my face into his thick, damp fur and take a lungful of the smell that is entirely him. He smells like the woods and the dirt and love.

He immediately purrs, a reward I have rarely received. When I look down, the orange cat is gone. She's run off into the woods, or just vanished like a messenger or a guardian angel might.

I wrap him in my arms, noting he's thinner. The week's journey to get to this place has been a hungry one. I don't know how he found me, but gripping him makes everything better.

As I climb the stairs to my dorm, one of the girls I met the day before—Angie, an exchange student from the UK, Scotland specifically—smiles wide. "By the gods, that's a cute cat. Look at that fur!" She reaches for him without asking my permission. Or Binx's, rather. But he doesn't care. He leans in, letting her love him up. His purring stops, because that's just the sort of cat he is, but his eyes close because he knows he's safe.

"What's the wee highness's name?" Her thick accent makes me smile.

"Binx."

"Like Thackery Binx?"

I nod, completely baffled at her knowing *Hocus Pocus* well enough to know the cat from the movie. "Yes. Exactly."

"One of the very best American movies ya Yanks have ever been able to pull off. Yer theater is lacking, largely, but that movie is a classic." Her grin widens; she seems like an old soul. Too old for college, but I can tell that is just the look in her eyes. She knows too much of the world to be a wide-eyed college girl. Somehow she is older and wiser than the rest of us and yet fits in with me; maybe it's just me, though. "The way yer people go about hiring an actress for her tits and ass is offensive to the real artists of the world. Ya will note that we in Europe hire an actor for skills. Yeah, they all have raggedy teeth and crazy hair, but at least they can get around a stage."

I snort, and it shocks me. I don't remember the last time I snorted.

Her gray-blue eyes and dark-red hair are an amazing combination. I haven't ever noticed a redhead with blue eyes like hers, except Mrs. Ridge at the post office, but her red hair is the bottle variety.

"Ya taking him back to your room then? He'll live here with ya?"

I nod carefully, watching her gaze. She could be a professor, her eyes are so old compared to the other kids in the hall I've passed by.

"Interesting. Well, if ya need someone to watch him let me know." She winks and turns, leaving with a wave. I clutch to my cat and scurry to my room. I lay him on my bed and stroke his back. He accepts a minute of love before turning and starting his exploration of our new space.

I catch a glimpse of my face in the mirror. The image flickers, maybe from the light or maybe my vision. The reflection is there until I blink, seeing the face of a girl with dark hair and different-colored eyes. It flashes for only a second. She's screaming and scared and then gone.

I open my eyes, suddenly shaking and cold.

The door opens to the hallway and Michelle walks in, instantly stopping when she sees the cat. "Seriously? Another one?"

I am still cold from seeing the weird image that doesn't feel like a memory, but I can't explain where else it might have come from.

"I said you can't have him in here. It's my room too, Ash. This is shit."

I open my mouth, but Angie is instantly behind her. "If ya want, we can change roommates. Mine hates the bagpipes, and she can't stand the way I sing The Stones. If you can live with that, then we can share and they can share."

She's like a guardian angel popping up, like the other cat bringing me to Binx. It's all so perfect; I have to wonder if I'm dreaming. I nod. "I don't care about singing."

"Wow, a match made in heaven." Michelle rolls her eyes and storms off, shoving Angie with her shoulder as she leaves.

"She's pleasant. Reminds me of a slag from my hometown. Another gem of a lass." Angie's eyes go to the photo on my bedside table. "Mother of God in heaven, who is that sexy beast?"

I scowl, looking back to make sure we both are seeing the photo of my brother Simon. I wrinkle my nose. "That's my twin brother."

"Does he go here too?"

I shake my head. "Portland State."

"That's not too far. What—an hour and a half drive?" She folds her arms across her ample chest. "He should come visit."

"It's three hours." The chill crosses over my spine again as I shake my head. "And he's pretty busy."

She shrugs, clearly not discouraged. I want her to be. I want to discourage her and convince her he isn't the right type of guy for her. He's a player, I think.

He's always been the one who gets in trouble and lies, dates more than one woman at a time, and uses his status as a sports star to get what he wants.

"Well, let's pack you up so Leona can move in here and you can move in with me."

I scowl again. "Did you ask your roommate already?"

She nods. "I saw yer roommate bitching about ya down the other hallway. She called ya a crazy cat lady and said she was telling if ya brought the dirty cat to the room." Her eyes turn to Binx in his new nest made of my pillow. "I knew he would be out before ya could even enjoy a good snuggle. Did yer parents bring him for ya?"

I shake my head. "He found his own way here from home."

"He's a special cat." She walks to him, picking him up with my pillow. "How far is it from home?"

"Half an hour drive."

She gives me a look. "Surely he didn't walk that far to come find ya."

I shrug. "He must have. He's here."

"He must have been in the car, hiding in yer bags." She winks, but I don't think it's funny that he's here. I'm still panicking that he was out there alone and scared and looking for me. I can't think about the things that might have happened.

She chuckles and starts packing my side of the room in the totes I had used to bring all this stuff in here.

It takes us all evening to trade rooms. Angie natters and sings and never really stops talking or moving. I feel like I should join in on the conversation, but I don't. I don't know why. I guess I don't feel much like talking.

She places the picture of my brother on her side of the room and stares at him longingly. "That is a mighty fine bloke. I think for saving your adorable cat, I should be rewarded with meeting him."

I roll my eyes and grab my phone. I send him a text.

Come visit me.

He texts back right away.

Can't. Have practice all week. How's Saturday?

Good. Come then.

Done, but if this is some bullshit about your cat, I'm not helping look for him. I told Mom to let you take him.

I add a tongue-sticking-out emoji.

He's here already. Found his own way to me.

See you Saturday, crazy cat lady. <3

It makes me smile to be called that. I already know it's true. I'll be a crazy cat lady to the death. It will likely be the reason I don't marry, but I don't care. "He says he'll come Saturday."

She grins wide. "Excellent. Now I need to lose five pounds before then so I can steal that gray dress of yours. The Victoria's Secret one." She jumps up and walks to my open closet, holding the slinky dress against her body. Her breasts are much larger than mine so the dress looks like it might not cover everything. But then again, that might be her desire. If I had her boobs I would rock them, and the gray dress is a prime example of how I would go about it.

The thought makes me uncomfortable, but I push it away. The weird, self-conscious quiet girl I have become here is driving me insane. I had more confidence than this in my pinky before I left home, and it's not like I grew up in the sticks. "Be right back. Can you make sure he's okay?" I point at the cat.

She rolls her eyes. "He's fine. He'll adjust to the new room." She waves at me, so I leave and saunter down to the bathroom. I wash my face and look into the mirror at my dark eyes, thick lashes, and perfect chestnut hair. I cock a delicately manicured eyebrow and scowl. *Have I always looked like Barbie's best friend?*

I shake my head and sigh, forcing a silent vow to be more like myself and stop worrying about everything. I dry my face on my shirt and stroll back to the room, earning a weird glance from a girl I pass who notices the water stain on my shirt.

When I get in the room Angie is twirling with my clothes. "Can

I borrow this purple scarf with the gray dress?" She wraps it around her throat, making my skin crawl. I nod, ignoring the terrible feeling inside of me, and honor my vow of being the cool chick I once was, a whole week ago.

"I have heels that match the purple scarf." The words are choked out. I climb on my bed and lie back, realizing it's more comfortable than the mattress I had in the other room with the ever-crabby Michelle. I would feel sorry for Leona but she doesn't sound much better than Michelle.

Who doesn't like bagpipes?

"Want to go get pissed?" It takes a second to realize she means get drunk.

I grin. "I do." It is just the thing I need to relax and get used to the new life here on campus. Simon and I used to have epic parties when our parents would take their adult vacations.

"There's a bar in town that serves minors. Ya just have to be a pretty lass and the dirty old bouncer will let you in. Once you're in, they don't ID."

I grin wider, reaching into my Coach wristlet. "I have fake ID."

Her jaw drops. "I knew ya would be the better roomie." She reaches into her own purse and lifts out an ID as well. "I still want to dress slutty, though." She grabs a red dress from her closet. "Yer what—a four?" She tosses me the super-cute red strapless dress with a white lace waistband. "Ya can keep this; it doesn't fit me anymore. I'm an eight, and there's no going back. Every time I lose too much weight I lose my boobs. It's not a sacrifice I'm willing to make. And no one wants to see the weight-loss rock-in-a-sock boobs. I'm too young for that shite."

To my surprise I snort again. "What is this, a prom dress?"

"Prom must be sad where yer are from. That is not fancy enough, not even close. Were ya raised on a farm?" Her eyes glisten.

I open my mouth, not seeing a farm but a nun. It's the strangest flash, and I swear it's a memory, but that's not possible. I narrow my gaze.

"Gods, how horrid it must be if ya have a mug like that one on ya when asked about home. Tell me, was it terrible?" She leans forward, her eyes widening.

I swallow and fight the shudder ripping through me. "No. It was bliss." The words feel like a lie. "Small town, great parents, suburb life. Very perfect. Close to the city." There really is nothing else.

"Dull. I sort of hoped you'd be a serial killer or something fascinating. That cat makes you more interesting than you are, by far." She loses all her excitement with a sigh. She's joking, but it hurts my pride just a little. She gives me a smug grin. "But I can tell, ya haven't been out here—have ya? Partied here in Seattle?"

I shake my head. "We never made it. We had plans, but the party at home was always better. My parents went to the city all the time to have their version of an escape."

"It's a goddamned fashion show. Now pull that on." She strips her T-shirt off, revealing her perfect breasts and tight body. I could actually hate her, but the dress in my hands is too pretty to focus on her stunningly curvy body in envy.

We dress quickly, as if we are actually going to a fashion show. Heels too high and dresses too short. I don't think I'll be able to outrun anyone, but I have a feeling it won't matter.

I dab a final coat of gloss over my lips and take one last look. My teased-up hair is sexy with wide dark curls and a ton of shine.

Angie has on a sexy black cocktail dress that flares at the hips, showing her long, lightly freckled legs—tanned and slightly freckled like her face. Her ruddy skin glows in a way only a redhead's can.

"Ready?"

I feel way too dressed up but I nod. When we leave the dorm room, I blow a kiss at Binx as I watch Angie lock the door.

When we get outside, we receive several looks crossing campus from the girls in sweats and tank tops. The warmth of summer is still upon us. It's a warm autumn here, but not too hot. At the curb, Angie hails a cab, taking us into the city.

I don't know this city as well as I should, having grown up nearby. The Northwest University School of Nursing was my reason for moving here from Tanner, which is a suburb of the city. Simon went to Portland State University with some friends. He wanted to be away from Seattle. I don't understand why.

When we get to the bar, the cab parks, and I take a deep breath. The line is loaded with girls in dresses and men in suits. Everyone is overdressed the way we are. I lean into the window of the cab, watching the lights in the line flicker off the smiling faces, flashing on all of their beautiful faces.

Why can't I get excited? Binx found me, even if it still feels like a dream. I got rid of my evil roommate and landed the best one at school, hands down. My day has been fabulous.

I push away the worrywart within, hating the way school is making me crazy and the exams haven't even started yet. I give Angie a look as she climbs out, grinning like she's got a secret. She reminds me of a friend back home; I just can't place which one.

"You ready to get this night off to a good start?"

I grin back. "That's a pretty big line."

She winks. "I have it covered."

I climb out, following her to the front of the line. Every girl in line is as pretty as we are, if not more so. They are dolled up, and their dresses look more expensive than ours. I wrinkle my nose, wondering if she's going to flash cash and get turned away. By the looks of every person lined up, they would have already tried that trick.

But as she approaches the tall man built like he might also be a wrestler or a hit man or a small building, his wide lips lift, and he nods as he pulls the crimson rope aside for her. She nods back at me. His eyes don't even flicker on me, but he stares at her in the strangest way. It is almost as if he doesn't see me.

The music starts to light up my body, flooding my head and heart with the beat. I swallow and swear even my throat moves to the sound of the loud drum and bass. It sounds like a rave as we enter, since the DJ is live, but the crowd isn't high, not on drugs anyway. Everyone is dancing in a wave; even the people lingering and waiting for drinks at the bar move in sync with the others.

The lights flash, complementing the beats and the glittering crowds.

One small part of me relishes the sight of the writhing sea of glittery people. But only a small part. The other part just wants a drink. But we don't have just one, and we don't have the thing I want. Being a red-wine girl, I never expected Angie to be a shot-drinking girl.

After several, she pushes the final shot at me, as I nod and choke on the previous one. She knocks her glass against mine, spilling Fireball on my fingertips. I toss it back, placing the glass down and shaking my head back and forth. "No more."

She grabs my slippery hand and drags me out onto the dance floor.

The song twists in my mind and my body, and everything feels right. In the midst of shaking with my hands in the air and a permanent grin on my face, I forget to be scared or confused. I have fun, like an idiotic college girl should.

3. TALL, DARK, AND HANDSOME

We stagger from the bar, gripping each other.

"Top night, Jane."

I laugh, shaking my head. "My name is Ash, crazy girl, who's Jane?"

She slaps her hand against her head. "Och, I'm drunk. You remind me of a friend I had, back home. Her name was Jane."

I giggle, then cringe as a sour burp fills my mouth. I realize the shots are not staying for the whole night. I stumble to the alley next to the bar, dragging Angie with me. "I think I'm going to be siii—"

"Jesus!" She jumps back just as I decorate the brick wall. I'm trembling and heaving but I can't stop throwing up, and I assume it's bad from the commentary and laughing of the people passing by us.

"Are you all right?" a man asks in the mix of my being sick and Angie shrieking. She says something, but I'm heaving so hard I can't form the words to explain that I'm fine. The alley starts to darken as my eyes narrow. Everything goes to tunnel vision in the form of a pinhole as I grip the building, my fingers scraping down the bricks trying to steady myself.

Warmth surrounds me as the deep voice gets closer. "Are you all riiiii—?" His voice blends into the other noises as darkness envelops me completely. I am there, lost in my own blank space and then I am unconscious.

I wake with a gasp. Pain hits first, not warmth or the sound of my mother, or the feel of Binx getting pissed because I moved. No, it's pain, and there's plenty of it. A truckload. It starts at the back of my head. I twitch from it as I attempt opening one eye. The pain immediately shifts from the back of my head to my eye. I wince from the burning and pressure.

There is no light blinding me like I expect, like there was the one time I got drunk with my brother to care for me when I passed out. I woke naked and wet, apparently having taken my clothes off, and spilling the water Simon had brought me.

That was not even close to this level of hell.

I wince and open the other eye, letting the consequences hit me with a baseball bat of pain. A sound escapes my chapped lips as I glance around the dimly lit space. It isn't my house.

I live at college.

But this isn't my room. I don't know where I am. It takes a second to remember we went out. The room is small, not a bedroom and not a sitting room. I'm on a couch in what looks like an office or den. I wipe my pasted hair from my forehead and make an attempt at standing.

At first I think it's me just sweating, detoxing from the shots, but then I realize it's the heat from the vent in the ceiling above me. I'm in a stranger's house, and they have the heat cranked during the worst dehydration I have ever faced.

On shaking legs and a tense stomach, I push myself up, trying to piece together the last details, but they're the hazy ones. I recall the bar, the shots, the dancing, but the rest is gone.

Voices come from the cracked door opposite the windows.

Angie?

Where's Angie? Is that her?

The voice sounds deeper. I stagger to the frame, peeking through the cracked door, hoping to catch the talking again, but it's a laugh I hear. I think it's Angie's so I step out into the hallway where there's light and a smell—bacon. It calls to me, dragging me down the hallway on my stiff limbs.

I round the corner of the hall, feeling instantly better when I hear her laugh again, certain it is Angie. Her flash of red hair brings an attempt at a smile to my lips. "Angie?"

She spins, wincing when she sees me. "Ash, darling, you look hideous." She looks back at the guy standing next to the stove. His dark-blond hair reminds me of someone, but I'm not sure of whom until he turns. Then it all comes back. He's the guy from the alley. He smiles, shaking his head. "You poor thing. Here!" He hands me a glass of orange juice as he stirs it.

I give Angie a look but she nods, so I take the glass and lift the glass my nose and fight the urge to be sick. From the feeling in my mouth I have to assume I have already been sick, several times.

Not smelling or even thinking, I lift it to my lips and drink as much as I can of the sweet juice. It stings a little on the way down, but eventually the gulping becomes less forced and more desperate. I lower the glass, gasping a little, and pass it back. "Thank you."

"Derek."

Angie waggles her brows. "Professor Derek, actually."

My eyes widen, but he chuckles like she's lying, or it's just a title and he's not really one of my professors about to have me kicked out of school for—for—for things I don't remember.

"It's just Derek." His green eyes and tanned skin are a perfect contrast to his dark-blond hair and wide smile. His lips are a little crooked, lopsided. When he smiles I see he has vampiric fang with just one of his canines. The oversized look of it makes his lip stick out a bit there. Something that encourages me to stare and day-dream about sucking his lip or dragging it slowly in my teeth.

I cringe, looking away. He's got something about him that makes my insides twinge in a good way, but just a little. I'm too hungover to feel anything else.

Angie giggles, giving me a look that would suggest she might have read every inappropriate thought I'd just had. My cheeks blush as his eyes lower, but I can tell he saw. The way the corners of his lips play with a grin that he won't let himself commit to makes the blush darken. I can feel it spreading across my face, and I don't even know why. Beyond being caught thinking lewd thoughts, I've committed no crime.

Angie gives him a wry grin. "You owe your night to Professor Derek. He saved us in the alley." Her eyes find their way back to me. She winks and excuses herself. "Be back in a moment." She exits the room, leaving me leaning on the counter, praying I don't fall over from exhaustion and dehydration. Not that I would mind being carried by him, though I suspect I have been already.

It's his turn to blush. "You don't owe me. I didn't save you. I just didn't want you to be alone. Angela was also incredibly drunk, and it was either the hospital or here."

I flinch.

"You weren't that bad, just sick." His hands lift with his eyes, defending me, but I can see the exhaustion all over his face. He's stayed up watching me, worried I would die on his spare-room bed. The thought of him in the room doesn't even bother me; the fact he's a teacher does, though. I almost heave again, hating myself, and Angie just a little. "I swear, you were just throwing up so much, I didn't want you to choke and die. It's no bother. We've all been there."

He doth protest too much.

"Thank you."

He shakes his head, really only making me feel worse because I know it was so bad he's making it seem like nothing. But I know my truth: I've likely barfed from one end of his house to the other. And more than likely in his car. And instead of being pissed and getting me kicked out of school, he's cooking bacon. If he were ten years younger I'd ask him to marry me. He grins, glancing at the bacon, and gives me a wry look from under his lashes. "A greasy breakfast will fix you. It's a scientific fact based on years of studies."

He makes me smile, even through the sickness in my pounding head. "You have read of these studies, I assume?"

"Yes, I enjoyed being part of the initial case study during my freshman year. We worked hard to prove something greasy cured all that ailed you." He lifts a plate, adds a couple of pieces of bacon, and nods at the oven. "There are pancakes in the warming drawer."

I take the plate, feeling exhausted and dizzy as I spin and bend to get the drawer. I pause, hating the sensation washing over me in heavy waves.

He bends next to me, making a warm jolt replace the nausea. He reaches and opens the oven drawer and grabs two pancakes and my plate. "Just go sit; I can make this for you."

When I turn my head his face is close, too close, and yet just enough to get a waft of his deodorant. He reminds me of a guy I dated, but his name slips my lazy tongue. A shadow crosses his face, changing his look completely, but only for a second. He looks like the guy I dated once, the one who wore the deodorant I can smell.

I nod, lost for the entire second he reminds me of that other guy, but when I back up a bit he looks like himself again.

I shake my head, wondering if I am actually too hungover to survive, and push myself up. My legs shake on the walk to the table, as I plunk down into a seat.

He places the plate in front of me and turns back to the fridge. "You need the whole array, trust me. This science is based upon a careful balance." He brings orange juice, coffee, cream, sugar, a stack of sausages, and a bowl of fruit salad. He winks at the fruit. "Stops the scurvy."

I laugh again.

He places two pills in front of me, next to my orange juice glass. "For your head."

"Thank you." I don't hesitate; I gulp them back, savoring the sweetness of the fresh-squeezed orange juice. "How is it we ended up with you?"

He sits across from me and starts serving himself. "Your friend Angie and I have been friends for a couple of years."

I cock an eyebrow, taking a piece of bacon in my hand and chewing slowly. The flavor of the salty meat takes over everything. My world becomes entirely about the meal. The butter is soft and real, not margarine. The syrup is Canadian maple syrup, the kind you find at a souvenir shop. The bites of bacon and sausage become coated in maple syrup, making the meat that much tastier. All the while he laughs and tells me funny stories about being a freshman.

"Then this one time we thought we were so clever, we went across the Canadian border and bought fake identification. I was from Hawaii, a state no one had really seen an ID from, and my roommate, Glenn, was from Missouri. We tried them the first time at the campus bar in Portland. Of course we were figured out instantly. The bartender was from Missouri, apparently. He spotted the defects before he even held it." He laughs to himself, chuckling like my father does, and shaking his head. "So both IDs ended up on the wall of shame, right behind the bar. They're still there, in fact. I was on campus a couple of years ago, and they were the older of the bunch for sure, but there nonetheless."

We both laugh, and I immediately notice I am feeling human again as Angie comes strolling in. She stretches and yawns. "Sorry about that. I ended up needing to lie back down a little. It was a late night." She gives me a grin. "You look better."

I beam at Derek, unable to fully contain the crush I am developing. "Science saved me."

He laughs, but she gives me the strangest look, totally unaware of my meaning.

"I think we might need to find a ride back to school, Jane."

I scowl. "Ang, you called me Jane last night too. Who is this Jane?"

She struggles with her thoughts. I can see the confusion on her face. "I have a friend from back home who is named Jane, and you are very similar. You remind me of her."

Derek sits back, sipping his coffee. "I like the name Jane. I always think of Austen or Lady Jane."

Angie rolls her eyes. "Before you go thinking too much of him, he teaches literature. He isn't just some nancy who likes chick flicks."

He nearly chokes. "I do like them; every man likes them. We just aren't fond of feeling things in front of you ladies. It makes us look weak. No man wants to look weak." His eyes dart to me. "Not in front of ladies we want to try to date, anyway."

A stupid grin slips across my lips. "We sort of like it when you put up a fight about those movies. The fuss guys make is kind of cute."

His lips lift even more, setting a dazzling glow in his green eyes. "That's because you always win. We always cave."

"That is my favorite part." Angie laughs. She serves herself a plate of food and starts eating, but my eyes are locked on his as if we are telling each other secrets without speaking. She doesn't see it, but I know he does.

I just don't know what it means.

4. WHY DO I HAVE TO BE THE BAD GUY?

Binx's purring and rubbing against me as I fill his food bowl brings a smile to Angie's lips as she climbs into bed after her shower. "Look at all that love and affection. Even Derek didn't rub against you quite that much."

I roll my eyes. "Whatever. He was being polite. He's a prof, not a student."

"No, he wasn't. He likes you. I can tell. And he isn't an instructor at our school, so the whole teacher-student thing isn't applicable."

That perks my ears up. "What?"

She sighs, smearing lip gloss over her lower lip. "Were you not listening when I said that he teaches literature? That's not a class here, dumbass."

I bite my lip, giving way to some unsavory thoughts, but Binx disturbs them with his after-meal grooming. Something feels off, but I ignore it, petting his fur. I glance at Angie, puzzling at the way things feel in my head. It's still fuzzy from the drinking, I think. "How did we end up with him?"

She shrugs. "You started getting sick, and he came and carried you to the car, saying you needed a doctor. I told him you just needed to sleep it off. So he said we should stay with him."

"And you agreed?" The whole thing makes no sense.

She sighs. "I know him—he's a good guy, so of course I did. It was better than going home in a cab with us girls both being drunk."

I close my eyes and snuggle into my surly cat. "Still seems like a risky idea over a cab ride alone." The purring of the cat and the warmth of my bed make the swirling in my brain cease, and I feel a deep sleep on the horizon. My mind wanders like water flowing down a drain, and it's then I realize I am losing her. No, I'm pulling away. I'm leaving on purpose. I'm staring into the wooden box with the clovers, getting lost in the darkness.

I blink three times and the room is no longer my dorm. I whisper to the crumbling walls and cracked ceiling, "Tell me about the swans, the way the swans circle the stars and shoot across the sky." It becomes like a painting as I step back somehow, moving away from the world that Ashley Potter belongs in. It becomes smaller, twirling and swirling in my mind like a top. It gets smaller and smaller as I leave it all behind, leave her behind, trapped in the awful painting that was her life.

When I blink for real in the warm room, I am Jane, and Ashley is next to me.

Angie is there, wearing her white coat, but there now are the beginnings of laugh lines on her face, reminding me she is in her thirties and not at the end of her teens. We are not freshmen, and I am not Ashley Potter. I blink as whatever I ate last crawls around in my throat.

She smiles but there is worry in her eyes. "Ya all right? It's only been fifteen minutes since the last time you woke up."

I swallow the acrid taste in my throat, shaking my head.

"Can ya talk yet, or do ya need a minute?"

Immediately anger wells inside of me, adding to the fire burning in my throat as I rip the headphones from my ears. The soft voice in my mind is not the right one. "Where is he?" I know Dash has somehow meddled with the subliminal messages and hints and pictures I am meant to be seeing in my mind. The whole point of the recording is to bring me to the places she's been, get me comfortable. The series of words spoken, including Dash's name and the description of his face, are meant to help me bring my triggers with me. If we have anything on the patient, it is whispered in my ear with a series of subliminal messages, helping me to find the keys in her mind.

If someone tampers with that, they can change the entire outcome, including the patient's experience.

"Where's Dash?" I ask again in my croaking voice.

She pauses. "What the bloody hell are you on about?"

"Dash!" I shout with my croaking voice.

The door opens, revealing his worried gray-green eyes. "Jane?"

"What did you do?"

He blushes, and I can see the guilt all over his face.

I glance over at the wall of two-way mirrors and manage to speak about the facts I have gleaned thus far. "The bad guy might be a professor, but I suspect he was never her teacher. The man we are looking for could be a teacher at the university in Seattle—start there. Literature maybe. Or associated with the lit department." I turn back, glaring at Dash. "You messed with something. You made a change in my story. Your face flashed, and one second you were Rory and the next you were you. I made up a lie in her mind to cover, but she could close up on me if she gets scared."

He winces—so subtle that I barely catch it. He licks his lips, and I see the guilt everywhere, plastered across him. Even the way he leans against the door frame and nods at Angie, like he's dismissing her, lacks all of his usual confidence. She hurries out, shooting me a look and brushing past him. I struggle with the strength in me coming back after a fifteen-minute slumber that felt like days.

"I didn't—"

"Don't lie." I climb off the bed and stagger to him. "I have a setup. I have a way it goes. I let her lead me, and this made it more like it was me leading her."

He wrinkles his nose. "I didn't think it was a big deal. I hate being the bad guy. You make me the bad guy every time. I hate it. In your mind I have raped and killed and been a full-fledged psychotic. Imagine if I made *you* some kind of evil in my mind?" He offers a soft look. "I don't want your subconscious to see me, your future husband, as a murderer or a pedophile or a serial killer. I don't want to be that in your head." His eyes lower to the floor. "Or your heart."

I wince too, far more annoyed that he knows the secret to my success. It's as if he's seen behind the curtain. He's seen the friggin' wizard. In a tone that expresses the level of my annoyance, I mutter, "You've basically wasted my time. Now I have to go back in and try to convince her that everything is normal in her changing mind. If she panics, she shuts it down. Not to mention, she isn't exactly getting healthier here. She needs to go back to the hospital."

"We have a better medical team here than any hospital. She's fine." He sighs. "Pick someone else to do the dirty work."

"No. How did you even do it?"

He grins. "I didn't."

"How?" I growl.

"Changed the recording." He chuckles like it's nothing, but we both know it's something.

I nod. "I gathered, jackass. When I woke to your voice in my head, I knew instantly the recording was changed and it was your fault, but how did you change my plans and her visions at the same time?"

He clears his throat and glances at the girl on the bed next to mine. "Changed both of your recordings to a different repetition. For you we read the triggers and the hints you knew, describing the scenery and campus and city, just like we always do. But then we added Rory's name in like a subliminal message the way you do with mine. It switches between me reading and Rory reading to confuse you. In the part where you describe him, I described Rory. It works every time to get you into the person's mind and to ensure they open up to you. So I figured, why not subliminal messages to you to pick a different bad guy? I thought about using a random guy you don't even know, but it didn't seem like a good idea to send you in blind. Then you could panic inside of her. But when we started making the new recording, Rory volunteered. It was a subtle change, my description for Rory's. It didn't seem like a big deal."

"Messing with my head isn't the big deal. But you said you messed with her recording, the one that has soft sounds and makes my voice a comfort and lets her relax and let me in? You know better than I do that her recording is the key. Hers lets me in and makes her trust me. She has to hear my voice, hear me speaking and describing myself, so when I get inside of her mind I am a familiar face." I squeeze my eyes shut. "You changed the words to change my plans, but really all you did was show her new faces to pin the crime on. I have to be able to see who she's trying to show me, which is why I use your face. For me it's the constant. Rory is always a brother or a side story. I need her to show me the bad guy. And guess what, genius? She doesn't want to see his face. She doesn't want to let me see. Can't you imagine why?"

"I know, Jane. I taught you all of this. One face isn't a big change. It's a very minor change—just so that the man you would love wouldn't be the man who took Ashley. I wanted it to be that maybe I would be the hero who saved you." A slight smile twitches on his lips.

"You wanted to be the hero?" The words leave my lips in a breathless tone that mocks him, even though his words are sort of sweet.

"I did." He glances down, folding his arms. "I hate that I'm always the bad guy. I've read through the files, the other seven mind runs you did. I am always the bad guy."

I bite my lips, completely scared of what I am about to say. In a moment of clarity and possibly hand-of-God action, I pause and stare at the wall of mirrors before us. "Can we take a quick walk?"

He sighs and makes for the door. I can see he wants to say more, but he doesn't. He saunters through, sulking almost. It's the strangest experience for me, but I honestly fear the things he thinks of me. Not that I haven't spent my entire life wondering and worrying what people think, but with him it's everything. He does normal things like reads the paper while he eats or sorts the contents of our house, which I notice are rapidly growing since he moved in with me. Everything is expanding, creating clutter in our house as we become a couple—a thing—an entity. I try to look busy like he does, wiping counters and sorting papers, but I don't know how to look busy and yet still watch him for his reactions to things. Every move he makes is natural. Where my movements are deliberate. I copy him and others like a sociopath might. Because regardless of always making him the bad guy, I am the one most likely to be a psycho, I am the one who is detached and damaged. He is the epitome of normal.

Following him out into the hall feels natural, as does the annoyance in his meddling in my run through her mind. But the part that feels forced is wanting to talk about why he can't interfere with my mind run.

I don't want to talk about it, but I have to. Even if it will embarrass me.

He folds his arms, cocks an eyebrow, and clenches his jaw. He has no idea how hot I think his annoyed face is. It brings a girlish smile to my lips, making me immediately feel like a schoolgirl. "Why do you always make me be the bad guy? Are you unhappy?"

And there it is. The difference between us. He can just ask, but I can't just answer.

"Do you want me to be a bad guy? Do you want us to fight more?"

I grimace, wishing the words would just fall out. I'm not the simpering mess he makes me. "No." How do I explain without sounding like a sissy?

"What then? Why can't you just use a random guy as the bad guy?" His tone is impatient, which somehow always makes me feel like a child.

"I need to be safe when I'm in there." It's the best I have for an explanation. "The people in their heads are what nightmares are made of, but it is impossible for me to have a nightmare with you as the bad person."

He pauses, stopping himself from saying whatever he was about to. The answer pleases him. I can see the look on his face. "Safe?"

"You are the safe bad guy. If you're him, I'm not scared, not truly. Not in my heart. You could do anything, and I would never be scared. Except maybe leave, I suppose. If you left me I would be scared."

"Leave? Are you crazy?" He melts as every one of his muscles loses its tension. "So you want me to be the bad guy to keep you safe in there?"

I nod, hating that I've shown him this piece of it all, but loving the smile that's spreading across his lips. "So you want us to be the way we are? We don't have to change it up? You aren't bored? You don't want me to be a bad guy?"

"Of course not." I shake my head slowly, unsure of the reaction. *Is he mocking me? Or is he high?* Clearly he hasn't ever thought about what it's like for a girl to meet a guy like him. I could never be bored, except when I take the job with the profiling section, but that won't ever be about him.

He scoops me up, pressing my lips against his. I sigh into the kiss, wishing we could stay here, but knowing I have to have the answer. I need the happy ending. I need to know why and who and where. His tongue lazily slips into my mouth as his hand lowers, gripping my butt cheek. "Tell me."

I have to close my eyes to say it, because it's like wishing when you blow out a candle; if you peek, the wish is broken. "I love you."

Dash smiles, changing the way his lips sit against mine. "I love you more."

I smile back, scared of the thing I'm about to say. "Except I made you the safe guy way before we ever dated. So clearly, I love you more, Benjamin Dash."

He shakes his head. "See you after?"

"Yup." We kiss once more before he puts me down. I turn, waving backward and stalking back into the room where the small girl is slumbering after being brought in with severe hypothermia and more broken bones than anyone would think they had in their body. What a way to spend Thanksgiving weekend, dying in a medical lab while being experimented on.

I climb back onto the table as Angie comes hurrying back in. "I need ya to focus, Jane. This is going to be a quick reinsertion. A third time in the same girl is unheard of." She leans forward, whispering, "And between me and you, we don't think she's going to make it. She's being switched to life support. Her brain activity flashes only when yer in there. She's a vegetable, and I don't know how easy it's going to be to go rooting around in a dying girl."

I give her a look. "You know it feels different this time. Like I know too much going in. So maybe it's that she's brain-dead, and I'm just making up the story."

She turns back to the large mirror where everyone is watching. "Right, and I suppose having a jackarse mess with the recording because his moronic friend pointed out he's always the bad guy doesn't help. Does it?"

"Rory brought that to Dash's attention?" I whisper and shake my head, looking at the glass. I'm sure my face betrays the fact I don't understand what she means, I don't understand why he would do that to me, he's my partner.

She rolls her eyes. "Och, ya dinna think that Dr. Charming found that information all on his own, did ya?" She leans in, whispering so they can't hear us. "I'll whip Rory later for ya. He's really just a meddling old woman in that sexy body of his." She winks and attaches the monitors to my chest and head. "Must be some of that Irish treachery brewing in those veins."

I swallow hard. "Why would he do that? He was the only person who knew everything."

"Welp, I imagine he thinks he was trying to help, doesn't want ya two to break up. Says he's never seen either of ya so happy. Not sure what he would know on the subject, scowling bastard."

A nervous smile crosses my lips as I lie back, wishing he'd keep his greasy paws off my damned records, but at least Dash knows the truth of it. Something Rory and his snooping won't find in my records. I never wrote down why I made my bad guy the way I did. No one knows that Dash makes me feel safe. Well, except for Dash, thank God. The odd bit of vulnerability with him isn't so horrid.

I close my eyes, giving a loud sigh.

5. PROFESSOR CHARMING

The cold air stings a bit on my nose, not frosty but windy and bitter. I close the window to suffer through the smell of hairspray in the dorm. I hate the coastline. I prefer to be inland, where the wind has less of the damp ocean in it. The cold salt water makes the very worst wind I've ever felt.

"You meeting him after class?" Angie asks from her bed, where she's curling her red ringlets.

I sigh, not sure of the answer. "I guess. He's sort of asked me to go away for the weekend."

Her jaw drops. "What?"

I nod. "He's got a cabin or something, a family vacation spot. It's a few hours from here, rugged and romantic, apparently."

"Then what's the problem?" She gives me a dubious look.

"Something I can't shake. He's just *too* awesome. He speaks slowly, with purpose, and enunciates every word. He's handsome in a way that makes me sweat. He's sweet, he cares about everything I say, and remembers every tiny detail." My eyes lower. "It's like he isn't real. He hasn't even tried anything with me. He's always a gentleman. We've been on like ten dates and only kissed."

She scoffs. "Och, this is the honeymoon. All men are on their best behavior for the first year. It goes to shite then. Then it's a quick shag and they got one eye on the football game while they do it."

A laugh and a snort slip from my lips. "It just feels like too much for eighteen, don't you think? He's overwhelming for someone like me."

She winks, dropping a curl and spraying it. "Ya know I do. I love me some intense men with obsessive qualities." She laughs and curls another piece of hair on her wand. I know she's talking about my brother. She likes him a lot, and he seems to think she's charming. He just hasn't heard one of her racist rants about the English or the Irish.

I want to say that I don't like men who are that way, but instead I just make a mental note to break things off this weekend if he doesn't chill out.

At the end of the day, class drags on. The teacher actually sounds like Charlie Brown's teacher. The name Charlie Brown sits funny in my mind. I can't seem to make out his face, but I know it's a cartoon. I just don't know where I've seen it before.

As it ends and I make my way out of the building, I see him. He's leaned against a tree, smiling at me like a cat watching a mouse. He makes me nervous, and regardless of the obvious attraction I have for him, I can't stop feeling uncertain around him.

He waves with nonchalance. I grin, walking over to the tree. He doesn't wait for me. He turns and walks to the car, a gesture I don't appreciate. He says it's because he's a professor at another school and we shouldn't really be dating. We keep it secret, except for Angie. She knows everything. Without her I think I'd go crazy. She and Binx are my sounding boards.

I follow him to his Jeep, climbing in and wishing for a moment he would open the door for me or hold my hand or carry my books.

But he just grins as I struggle to climb in with my books and purse. "Hard day at the office?" he asks with his intense way of speaking. I get lost for a moment in his eyes. The stare whispers to me that I'm foolish to doubt his love for me. He's sweet the moment we are off campus. He just doesn't want anyone to know he's dating a student. It's logical.

I shake my head, placing the books on the thick rubber mats on the floor. "Just did a few theory classes and English."

He doesn't bat an eyelash at the mention of his favorite subject. "You ready for the trip?"

I nod. "My bag is at the dorm, ready to go."

He looks out the window like he's struggling with the sentence. "Why don't you run back to the dorm, get the bag, and meet me down the road a little?" The question makes my stomach ache, but the idea of being on a mountaintop with him, alone and able to be together, makes me nod again. "Okay." I leave my books and climb out. He points. "Take those." The way he says it makes me frown, but he just grins more widely. "You won't be needing them."

I grin back, picking them all up and hoofing over to the dorm.

Angie isn't there when I get back, but I know she'll be watching Binx. I sniff his thick fur, pet his chin a bit, and leave, carrying my heavy bag out into the hallway.

"You going home for the weekend?"

I glance back, seeing Michelle and Leona in the hallway. They have hit it off as well as Angie and I have. "I am."

"Have fun." Michelle rolls her eyes, dragging Leona off down the hall with her. She really is a miserable twat, as Angie would say. Has said.

I offer a weak wave and strut down the stairs and out the door. The cool wind bites at my fingers as I send Angie a quick text to remind her to feed Binxy. She responds with a happy face.

I almost text my brother to tell him where I'm going, but the realization I'm an adult hits me. I don't need to check in with anyone. He wouldn't tell me he was going to shack up with an older lady for a weekend. He would do it, have fun, and maybe text me when he got home to fill me in on the gross parts I prefer not to hear.

The bag cuts into my hand with the weight of my hiking boots and a thick coat. I have to assume a mountain retreat isn't going to be as warm as it is down by the sea, and it's friggin' cold here.

I round the corner, leaving the nursing college completely, and see his vehicle. He jumps out, opening the door like a gentleman. He's like Dr. Jekyll and Mr. Hyde that way. He scoops me up, kissing me after he's tossed my bag like it weighs nothing.

He buries his face in my neck, and I know it's going to be a wonderful trip.

He drives for what feels like forever, just to get out of the city. He offers me hot chocolate, my favorite drink. I sip it slowly, staring out at the people bundled up on the sidewalks. "It's so cold out," I mutter as I close my eyes and let myself drift off.

I don't know how long we drive. I don't know how long I sleep. But I wake as we're making our way up a hill. I have a slight headache from the nap; I never nap anymore. The sun has set, and the headlights of the Jeep bounce off the road ahead of us. It's gravel, and the only other lights are coming from random cabins we're passing.

When we get to what seems like the top of the hill, he stops and turns onto a wide driveway with a large barn next to a beautiful cabin. The back side has no windows, just a door and a porch, but I can tell it's stunning just by the architecture. The roof is a dark tin, and there are several eaves. But instead of logs, the cabin is covered partially by regular siding and rock. It looks like the back side of a mansion, all closed off so the public sees very little.

"This is your family cottage?"

He grins wide, nodding and sighing. "This is my favorite place in the whole world." He leans in, kissing softly on my cheek. "And you are my favorite person, so you can see why I was excited for you two to meet."

It makes me blush and embarrasses me. Even in the dark car where I know he can't see my cheeks glowing, I hate it. He hops out and runs up to the main door at the front and opens it, leaving it ajar. I grab my bag from the back and hop out, walking to the door he's left ajar. He points at the barn. "I have a few things in here I need to tend to, mechanical crap. Why don't you head inside, snoop around, and find the hot tub. It's on the back deck, overlooking the woods and mountaintops. I'll join you in a moment."

I don't feel particularly comfortable going, but I just shrug and walk inside, closing the door behind me. It's dark, but even so I can tell the home is magnificent. It's not a chalet or a family cottage— it's remarkable. The foyer is large, opening right up into the massive great room. A river-rock fireplace climbs the wall to the left, and the kitchen is to the right.

I drop my bag and stumble in, stunned at the beautiful house. It flickers in my mind, contrasting with the stone walls of a building I'm not sure I've ever seen. It's a barren place with children running and playing, making up for the lack of joy in the air.

But this, it's something completely different. It's like a whole other world, and I don't know how to be in it.

A vision of my childhood bounds into my brain. My house is nothing like this. There's warmth in my house, surrounded by clutter, and my mom shouting at me to bring her the thing she's looking for. And yet, the place with the stone walls and running children feels like home for a second too.

Walking into the living room I reach to flick on a lamp, but the moon surprises me, rising above the mountains. It's so large and bright that I stay my hand and watch it fill up the room.

It's cold and silver, a perfect moon for the dark night. As it crests the hill across the valley from me it lights up the small valley. All of the hills fill with shadows, crevices I imagine are dark places someone could hide. Or places where something could lurk.

I shiver, lost in the captivating brilliance of the cold moon, realizing I'm cold too. The fireplace on the wall is a wood-burning one, and even though I don't know how to start it, I walk to it, dropping to my knees in front of it. And then, as if the silver light of the moon gives me knowledge I can't possibly have, I light the fire. I make a teepee of sticks, and stuff the paper I've rolled up under it, lighting and watching as the soft sparks lick at the paper and then build into orange flames. Immediately I feel the heat from it, realizing how cold the room actually is. I leave the glass doors open as the fire increases, giving off a slight scent of the smoke coming from the hardwood crackling inside the fireplace.

I turn and walk into the kitchen, leaning on the large, pale-marble island. There are pictures on the fridge of small kids and Christmas cards, but when I blink they vanish, leaving behind only a steel refrigerator. The Christmas cards and pictures and old coupons are on my mom's fridge, but I don't know what made me think of that. Except maybe because the house is so cold in some ways, and yet homey in others. It's staged to be inviting and warm, but it lacks life. It is missing people.

That doesn't take away from the beauty under the silver moon.

"She can build a fire—who knew?"

I turn, smiling as I see his lips curling up into a grin. He's a bit out of breath, and he looks like he's been running or working at something hard.

"Do you like it?" He tilts his head, staring deeply into my eyes.

I nod slowly, realizing this might be the first time for us. We may actually make love.

The mischief in his eyes tells me we won't be kissing and admiring purity rings much longer, that tonight I might be in for something I have never had before. Sex with an adult is amazing—in my head. I don't know how it'll be in real life, but my expectations are quite high. Teenage boys are not great at it. I have experienced that a few times and have never come away feeling like I understand the greatness that is sex.

He crosses the room, lifting his hands to my face, cupping and lifting to a nearly impossible angle. He kisses my forehead and stares out the window over top. "I want your permission to make—love—to you."

I gulp as an involuntary twitch between my legs jolts through me. I nod, not saying it aloud.

"Say it."

"I give you my permission." My voice shakes but it isn't nerves, it's excitement. *And about bloody time.*

"You give me permission to ravage you in every way I know how?"

I nod again, not even sure what the fuck I am agreeing to. *Don't cuss!* I reprimand myself.

He lowers his gaze and mouth, crashing it upon mine. The feeling of his lips engulfing mine is unexpected. He kisses like he might actually devour me, and I don't know if I like it or if I think it's weirdly fetish-like. His saliva coats my lips, greasing the way for our kiss. I'm not sold on the way he kisses. I'm not sold on anything as he lifts me into the air and carries me into the dark. I have a terrible feeling he is taking me into the dark in more than literal ways.

Gently I am placed on the bed, gently my shoes are removed, and gently my hands are kissed.

That is the last of the gentle acts.

His lips pressed against my palms are deceptive. I let him lift my hands into the air after each kiss, locking my wrists into something, something I don't understand until it's too late. I'm too excited. His cock bulges from his jeans, rubbing against the inside of my bare thigh; my pants have been removed in the fluid acts he's committed without really moving much. He's smooth and efficient at locking me up tightly. I try to reach for him as my fingers tingle, desperate for the touch and feel of what I imagine is smooth skin. But he doesn't allow it.

My hands are pinned and my heart is pounding when I realize what has happened. He lifts something from the dark bedside table. It's then I realize the entire wall next to the bed is glass and the cascading mountains are almost in the room with us, they are so close. I can taste the moonlight in the air, the still cold air. The thing in his hands flashes a bit of light as the moon grazes it slightly. My eyes widen when I see the scissors. I don't know where we're going suddenly; my hands are bound and the scissors seem sharp, like kitchen shears. The way they catch the light and shimmer is cold and frightening.

"Do you trust me?" he asks softly as he rests the cold metal of the clippers against my stomach. I nod again, but it's a lie. The grin on his lips and the gray his eyes have become make me even more nervous. "You don't have to lie," he whispers as he cuts once, making me flinch and wait for the pain. He cuts again and again until my bra and heaving chest are bared to him and the cold air. He drags the blades down my skin, barely a whisper of touch. "Are you scared?"

I nod. *Fuck it!* I can't deny the fear in my eyes or the near-tearful stare I am certain he sees.

The grin on his face should have been my warning, but I eat it up like it is the most delicious thing I have ever seen. I eat him up; everything about him is beautiful and enchanting in all the wrong ways yet striking all the right places.

He lowers the shears, clipping away the sides of my underwear and then the middle of my bra. The cloth falls away from my skin, leaving me lying on a mat of my removed clothing. He cuts away the sleeves and flicks the bra from my breast. Even I can't deny the beauty of my body as the shadowy silver light hits one side, casting abstract contrasts on the other. He runs the closed metal scissors across my nipple, making what is standing at attention grow even more.

He bends his beautiful face, replacing the cold metal with the heat of his mouth. Again he kisses with too much moisture, leaving my nipple wet and aching for more attention. But he leaves that one, sucking the other in a way that makes it feel as though there is a string from my clit to my nipple, and when one gets touched the other tugs.

He runs a finger down my belly as his tongue circles my erect nipple. The other is freezing cold and begging for more attention, which he grants it when his finger makes its way to the destination I have been desperately, but silently, begging from him.

As he inserts a finger roughly, his mouth lands on the cold nipple, both earning a gasp from me. He doesn't hesitate to see what I like—he immediately saws his finger in and out of my wet opening. I cry out from the shuddering bliss rocking me as he bites gently, no worse than the cuffs do on my wrists.

I can't touch or move, really. He's pinning me to the bed and abusing me in the best ways I can imagine. It all feels wrong and right, conflicting my opinion on an appropriate response. I don't know if it's the second finger he inserts, or the clenching of his teeth on my nipple as his tongue flicks rapidly, or the cuffs pinning my body at an unnatural angle, but I orgasm in the most violent way I ever have. A scream tears from my lips as I arch my back and tremble, clamping down on his fingers, which don't slow in any way. I twitch and ache, but he doesn't relent.

"Please! Please!" I beg for him to stop but my lips betray my body, they won't utter the word *stop*, and so he continues his assault. I don't imagine the word *stop* would end the pulsating in my quivering pussy. I don't imagine my begging does anything but feed his frenzy.

His pants rustle. I assume one thing and yet receive another. He grabs his cock, rubbing it between my pussy lips and yet never entering me. Again I beg, but not the way I thought I might in a situation such as this one. "FUCK ME!"

But he doesn't. He pulls his fingers from me, rubbing his cock between my lips with several aggressive thrusts before orgasming all over my stomach. He twitches and sighs, looking confused for a moment. He smiles and nods. "I got a bit excited."

I'm heaving breaths in desperation and lost in the glistening fluid all over my bared belly. He climbs off me, making my hip ache immediately at the awkward angle.

He leans forward, dragging his cock in the mess he's made as he unlocks my wrists. I whimper a little as he releases them and lowers my upper body to the pillow again. I hadn't realized I was nearly suspended.

He's up, no cuddle, no talking. Just straight to the shower. He doesn't even turn on a light.

I lie there a minute, not sure if I should laugh or cry. It is hands down the weirdest sex I have ever had, and yet I have a feeling it might also the best.

6. PROFESSOR HYDE

Angie gives me a confused stare. "So he just rubbed his wanker on ya bits and came, never entered ya?"

I shake my head.

She cocks an eyebrow. "He's a freak. Jesus, Mary, and Joseph. He's one of them Bates Motel types. Ya need to get out. No one needs that sort of shite. All the mess, with none of the sex? Feck that." She shakes her head again, almost blankly. "Fecking weirdo, that's what ya got. He breastfed from the tit till he was seventeen, I bet my life on that one."

I snort, still feeling the odd bit dirty from the encounter.

"And you never did it again after that? Ten dates, and he uses ya to jack off?"

"Don't get me wrong. He made me come twice before he came. We had mutual orgasms. He just never entered me with his penis." I make a driving-forward motion toward my vagina, like I need to explain it better.

"Fecking weird."

"Agreed." I nod and contemplate what will become of us. I know I have to break it off, but I desperately want to have him. It's perverse, but I can't stop thinking about what it might be like. He's obviously weird. Who just happens to have handcuffs on their bedpost? Does his mom know they're there? Does he even have a mom?

"So what did yas do with all that free time the next two days?"

The memory of that brings a scowl across my lips. "Played games, hiked, and made gourmet meals." I give her a look. "Pretty dissatisfying, actually. We cuddled every night."

She wrinkles her nose. "Like friends or sisters or some shite like that?"

I shrug. "He seemed all sweet again when he got the shower over with. I had one, and then he warmed up the house and made a meal, and we watched a movie." I flash the welts on my wrists. "We pretended this never happened."

Her eyes widen. "He'll tie ya up, but he won't shag ya? Not worth it." She starts filing her teal-colored nails. "I don't mind a bit of tie-me-up tie-me-down, but it better come with a rock-hard shagging. I better not walk—"

"I get it!" I clear my throat. "He's fairly good at everything else."

"Yeah. He'll be wearing your shoes by Christmas, trust me. This has *Mommie Dearest* written all over it." Her words ring through my head, like a bell in a courtyard, chiming the hour.

I curl up in my bed and snuggle my cat, or rather struggle snuggle, until he eventually gives up.

I leave for my parents' house the next day, for Christmas break. The nutty professor doesn't text or call for the entire break. My brother mocks me as a crazy cat lady, and my mother defends my odd obsession with my feline companion. They all assume I'll end up old and alone. But even then I don't tell them about Derek. I don't dare utter a word. How would I explain our relationship? *Sometimes he ties me up and comes on my belly, and I'm not allowed to be seen with him in public, but he reads poetry and tells me impassioned tales of traveling through Ireland and his fondness for the place.*

There is no way to explain Derek and me to myself, so I can't imagine trying to explain it to my family. I nod and let them chide me.

I do notice, however, there is animation in my house that his lacks. His entire life lacks it. He's dry and funny, but in a way that always seems to keep me at arm's length.

After Christmas break, on the ride back to Seattle, I notice the rain hasn't stopped. The fall was cold and damp, and the winter doesn't seem to be improving. I hate that we might not see a flake of snow this year. It's weird. We usually get a bit, just a bit.

I like to stare up into it, letting the flakes fall on my tongue.

When I get back to the dorm, I notice his Jeep is parked in the lot where all the girls park their cars. His silhouette is there, hiding in the shadows of the dark vehicle. He doesn't open the door or climb out. He doesn't wave. He just watches. And like a fool I walk to him. I don't drop off my bags. I don't tell anyone I am there. I walk to his Jeep and open the passenger door.

He looks rough, different. I never noticed before how much he resembles my brother. Tall and broad with dark hair and dark-blue eyes. He's chiseled and ruggedly handsome. In the moonlight I lean in, squinting at the dark blue of his eyes I could swear were always green. Gray green when he was emotional at all. But now they're dark blue, and his eyebrows seem a bit different. The boyish good looks are gone. In their stead are rugged features that make him handsome in a way that intimidates me, as if it has made him older.

I blink, wondering if I have the right vehicle. But he turns and smiles, and all my doubts are gone.

"I missed you all Christmas." The word *Christmas* sounds funny the way he says it.

I climb into the vehicle, dropping my bags on the ground next to the door I leave ajar. I slide into his lap and wrap my arms around his neck. It's hard not to kiss him with every bit of passion I have in me. I want everything he's willing to offer, and I don't know why.

TARA BROWN

He cups me in his lap, holding tightly to me. His fingers tremble just slightly, like they're straining too much or holding back maybe.

I rock in his lap, grinding against the erection I can feel there. I sit back, reaching between his legs to free the beast I think is beckoning to me. As I open the zipper and button, it springs from the pants and underwear. I don't think. I don't even consider what I am doing. Instead, I kiss him and wrestle with my own pants after kicking off my shoes. There, in the parking lot, I lower myself back over him once I'm bared, sliding my wet sex over his rigid cock. He freezes, not touching me, not breathing. He's perfectly still as I ride him, rocking my hips and rolling my stomach, working him like a joystick.

I increase my pace, biting down on his quivering lip and gripping his shoulders with my greedy fingers that want too much. I force him to move with me, force him to fuck me. It's better than I imagined. He fits inside of me like he was made to be there. I orgasm, clutching to the headrest as he pants softly in my ear.

When he climaxes, he loses all control, just like at his cabin. He grips me too hard, his fingers digging into my hips and butt. He forces my pussy up and down, forces the riding and the circular motion. He comes moaning in my ear, biting down on my lobe. I hadn't noticed he'd bitten me, but I cry out as he bites harder. He jerks his finish inside of me and pauses, again frozen.

"I think I love you, Professor."

He shakes his head. "You can't," he mutters with a strange accent and shoves me off him, pushing me from the Jeep with semen dripping down my bare legs. I just land on my feet, and he's driving away with the door open. I yank my pants on but have lost my shoes, for what I assume is forever.

I think this because I don't see him again. Not the way I did.

My heart aches when he doesn't come to see me, or call me, or text me. My insides tighten and burn when I think about how

48

I let him use me. I try not to linger in that place, the one made up of shame. I worry that I might have gone too far to that bad place where you can't ever have normal again because you are addicted to the twisted darkness.

I try to not to think about him at all.

It doesn't go well.

7. FIRST DAY OF SPRING

It doesn't feel like spring. It feels like fall or early winter. It's dank and cold, and my hopes of seeing snow are gone. I know I will not see a single flake for the whole year until next winter.

My phone vibrates as I reach the steps of the campus. I glance at it before I realize where I am. I'm at the campus of the university in the city. I had gotten on the bus to go to the mall, and yet, here I am. It's happened before. I have gotten on board to go somewhere, and my body instinctively goes looking for him.

I climb the steps, knowing exactly where the literature department is. It isn't my first time making it all the way here before stopping myself.

When I get inside I pause, looking for the information office. My insides tighten as I walk to the silver-haired lady with the granny glasses and a terrible winter sweater on. I grin when I see her name, Anne Holle. She is Ms. A. Holle, and my brain is just infantile enough to enjoy that. When she glances up I turn my grin into a soft smile. "Hi, I'm looking for Dr. Russo."

She cocks a brow. "Who?"

"Dr. Derek Russo. He teaches literature."

She tilts her head to the side, giving me the oddest look. "You mean Professor Hanson? Dick Hanson?"

I purse my lips. "Nooooo. I think I mean Russo. He's a professor here. Perhaps he's changed subjects."

"Oh, if only it were that easy. I can tell you that there has not been a Dr. Russo on campus as a teacher since I started twenty years ago, and Dr. Hanson, the literature professor, has been here since Jesus was in short pants." She chuckles. "He's older than Methuselah's bloody goat." She sees the look of pain on my face. "I assume you are looking for this professor for the wrong reasons. Well, our lit prof is gay, very gay. He's been to Canada to marry the theater director from the playhouse downtown." She winks. "Go figure, a gay lit prof and a theater director? Who would have guessed?" She chuckles again.

My insides twist and turn. "Who is Russo then? Who's Derek Russo?"

She shrugs. "Honey, I have never heard that name before. I think you might have been messed with."

My world spins, and my mind goes for the most logical explanation. She's a fucking liar. I turn and run down the hallway, my Hunter boots clomping on the tile floor. When I know I'm lost I stop and stare at the map on the wall. I go down a set of stairs and down another hallway. The sign for the literature hall stops me dead in my tracks. Dick Hanson is the name on the plaque. I hurry to the wall, peering into the room through the slim window in the door. An old man wearing a very feminine purple scarf leads the class. He has gray hair and a bit of a mustache that matches his head. He's a little chubby and definitely not Derek.

I back away until I hit the wall and slump onto a bench.

I don't know what that means, and I don't know how to respond. He's not a professor?

I pull my phone out, texting Angie in all-caps rage.

WHAT THE HELL? YOU SAID YOU KNEW DEREK! HE'S NOT A
PROF! HOW WELL DO YOU KNOW HIM?

She doesn't message me back. The text doesn't even deliver.

I close my eyes, wondering how I got here. I need to go home.
Not just my dorm but my house. I left Binx there after Christmas;
he wasn't enjoying the dorm life at all. I need a furry snuggle and
maybe to reevaluate my life and classes and career ambitions.

I stand and stagger down the hallway, wishing I'd just stayed
home for a year like half my friends. Or gone to Portland with my
brother.

But I don't end up back at school. I end up in a bar with a stiff
drink and a plate of cheese fries. I drink a second glass and sit back,
realizing I have been played. I have definitely been played. I message
Angie again, but as before it doesn't deliver. Her phone must be off.

I hate that I don't know who he is or where he works. I hate
that I let him cuff me on a lonely mountaintop and that he has seen
me orgasm in the silver light of the moon. I hate that I have wasted
my time—my precious first year at college—on a wanker like him.
Wanker? God, I sound like Angie.

I lift my phone again, and in the reflection I see a face I don't
know. A girl I don't recognize. She looks pretty but different from
me in every way. She's got dark hair and puffy lips, the kind people
pay for. Her different-colored eyes are sad, like empty pools. I blink
and she's gone. Then it's just me and the annoyance that's plastered
on my brow.

"Ash?"

I lift my head, smiling when I see Michelle. She might be the
devil, but I could use a familiar face. I wave at her and Leona, realizing they're holding hands. Not something I expected, but it seems
to fit. They both seemed like they were in the wrong place at the
wrong time in the dorms, to me anyway, as if they were fighting to
fit in. Mean girls are always that way—conflicted and angst-filled.

"Hey, girls!" I hold my hand out to the empty table in front of me. "Have a seat."

They plop into chairs, and I swear for a half a second Michelle gives me a challenging stare. But I smile, because her evil mean-girl antics are nothing compared to being handcuffed and masturbated on. Nothing. Not to mention my reaction to said masturbating and handcuffing.

Leona grins. "You're here alone?" She reaches across and steals a cheese fry.

I nod, sipping my overly strong drink. "I am. What brings you two in here?" It is the saddest place on earth, possibly. There's me and one other guy in the whole place. He's been at it longer than I have and is considerably drunk. He has grinned at me a few times, but I haven't returned his smile. That hasn't been super lucky for me lately.

"We were headed downtown for some drinks and some dancing. You wanna come?"

Michelle gives her a look, making me smile wider and nod. "Sure. I don't have any plans."

"What about your mystery man?" Michelle's eyes narrow.

I almost congratulate her on the exact wording one would need to describe the piece of shit in my life, the lying sack of shit. Mystery man is bang on. But then I would have to talk about the masturbating, and that might get weird. Not to mention, I would also have to reveal just how naive I am to a girl I am certain despises me because I have a cat. "He's actually not in the picture." I wink at her and chug back my drink. "Too mysterious."

Leona laughs. "Dudes suck."

I lift my glass. "If only we could all be gay. You girls have it made. Two chicks, no nonsense."

They roll their eyes exactly the same. "Twice the nonsense is what you mean." Michelle nudges Leona, and they grin at each other, having a full moment. One where I doubt the validity of their claim of twice the nonsense.

I lift my glass, signaling the lame bartender who hasn't even offered to listen to my problems. He brings a round of overly strong drinks, assuming my friends also want to get drunk.

Michelle wrinkles her nose at it but Leona tosses hers back like it's a shot. I realize then it is. That's why it's so miserable to sip. I shoot mine back and grimace. "Gross."

"You don't like liquid cocaine?" Leona asks softly.

I don't know what she means, and nearly look behind me to see if she's talking to someone else.

"The drink is called Liquid Cocaine. It's a couple of types of schnapps and something else. It's a shot." Michelle rolls her eyes again and shoots it back calmly.

"Oh, no. I'm not a fan. I told him to bring me something strong and he did. He said it was trendy with the ladies."

Leona's eyes glisten as she nudges Michelle. "It's my favorite. It makes her sick, though. Drank too many. And Jägerbombs too."

I know that drink, and it makes me cringe with Michelle, who slaps down cash and nods, getting up quickly. "Let's do this." She walks out, not even checking to see if she's left enough money. I scramble to keep up and follow her out the door. The weird guy with the grin waves, but I try to ignore him.

When I get to the sidewalk I realize where we are going—it's the bar across the street, the one we went to last time. I still cringe when I pass it. The feel of getting sick haunts me.

She walks right in, nodding at the bouncer. It's early and there is no line, not yet. The music is playing already, though, when we get inside. The lights are flashing too, lighting up the near-empty bar. I almost stop and walk back out, but Leona laughs at my face. "It's going to fill up in like half an hour. Line around the block. If we come now there's no cover and we get a booth." These are things I would know if I didn't spend my weekends with a psychotic douche.

We sit at a booth, and immediately a couple of servers are there. They're clearly desperate for someone to talk to. Michelle orders three beers, just assuming I want beer. I don't care, but the option to have water might have been nice. It's then that I realize I'm downtown with the two girls I had to assume hated me, all because I wanted to change rooms. But here, in the flashing lights and weird smells, they don't seem bad at all. I send Angie a text, telling her where I am. The message finally delivers. I get a read receipt but she doesn't answer.

Half an hour later, it's just like Leona said it would be. The bar is shoulder to shoulder, and everyone is dancing. It's only ten thirty but the place is crowded. We dance, meeting up with a couple of girls from class. We drink and we laugh. The night isn't at all how I expected it to turn out. When the fourth beer lands in my stomach with a thud, I know I've had too much. I give Michelle a look and nod toward the door. "I need air and maybe a hot dog from out front."

She laughs. "Me too. Let's get a stamp so they let us back in. They have a spot for people who need some air, over this way." She says something to Leona and leaves with me following. A crabby-looking girl gives us a stamp, and we mosey out into the cool night air. It's damp, because apparently that's the only season we are getting this year. Michelle reaches a ten-dollar bill across some ropes to the hot-dog guy and gets us both one. I slump into the patio furniture and take the hot dog. It's awkward with just the two of us. "I'm sorry about the cat," I say, not comfortable at all.

"No, I am. I get it. Being in the city and having no friends is tough. I should have been nicer. I was pissed when they roomed us together. I had specifically asked for one of my friends."

I nod, taking the most delicious bite of food I have ever had. I close my eyes and moan into it. When I look at her she seems angry or annoyed, but when she speaks again I understand why. "I thought you and that girl you're roomed with wanted to switch because you guys knew me and Leona were lesbians."

I desperately swallow, wishing I could get it all down faster to explain. I shake my head aggressively. "Not at—all." I nearly die, but I manage to get it out. I take a deep breath as the huge lump painfully makes its way into my esophagus. "I didn't know. I actually didn't know until you two walked into the bar."

She doesn't look convinced.

"I swear, I thought you hated me because of the cat. I felt awful."

She rolls her eyes. "So your mom snuck a cat in the room, and you think I'm that crazy that I can't adapt?"

I don't say anything. Not because I don't think she's adaptable, but because that's not how I recall it at all.

"Fine, I acted like a dick. I hate cats. I'm a dog person. But you switched, and I thought it was because you had the whole anti-lesbian thing like that girl in your room. She called Leona a dyke."

My jaw drops. "Angie would never." I don't know that I believe my statement or hers. While Angie's prejudiced as the day is long toward all other Europeans, quite savagely too, I have never heard her mutter a word against gays. It's possible she is also homophobic, but unlikely, as all her rants involve nationality and their inferiority to Scotland.

Her brow furrows. "No, Steph is the one who did it."

"Steph?"

Michelle shakes it off. "It doesn't matter. I'm glad we talked about this."

I'm stuck on Steph, but she leans in and hugs me before I can rationalize why Angie lied about her name to them. Her name is Angie, I've seen her real driver's license. She stands up abruptly and points. "I'm going back in. You coming?"

I shake my head, feeling weird and sick, and the hot dog isn't improving a single thing about my situation. I suspect that huge bite might try to come back up and that is how I will die. My greatest fear ever, choking on throw-up alone in the bathroom.

I nod at the street. "I think I'm gonna jump this rope and head home. I feel like ass. Really nasty ass too."

Michelle chuckles, giving me another hug. "I'll come with you to get a cab."

"No, it's fine. I can walk." I don't know why I don't want to be vulnerable with her, maybe because she hates my cat and all other cats. It's suspicious to see someone not love cats. They are the greatest companions a person could ask for.

She tries to argue but I get up and climb over the rope, waving my hand for a cab. The bouncer here in the roped-off area waves at the cabs for me. When he gets one, I climb in, waving back at Michelle as she goes inside.

I mutter my address and sit back, hoping I don't get sick and die in the cab.

As the car stops in front of my school on the quiet side of town, I pay the man and climb out, working hard at not staggering. The staggering drunk coed is always the one to get raped and murdered.

"Ashley!"

I cringe when I hear the voice, and not because I just thought about rape. I take another step away before I turn back, giving him a scowl. He's hurt my heart and now my pride too.

"Ash, wait up. We need to talk." When he gets closer I step back again, trying to get a bit of distance. He stops about three feet away from me. "I haven't been honest." His eyes narrow, and the hint of the accent I have caught before is completely there.

"I know."

He nods. "I saw you go to the school today—"

"You followed me?"

He winces but doesn't back down. "I had to. It's my job." He takes a step closer. "I am trying to find someone, and I trailed you because you fit the person's taste in women."

His story sounds insane, but I don't say anything. What could I even add?

"Me and a few others have been hoping the guy would try to grab you and we would be there. We would keep you safe. But it hasn't happened. He hasn't tried, even though this is his favorite city and you are his favorite type of girl."

My stomach slips from its usual spot right into my bowels. "You have been waiting for me to get abducted? Are you insane? By who?"

"Whom. And we don't know. That's why we've kept close tabs on you and a couple of other girls, and so far nothing. If we knew him he'd be in jail."

My skin crawls, and the liquor makes my reaction to this ridiculousness painful. "Who is 'we'? What do you do for a living?"

He clenches his jaw and looks down. "I work for the government, in surveillance and undercover work."

"What's your name?"

"Rory Guthrie. I used to be Irish intelligence, and now I am American." He looks down, fighting something, his words maybe. "And I have made a mistake telling you this, but I need this to end. The guy isn't ever coming to grab you. He isn't ever going to take you, because I'm always here. I ended it because I needed to do my job, and I wasn't."

I feel sick, but scared of the hot dog piece that might actually kill me. "Is that really your cabin?"

He nods.

"So you took me there against the rules then? Against the plan?"

He doesn't need to nod; the guilt all over his face is enough.

"But Angie knew you. You said she knew you. Is that why I can't seem to get hold of her? Is she one of you?"

He swallows. "She is. She had to go back home for something."

"So she is a liar like you?"

He chuckles a little under his breath. "We lie for a living."

"How do I know you're not lying now?"

His dark-blue eyes meet mine, and I know. "I'm not. I love you, and that's a problem for me. I need to get past you. I need to let you go." He pauses and gives in, ending the battle I have seen with his will. "And I can't." He looks so vulnerable, like the struggle to not be with me is real.

So I jump him.

It isn't the most rational choice, and it makes almost no sense to me and clearly none to him, but I do it anyway. He lifts me into his big arms, cradling me and taking away all the pain. I believe his lies and his bullshit. I believe because I don't want him to be crazy, which makes far more sense. All of it makes more sense this way. How I ended up at his house when I was sick. How I never see him in public and am not allowed to tell anyone who he is. How he doesn't actually do the job he lies about doing.

Yes, this makes sense. He kisses, sucking my lips and grinding my body into his. I let him carry me back to the Jeep. We don't make love there. He places me in the seat and does up my belt. He closes the door and walks around to the other side, getting in and starting the Jeep. I watch him drive as long as I can before I pass out into the blackest oblivion I have ever been in.

8. THE DUGOUT

I remember very little, but I know I fell asleep in the black oblivion, and when I wake I'm still in it. Only I don't feel like I'm in the Jeep. I'm somewhere else.

The air is thick and cold—heady, if that's a possible trait for air. I feel as though I exhale and then inhale the very same air. My lips hurt when I open my mouth. I honestly don't know what to think.

My eyes fuzz in and out, unable to catch one thing to focus on here in the dark. I shiver and lie back on whatever surface I am on. My fingers come back to me, finding their senses in the black, and discovering a blanket. I brush my fingertips across it, feeling the soft fuzzy cloth and wishing I were home with my cat.

The ache in my body and the apparent swelling on my face have me frightened.

I roll over, griping and groaning as pain shoots through me.

We must have had an accident.

I must have fallen asleep and we crashed.

But where am I?

Something moves in the dark, but I sense it's behind something or in another room. I feel like I am alone in here, and the space is small.

Is it a hospital?

My insides clench, sending me on my side and then off the bed I didn't even realize I was on. I land with a painful thud on a strange-feeling floor. My fingers grasp the surface, tickling almost until I recognize it as straw. I'm in a room with hay.

Not a hospital. Unless it's an animal hospital. Did he carry me here, and this was all he found on the way? Where is he, Rory Guthrie? His name isn't Derek.

I lift one hand, breathing raggedly, and touch the bed. It too feels like straw beneath the blankets. I force myself up, pushing with my hands and legs until I am finally standing on wobbly feet and rubber legs. It's like having been on a boat all day and then stagger-ing up the dock.

"Hello!" I croak into the dark. I'm not afraid of what's here with me. I am afraid of being here alone.

"Shhhhhhhhhh. It's all right. Don't panic." The woman's voice is one I don't know, but I don't care. I'm not alone. I stumble to the wall, running my hand along the cool surface. It's wood, I think, but damp wood.

"Are you a nurse? Or a tech? Is this an animal hospital? Can you help me?" I call out to the woman. "I think I'm hurt, pretty badly. I think we might have been in a car accident. My boyfriend, Rory, is he okay? Is he here?"

She giggles, nervously. It's a strange sound to hear in the dark when you're scared. She sounds crazy. "He's my boyfriend too, and because of him we're all hurt. But survival is staying silent. When Rory comes, just lie there and don't fight him. The ones who fight don't last."

Tears stream from my cheeks instantly. "What?" The word is more of a ghastly whisper and less of a question. "Where are we? Can you hear me? Are you talking to me? Can you just open the door? My boyfriend is named Der— Rory, has he been here?"

"Oh, he's been. He's been and gone. He's the one who locked you up, you idiot. He's gone most of the time. When he comes back we do what he wants, and it gets better. We all start in the dugout, but now I have a full room. And he's not so bad. Just don't make him mad."

Another voice joins the conversation. "You have to be quiet. I've heard him moving about today since he brought her. He'll be down here soon. We have to be quiet."

I slap the wooden wall. "What is this place? Rory! You let me out! If this is some kind of fucking joke, it's not funny!"

A voice that hasn't spoken yet, but is very close to me, whispers harshly from a crack in the dark wall. "This is hell, and we are his. Just do everything he asks and be everything he asks. There's no escape. Only madness. He's locked you up like he did all of us. This is a prison, you understand?"

"No." I lift a finger to the corner where her face is and feel her breath as she continues.

"My name is Be— Jane. My name is Jane. I came here six months ago, I think. But I can't be sure. What's the date?"

My brain pauses, fully frozen, to try to answer her. "March 22, I believe."

"2014?"

I shake my head. "15."

A soft sob slips from the crack in the wall. "Oh God, of course it is. I've been here since last May. Nearly a year." Her voice breaks, and for a second I think she might fully cry. But she doesn't. She accepts it and moves on almost immediately. It's creepy and not very reassuring. It's much more a sign of what is to come for me than I think I can comprehend.

"I was in a car with my boyfriend. And now I'm here."

"A Jeep?" she asks softly, her delicate word ripping a huge hole in my stomach and heart.

"Yes."

She whimpers again, but it sounds like a laugh. "He's the best boyfriend ever, isn't he?" She giggles again, but it's as if someone is dragging a knife down her arm, forcing the pained giggle out. "Until he's not and you're here."

"Where are we?" My throat is dry and coarse.

"I don't know. It's underground—I know that. But there is nothing else. No water dripping, no traffic, no noise whatsoever. It's just us and silence and him. But he's not here all the time." Her voice is so familiar, like it's been inside of my head.

I immediately know where we are. We're at his cabin. The dank air doesn't smell the same in here as the crisp air outside, but I know that's where we are. I don't know how I know it, but I do. "Has anyone ever escaped?" I whisper back into the corner, feeling my own breath landing back on me.

"I don't know. A couple of the girls have been here longer than me. Some have left, but not 'cause they escaped."

I don't want to talk anymore. I need to find a way out. I rifle my pockets for my phone, but it's gone, so I lift my hands and run them along the walls the whole way around. I am truly in a dugout. It's a room surrounded by dirt and wood, and the floor is straw the entire way. My brain tries to whisper things about bugs and the stuff I can't see, but I don't let it. I sit back on the bed and wait. He will come, and I will kill him.

"You have food in the corner at the end of the bed. It's in a bar fridge next to the toilet. There is food and water there." The girl, Jane, whispers, "The light can be a friend in the dark."

I scramble to the end of the bed, feeling for the fridge. I had noticed the toilet on my circle around.

And there it is. I fling the door open, flooding the dark space with light. As my eyes adjust I am surprised by what I find. It's much nicer than I anticipated. Much.

It's cleaner and less like a dug hole in the ground. More like a cellar. The ceiling is cement, perhaps the oddest part of the room, and the floors are cement with straw covering them. Some of the walls are wooden, and others are old cement that's broken down and looks a bit like dirt. The bed is stacks of hay with blankets over the top, and the small white bar fridge is my only company. The crack where Jane whispers from is in one of the cement-and-dirt walls. The cracks are decay. In the dim light I can see her dark eyes in the shadows. I might not have seen the color if not for the ghastly state of her pale skin. She is white like I have never seen. Gray almost. When she leans in I can see she has different-colored eyes. One is dark blue and the other pale. She blinks and backs up, making them both appear dark again. Her face changes in the shadows, making me think I have seen her before, and then maybe not.

"The food gets refilled when he comes, so it's feast or famine, but he always comes." Her puffy lips are cracked and sore. She looks exhausted and hollow. Her oddly colored eyes reflect only blankness.

"Do I know you?" I ask, thinking I can't help but feel like this Jane has crawled around inside of my head.

She shakes her head slowly. "I don't think we have ever met. I'd remember."

I shrug. "What does he do with us here?"

A single tear slips down her cheek, washing away filth and leaving an even whiter streak of skin that glows in the muted light. "He will bathe you, show you how much he loves you." She cringes. "Then he bathes you again and puts you back in the cell. Sometimes he makes us put on dresses and dance with him. Other times, when he thinks one of us has misbehaved or we've talked too much, he beats one of the girls, and we all have to hear it." Her expression tightens a slight bit. "Try not to be that girl."

I close the fridge and let the darkness rush back in. I don't want her to see me lose my self-control. Even if it is a useless cry for help, I make it as silent as I can.

9. HANDSOME PRINCE NUTBAG

I am still sore and frightened I have a UTI. I had one when I was a young teenager, and now it feels as though I have another. Being locked away and abused randomly has damaged more than my spirit. We sit in the dark and wait for him to pick us, frightened by either outcome. The suspense of possibly being chosen each time he enters the dungeon is horrifying, but it is nothing compared to the moment his fingers clasp the lock on your door. In the silent suspense, the sound of your lock clicking can drive you to madness.

Today it was my lock, my madness.

I blink away the remains of the drugs he filled me with. He does it every time he takes us out of our cage. I sit up and find my way to the fridge. It helps metabolize the drugs if we eat straight away.

The girl in the room next to mine stands at the crack in the corner of our shared wall that we have picked at, making it a little bigger day by day. Her face is odd, almost like she's Asian, but I can tell she isn't. She's pretty, though I suspect we are all pretty in one way or another. I swear I have seen her before, though—as if she's been my best friend or something so close I can't help but know her better than I know myself.

"So he gave you the spiel about being a cop or whatever? That you were in danger?"

I nod, eating the packet of cheese I've just grabbed from the fridge. It's not the best cheese, but after a while you get used to it. The fridge is loaded with healthy food. Sometimes I just want a piece of chocolate.

"The worst part for me is I nearly got away. He tried his bullshit, and I tried to run, but he caught me and knocked me out. A lady saw me trying to get away. I just remember how wide her eyes went when she saw him hit me. It was the last thing I saw."

I pick at the cheese with my newly cleaned hands and nod. "I was an idiotic fool. I fell for his story right away. I liked him." It makes me feel dirty now. The feel of his breath is like poisonous vapors. His skin is sandpaper against mine, stripping and sanding away the layers of dignity and respect. Even boundaries I worked my whole life putting up are knocked down.

"We were all idiots. And we are paying for our sins now."

I give her a look. "I don't think any of us ever did a single thing to deserve this. I know we didn't."

She shrugs, leaning against the wall. I can barely make out her shoulders through the thin crack. "One day we will be out of here, and it will all be a bad dream. A nightmare we share."

A slow and bitter grin slides across my lips. "We can all do a talk show about how we're survivors."

She parts her lips to speak, but there is a noise we don't expect, not so soon. He has only just left me. My insides twist and turn. Jane reaches a hand out to me. I close the door to the fridge so the light dies. I jump up and grip her fingers. "It's okay, Ash. Be strong and remember the smell of your mother and the feel of rain on your face." She says the thing I have told her that I miss the most. I was so tired of the rain that never seemed to end this year, and yet I would die happy if I felt it on my face again.

Tears stream on my cheeks as we hear the outer door open followed by his footsteps, bold and purposeful footsteps. They stomp across the gravel floor of the main hallway, taunting us as they pass the horse stalls, each filled with girls of every flavor.

We have discussed it once. Calling out what we look like in turn. Some are blonde and others are brunettes and one girl is a redhead. All Caucasian, which we know is most likely because Rory is a Caucasian. We all weigh around 120 pounds and are all about five foot five. Here in the dark we are all unnaturally pale.

He has a type, and we are it.

Now we sit in the darkness, each waiting for the sound of our doorknob and lock to click, each silently praying it is not our turn. We betray those girls closest to us, wishing horrors upon them instead of ourselves. When it comes down to it, human nature means we will all betray one another to survive. It's the basest instinct we have, survival.

The echo of his footsteps could drive you mad in the dark, if you weren't already there. But the sound of a doorknob being manipulated is worse than a blade slicing through the air.

When a lock rattles and it isn't mine, I exhale my hurried breath, realizing how desperate I am for air, even this dank air.

The girl in that cell, I think the redhead, starts to sob. She's newer, like me. She still cries every time, like me.

"Princess, are ya so happy to see me rescue ya from the evil prison that ya weep?" he asks in his full Irish accent, no longer hiding it from us. He closes and locks the door behind him until he gets his needle and injects her with the tranquilizer.

She weeps louder, stuttering the thing we are to say: "M-m-my p-p-prince, y-y-you f-f-found me."

"Aye, I found ya, and now I will free ya from this hell, my love."

I grimace, knowing exactly what is happening at this point. He's kissing her cheeks and dragging his hands up her arms.

I know he scoops her up, carrying her weak and slowly relaxing body from the cell and up a set of stairs to the washroom. He carries her up and pours a bath, cleaning her and singing his fucking songs. The words of one still haunt me.

Listen, listen to the sound that bullets make of blood and bone.

Those words are haunting me, and yet I don't know where I have ever heard them.

Then he takes her, trembling and cold, to the bedroom off the bathroom. When he gets her there he will make sweet passionate love to her, slow and soft. He will make her orgasm again and again, even if she doesn't want to. She can't help it. Her body will be relaxed and calm, and only her mind will be screaming as he thrusts in and out, rocking and swaying until she's certain he knows every inch of her body and soul.

The whole event will be nothing at all like what he did with me when we were in the real world. It will involve cuddling and a condom, and him telling her he's going to protect her and keep her safe from evil in the world. Then he will bathe her again, singing and loving and rubbing places that are sore and overstimulated. He will tell her that he will take her back to his kingdom and marry her. They will live happily ever after. It's a fantasy like no other, and it will last the whole afternoon.

Until he realizes he must put her back into the cell, but he will be back. And she should never doubt his love, because it is eternal.

Eventually he will close the door, leaving her there. She'll be sore from hours of sex, not to mention exhausted and confused from the tranquilizer.

Jane and I clasp each other's fingertips in the dark, the only part of us that can really touch through the thin gap. We always do it when a cell opens that doesn't belong to either of us, we sigh simultaneously with relief. He has chosen someone besides one of us, which means we will enjoy another day of safety and peace.

When he closes the door to the stairs, carrying the girl away from us, the cells reanimate as girls begin to breathe and softly whisper to one another. Jane's breath is upon my face when she speaks softly: "Just once I want one of us to fight back, to attack him and free the rest of us."

I nod, thinking how it would all be impossible. "That bathroom and bedroom aren't above the ground. I don't know that it would be easy to find your way out of here. And the daylight would blind you upon leaving. We've gotten so used to the dark. He would have the advantage. You would have to attack and lock him in the cell, but before the fucking needle." I need to stop cussing so much.

She sighs. "But if you could knock him out, you might stand a chance of escaping—and freeing everyone else. What's in that room that could knock him out?"

I shake my head. "I don't know. I've only been in it a few times. The bathroom has that massive claw-foot tub and the toilet and the sink. I don't think I've ever seen anything but a towel and some soap, the French lavender soap. If I ever smell it after we get out of here, I'll kill the person holding it."

She chuckles softly into the crack. "You know it. Same for basements. I will never own a house with a basement. I want a house made of glass so I can see the whole world around me, every nook and cranny, from my window. There will be no shadows."

We sit in the corner, holding hands and waiting for the sound of her cries when he puts her back into the cell. She cries a lot, that redhead. Her name is Jenny, Jenny Rutledge, and she cries more than any girl here. But for some sick reason, he likes it. He likes it when we cry.

Her screams wake me up and I think Jane too. She jumps and grips my hand. The door slams, and the redhead screams violently. I didn't even realize I'd fallen asleep, but I clearly have, and the afternoon has gone by. He has entertained himself, and now the redhead is back in her cell and screaming.

"Don't make a sound," Jane whispers so softly I can barely hear her. "He's pissed. She's done something bad." I blink, trying to wake up.

The girl screams again, and in the mix of her screams and raging words, he speaks in a low tone. I can't hear anything he says, but her sobs quit for a moment, and I hear the thing that makes her scream. He strikes her. It's the sound of a lash. Like whipping a person with a belt. She screams again, and every inch of my body feels her pain. I am so tight and trembling that my muscles are spasming from the exertion of holding myself this way.

He strikes again, and again she screams but I think a little less. At the next strike, she doesn't scream at all. He shouts something muddled, something I don't understand, and the door slams again. The lock clicks in anger. His movements are rough and overly done, making more noise than is necessary. He's snorting and spitting when he leaves the area, again crashing and slamming doors. His footsteps find their way back in; he rattles a lock. The door slams open and shut, and his grunting is obvious. One of the girls, maybe the fallen redhead, getting this violation is silent. She takes the grunting and the savagery without a sound. He's done in seconds, and the door opens and closes again roughly.

There is no sound once he's gone. The redhead is either dead or passed out from the pain.

We sit in the dark, waiting for something to change, something to bring us back to life.

Jane whispers to me, soothingly, "When I was a girl, I had a sister named Andrea. We were twins, she and I. She was the better child; my parents were always angry with me over small things. But Andrea was perfect. I rarely remember details of the life I had before the accident. I think I locked them away so I could make my parents perfect in my mind. But they were flawed in a few ways. When they died in the accident and I had lost my memories, I made certain I created new ones of them. I took pictures of my parents and told myself lies about them. Lies that made my life before the accident perfect. But then I went to the orphanage and I learned there were kids with stories so bad, mine seemed a bit sad, really. My parents had loved me, my sister was my best friend, and my house was clean and beautiful inside. The other kids from the orphanage had terrible lives. They'd been taken from their parents. Or they'd been left at the orphanage. I realized then that nothing about my life was as hard as theirs, and that I needed to be positive about my past and my limited memories. The nuns taught us that rarely is the truth of the matter the truth of the matter. Rarely do we see what's behind the story. They taught me not to pity the children left there, because they were safe and loved, in a way. And perhaps their lives were better than what they might have been." She lowers her face to my fingers and kisses softly. "This place and this life and this hell are the same. We cannot see the driving force behind what is wrong with him. We cannot pity the other people here, because we do not know the whole story. We can only be positive and hope for the best. That's what survivors do. We don't take on the shit we see and hear and suffer. It isn't ours. It's being done to us, but it doesn't define us."

I feel a tear slip from her cheek to my fingers, and nod. She can't see me or know that I have agreed with her, but I can't speak. My heart is aching, and my stomach is on fire.

We sit in silence and wait for a noise from the room. Part of me hopes the redhead is dead, freed from this terrible fate.

"Do you believe in God?" I whisper to Jane.

"I don't know. I believe in miracles. I believe in science. I believe there is something else. The nuns taught us to believe in God, and taught about the goodness of him, but in this place it is hard to see the light. One of my favorite sayings is that only when it's dark enough can you see the stars. And so we should be able—there is no darker place on earth. But I dare say the view from here is rather bleak and the outcome is rather hopeless. If I see the stars once more in my life, I will count myself lucky." Her positivity talk doesn't seem to have lasted long on her. I think it's a weak moment, made entirely from the fear we both feel for the girl named Jenny.

So I do the thing she does. "We will see the stars again, Jane. We will see justice for the things that have happened here."

She answers with a squeeze of my fingertips.

It is a long time, filled with tense silence, before we hear a noise. It starts with a whimper and then a shaky moan. Jenny cries out to us, "M-m-my b-b-back, m-m-my skin is t-t-torn." She heaves her words. I'm certain each face of the other seven girls is the same as mine. Scrunched and wincing in desperate empathy. "P-p-please help me." She starts to sob, and my need to help her worsens. I grip Jane for dear life, not sure what a single one of us can do.

One of the girls, one of the older girls, Lacey, speaks in a soft tone, "Jenny, you need to get the water from the fridge. One of the bottles of water, and pour it on the wound. Then lie on your stomach and let the air get at it. No shirt or anything touching it. You need to do this now. Don't touch it with your hands at all. It will be fine so long as it doesn't get infected."

"Okay." She sniffles and moves, making small noises.

Stumbled steps.

A groan.

The fridge—first she bumps into it and then opens it.

Water bottles and food are moved.

The fridge door closes.

The water bottle lid is unscrewed.

Water pours.

A cry fills the air, shaky and weak.

More water drops to the ground.

Actual sobbing.

A gasp as the water bottle falls to the ground.

Stumbled footsteps.

And then it is quiet again. I believe she has passed out from the pain. I only hope it was on her bed.

Jane sighs. "She's going to die."

I don't have a response to that.

Jane is quiet for a moment before whispering again, "What's your favorite thing in the world?"

I shake my head, not sure I can remember things like that. I make a throaty sound that's meant to be a chuckle but it comes out too much like a cry. "I think my bar has lowered for any sort of standard. I think being in my bathing suit, sitting in a friend's pool, with a drink in my hand and the sun on my face, could count as a top favorite now. Before it wouldn't have even made the list."

"Mine is the History Channel. I miss it, and I never even noticed I watched it too much. The last thing I saw on there was about the women who were spies for Bletchley Park during the second World War, in England. They were common women to everyone who met them, nine thousand housewives and simple shopgirls, but they ended up being discovered as varying types of geniuses. They saved the British armies from many attacks by code breaking and finding patterns in attacks." Her voice cracks. "I miss TV."

I nod, missing everything.

10. THE FIRST SNOWFALL

I force myself to do the push-ups and sit-ups. I force it every day. I don't like exercise, I never have, really, but the weakened state of my body is frightening. I can feel it. I don't fight him at all anymore. There isn't any point. He would win, no matter the effort I gave. So I play his game, I say the right things. I don't even cry anymore. I hate that about myself. I wish I could cry, but I seem unable.

Jane cries more lately. Sometimes when the fridge door is open I see the shock and horror on her face before she realizes I've seen it. She makes herself look calm again. We spend all our time huddled in the corner, giving each other private moments when we go to the bathroom. And even then sometimes we remain while the other pees in the dark. There are no boundaries. No walls. No defenses. He has broken them all, our mighty prince. He has torn down anything that stood between him and our total obedience.

"I don't feel so good." Jenny speaks softly, her words slurring a little. She's slowly gotten sicker and sicker. I did suspect infection, but now I think it's a lack of will to live. I don't think she's eating. Rory hasn't seen her since he beat her mercilessly, still the worst beating I have ever heard in this place.

"You have to eat and drink, Jenny," Lacey calls out to her. We've all been talking more since he nearly killed her. I don't know about them, but for me the realization that we might be dead no matter how we behave has made me chattier. If I'm dead either way, I'd rather have spent my last days talking to them and not being alone.

"I can't eat. I just get sick." Jenny's voice is so weak I can hardly hear her now.

"She's dying. She has an infection. There's no way she'll make it if he doesn't come soon," Jane whispers from her bed.

She opens her fridge and grabs a bottle of water, drinking some and passing the rest to me. I sit in the corner and nod. "I don't know if it's infection. It's been a while since she got hurt, and she said it's turning to scabs pretty well. I think she's just giving up."

In the pale light of the fridge that now seems as bright as the sun, she gives me a weak smile. "It's not so easy to stay strong here."

It's almost as if she has split personalities sometimes. She is strong and brave and almost badass sometimes, and then others she gives in too easily.

There are whispers amongst us, voices and noises of life, but the moment we hear the door we all stop. Like mice freezing when the cat enters the room, we sit and immediately start to pray to a God we don't believe in. Not anymore.

He saunters smugly to a door. Jane slowly closes the fridge, making the room black for us both. When his hand rattles the door and the lock I stiffen, holding myself so tightly I strain my muscles. But it isn't my door he opens. It's Jane's. I back from the corner just slightly; we don't want him to know about the crack we have picked open so we can see each other.

The light in the hallway outlines my door, making it seem as if something supernatural is there, lighting up the space behind it. In the crack, with my one eye I refuse to tear away, I see him walk into her room, casting a shadow like a monster on her.

"My prince, you've found me," she mutters weakly, smiling and staring right in his eyes.

He walks forward. "My beautiful princess, I have found you at last. I've searched high and low." He walks to her, sweeping her up into his arms. He doesn't do the needle with her or Lacey, not always. They've earned his trust. Their rooms are nicer too.

She's small and weak compared to him, but only for a second. Then she's savage. She bites his throat, stabbing something I haven't ever seen before into his shoulder. He screams and backs up toward the light in the hallway, but she kicks the door closed, making the room dark. She flings open the fridge, flooding light into the dark space as she snatches the key from his hands when he reaches for the wood stabbed into his shoulder.

Her eyes meet mine, and in slow motion I watch as she tosses the key at the crack. I reach my hand through as he pulls the thing from his shoulder. I realize then it's splintered wood, no doubt from the wall in her cell.

When the key lands in my hand, his hand drives the spike of wood into her back, changing the look on her face from hopeful to something else. Perhaps it's the end she knew she would meet. "RUN!" she shouts, and falls, tripping him as he tries to reach for me and the key.

The fridge closes and the light is gone. She opened it to save me, to throw me the key. She had a plan.

I back away, pulling my hand out through the crack, slamming my back against the wall of my cell as he punches the thing. I think he breaks it open enough that he reaches through, maybe with his whole arm. I can feel the wind and motion of him swinging it, and yet just missing me. Rage and screaming join the swinging arm and reaching fingertips. But it is all my imagination, for I see nothing.

I stand, clutching the key, shaking and sobbing. The other girls are screaming, he's losing his shit, and Jane is dying. Hot tears slip from my cheeks as slowly my hand lowers to the lock. I turn the key, clicking it once. It's so loud to me, even over their screams, that it echoes in my mind. I am accustomed to the sound being horrid.

I open the door a little, letting light flood the small room from the hall. I glance up, gasping when I see I am looking him right in the eye. I open the door wider, blocking him with it and slipping into the hallway as he screams, "Don't you dare, Princess! Don't you dare!" I pull the key from the lock and close my door again, locking it. I can't help but wince with the sound of the clicking metal inside of the door.

When I turn, there are so many doors and bright lights, I don't know which way to run.

So I start turning keys in locks. When I open a door to a blonde girl with a crazy look in her eyes, I toss the key at her. "Free the rest; I'll find the way out." I know she's Lacey.

I turn again, running for the main entry as far as guessing will get me.

One door is a closet, with clean linens, the ones we change our own bedding with once a month.

Another door is the stairs to the bathroom. I have been carried up it many times.

I turn and open the last door on my left to find a set of stairs I have never seen before. So I climb until I find a hatch. I push on it, my poor feeble arms failing me. Just as I am about to give up I feel a switch next to the latch in the ceiling. I press it, sighing as the lid that is the ceiling lifts and the floor of a garage, the barn next to the cabin, is revealed.

I pull myself out. My legs are weak from limits to workouts and walking, and my skin instantly tenses, maybe afraid of the elements that might be out here.

My feet are cold and bare, but I don't bother acknowledging the sniveling my addled brain is attempting.

Jane has died to free me.

When I get outside, the air around me is crisp and cold. I pause, taking in the breathtaking view of the mountains.

I glance back at the hatch in the floor, but no one is coming. I nearly walk back to see what they're doing, but something inside of me screams for me to run, just the way Jane said it. So I do.

I turn and flee from the barn, running down the driveway and across the street to the woods. I push myself hard, until the woods cover me.

The mist swirls, attempting to blind me, but I don't dare back down. I push through, sucking in air so heavy I can barely get it in all the way. Something in my back stings. It's the thick mountain air and the elevation in my lungs. I'm not used to exerting myself up here.

Branches stab into my bare feet, but I don't feel them the way I should. My whole body ignores the pain. My mind reels as my fingers reach for the branches to pull me farther along.

My panicked breath and heaving chest are like percussion instruments in my ears, where blood is racing through at a rapid rate. The crunching of the sticks and branches seems to scream of my trail. Even the rocks and dirt try to betray me by announcing where I'm running.

Light filters in through the green canopy as I slide over logs and branches to get deeper into the silent woods.

Then I hear it—the worst sound ever.

"Ashley! I know you think you can get away, but it's a hundred miles in every direction! Princess, we can talk about this!"

I duck, hiding behind a log and some ferns. I know my dark hair and filthy skin have to be shielding me, camouflaging me from his eyes, but the shaking in my aching body and groggy mind seems to make the woods move in an unnatural way. The trees vibrate with me, and the leaves crinkle and crunch even though nothing is moving, nothing but my beating heart.

"Ash, my sweet princess, I'm not mad, I swear! Just come out and let me tend to your wounds! Come on, Princess, come back!"

His voice grates on my skin, his accent driving me crazy. It doesn't matter if he whispers or shouts, the sound is the same. It nauseates me and haunts my mind with memories—all groggy. But his whispering breath on my rocking body is as clear there in my mind as it is in the woods. Him inside me, pushing harder, spreading me open to him as he violates even my soul.

I hold my breath as he enters the woods. "You're bleeding! Let me make it better! The animals will track you!"

I cringe, thinking about him, but I don't move. I don't dare run for it. I wait. He can't see me, and I might have run in any direction for all he knows.

His breath and heavy steps fill the forest with echoing noise. It's then I see the clouds rolling in behind us, over the mountain peaks. I realize the air is colder than I thought it was. It's winter, I think.

I hold my breath, straining my lungs and making the pounding in my head worsen, but it isn't worth it to let him find me. I force the image of him pinning me down, whispering his love for me with every thrust. It stops the pain, and it pushes it away with intense amounts of fear.

"Ash!" His voice sounds farther away, but I don't lift my head to look. I wait, because there is no way to be sure. My ears are still thick from the thin air and elevation.

A hot shiver breaks out, making me breathe again. The feeling of a fever and possibly a sickness of sorts starts to surface. I hope I'm not sick, but being in a dank cellar for months can't be good for anyone.

I don't know how long I've been here. I don't know how long I will last here in the woods, in the cold, bleeding from my feet and hands. I do know I will die here freezing, surrounded by trees, before

I will let him find me. I will lie back and stare at the stars for Jane and me. Together we will see the stars one last time.

His footsteps crunch, leading away from me, but his words are still there. "When I find you, you'll be punished for every day you hide! Make no mistake, Princess, I'll find you!"

The word *Princess* makes me want to vomit.

I sit, wondering if he's messing with me, waiting for me to make the mistake of standing. But I'm not that dumb. Not to mention, my legs are not that strong. They've sort of failed me, in either paralyzing fear or crippling weakness. When I needed them they worked, but now they're heavy like they're soaked or caked in mud.

My brain whispers something about adrenaline and lactic acid, but I don't care for the nurse's knowledge I have locked away from the three months of courses I've taken.

I care about getting off this hill and finding help.

When I don't hear him again I start to breathe normally. I don't move until I hear the Jeep. He skids away, driving like a maniac. The maniac I didn't know he was.

Then the adrenaline hits again.

I force myself to stand, pushing my feet to run from the forest, toward the barn. The road will allow an easier escape than the woods.

I turn from the woods, making my feet and legs move as I make my way to the road. The drive up here to the cabin revealed several cabins along the way. If I can get to one before he finds me, I might make it. I nearly go back for them, the other girls. But in my racked brain I know one of them gave him the key. They don't want to leave. They don't want to be free. They fear his wrath more than they desire freedom.

I hate myself for thinking it, but I don't believe they deserve the freedom my friend—no, my sister—died for. She became family in there, in that hole.

I run down into the ditch, splashing the frigid water up my legs as I make my way to the closest driveway. I'm out of breath and light-headed, but clear enough in thought to realize the closest cabin is a mistake. He'll go there once he realizes I haven't made it to the bottom of the hill.

I run past the second driveway, scrambling from the ditch and crossing it carefully. When I get to the third driveway I almost run up it, but my brother's voice rings through my head. "Three times lucky." I don't know why; perhaps because I'm a bit dehydrated and exhausted and my mental state is a mess.

The fourth driveway is a ways down the hill. The blind corners along the road frighten me. I struggle to get past the ditches and rocks. My feet have stopped hurting, with the cold water making them numb.

Breathlessly, I climb up into the fourth driveway, staggering and limping as my muscles freeze up.

I back up the driveway, forcing myself to watch the road and woods, in case he's there somehow. He's smarter than I am.

My legs buckle, dropping me like a sack of rocks to the gravel. I wince, feeling the jarring in my neck, but I grip the cold rocks and scramble back up.

A shrill noise rips through the air. It's an animal, but I don't know what it is. It sounds terrifying and close by. I hurry, limping brutally because the lower part of my left leg has gone totally numb.

The cabin is nicer than his, but has no barn for the ATVs and snowmobiles. I hurry to the back, trying every window and door. None are open or unlocked. I slide down the back of the door, desperate to rest a minute and listen for him. I'm just grateful the snow hasn't fallen up here yet. The path would lead him right to me.

Every sound becomes louder as my breath softens in hesitation. I expect him to run from the woods any moment, leash and collar in hand, to drag me back to my cell like a caged animal. I expect him to make me beg and make me tell him I love him and he's the man for me. I expect to die crying and begging for it—not his love but death itself.

My eyes long to close, my body whispers *Let's give up* as my heart aches from the memories that are filtering back in. Memories I will never be rid of or solve even. I won't ever know what it all meant to him, what I am to him. What I am representing or curing. What void I am filling. What in God's name could have happened to him to make him so evil?

A sound catches my cold ears. I glance up into the darkening sky as snowflakes begin to fall. A tear drips from my eye as I realize it's the first snow of the season. It's the first snow I have seen in a very long time. Each flake feels like a little burst of energy and bravery. Each one is a kiss from my friend, whispering for me to run more. Run down the hill. Find a vehicle. It's what Jane would have done.

The sound gets louder as I realize it's a vehicle making its way up the hill.

I push away the sound of the tires skidding around the gravel corners, and stare up into the sky as it becomes like a vortex. The flakes swirl, taking my care and depth perception away. I tilt my head even more, letting the fat flakes fall into my mouth and land on my lashes.

I don't close my eyes. I don't try to block out the sound as it gets closer. I stare up into the snow and force a memory, one of a time I was happy. It was a moment, fleeting and precious. Her face makes me happy. She brings me joy as she becomes all I see in the swirling snow. Jane laughing and talking and living. Jane the way she was before Rory put us in a cage and made us something in his image.

I close my eyes and whisper to her, "Thank you, Jane." When I open them I have a plan.

11. POISONED PRINCESSES IN A ROW

The cage is different than it was last time.

He's different too.

He's no longer my prince; he no longer loves me.

Now, hours later, my wrists tear a bit, dripping blood down them onto my shoulders and back. I hang from a meat hook, suspended for his pleasure. It changes daily. Sometimes it's the back of a hand, others it's the feel of a rope stinging my back with every whip. The room is not a nice place. It's not a proper cell. It's just a spot for him to torture. And there is light here, just enough that I might see the hate on his face when he strikes me.

Jane walks through the room. At first I assume I'm dead too, but then I realize there's just too much pain for me to be dead. Even God is not that cruel.

"Hold on, Ash. You are so close to being free." Her voice is a whisper on the wind, and her lips do not move. She smiles at me and then she's gone. She looks different now, peaceful and pretty, and for some reason I want to call her Bethany.

It's almost comical to me, and clearly her, that I am back here. I'd gotten away. I had to run for it.

I'd thought the vehicle was him, the one I'd heard coming up the hill. But it wasn't. When I snuck down the hill and stole a truck, he was waiting at the bottom of the hill for me.

At the turnoff to Granger Mountain.

I just made it to the road when he rammed me with the Jeep, flipping the truck down a small ravine. The last thing I remember was rolling down the ravine and then waking here, hands bound and hanging over his shoulders. He was carrying me down the staircase. I passed my old door, my eyes half open and my heart completely broken. It was the strangest sensation. I wanted to go back in that cell. It was a safe place for me.

Now I hang here, waiting to be freed like Jane has promised, but certain that even death will not free me from here.

My eyelids grow heavy, too heavy. Maybe the loss of blood, maybe the exhaustion, maybe the torture. I don't know which, but one of them claims me, and my eyes close.

Cold surrounds me, opening my eyes, but I don't see. Jane is there. She cups my face, saying something, but my ears don't hear. Everything is blocked and plugged and bursting. She lifts my face, and instantly in the light that's above us, I see him. He's covered in blood, but he's not clear. He's fuzzy, no . . . blurry. He washes his hands in the water above my face, looking directly at me. A sick smile crosses his face, his face that I can't make any clearer than it is—even though now I see him for exactly who he is.

It's then that my lungs try to explode inside of my chest and I realize *I'm* in the water. He's washing his hands and watching me sink.

I start to thrash, kicking and screaming for the surface. Jane helps, I swear it. She pulls me to her, pressing her lips against my panicked mouth, and offering up air. The current catches me, dragging me away from him.

The sick smile vanishes as he watches me sail away, away to a freedom he doesn't know I will find. He doesn't know she has stayed behind to help me.

Jane—no, Bethany—presses her lips to mine again, filling my mouth with air.

The world goes dark and then light, and it flashes so many times I don't know if it's day or night.

But suddenly there's sand and a man, and he tells me it's going to be okay. I close my eyes, and see Bethany who called herself Jane one last time. Everything swirls and vanishes. I open my eyes to a sky filled with clouds shaped like horses. I blink three times but they remain, so I whisper to them, "Tell me about the swans, the way the swans circle the stars and shoot across the sky."

I gasp my way out of Ashley, sputtering and coughing and choking from the river. Anger has built right up inside of me. The poor girl has relived every minute of that horror, and I don't have a clue as to who the man is.

Before I get a handle on myself I quickly blurt out in a croak, "Granger Mountain. The cabin's at Granger Mountain. The cabin with the huge detached garage off the side. Really fancy. The other girls are there still." Then I cough again and sputter a few more times as my body realizes it's not in pain and it's not drowning. The girl's monitors start going crazy. I turn my head, opening my eyes, and watch as a smile curls upon her lips, and the heart monitor stops completely, just flatlining.

A tear slips down my cheek as I watch her go.

"You all right?"

I blink, shocked to see Dash, but grateful. He wraps himself around me, lifting me off the table. "You're shaking. Last time, Jane. You can't do a mind run again after this one."

I hold tight to him. He tries to kiss me, but I bury my face in his chest. I can't do affection just yet. Not after the last moments of her life being what they were.

Angie comes barreling in, grabbing me and giving me a hard stare. "They need ya to debrief fast. She's gone, we've been keeping her alive, and I was scared shitless she'd die with ya in there. Lord suffering, you look rough. They want answers, Jane."

"I don't have any." The anger comes back fast. I lift my face, giving Dash a look. "You screwed with the results. She saw you and Rory as the bad guys the entire time. I never got a clear look at him."

Dash's eyes narrow. "Impossible."

"And yet not. She never gave up a single clue. The story started with you as the bad professor and moved into Rory, and his being a naughty spy." I choke a bit on the words. "My story got too mingled up in hers. I need to go with the team." Dash opens his mouth to argue but I snarl, *"If you hadn't touched the recording—"*

"It doesn't matter what happened. We have the local uniforms on their way. The team's been dispatched."

I glance about the room. "Where's Rory?"

"He's headed there with them. They're leaving in a minute."

I pluck the monitors off me and jump from the bed, struggling for a second before my legs remember who they belong to. I blast through the door with Angie and Dash shouting at me, but I don't listen. I hurry out the front of the building where the helicopter is, waving at them when I get close. They look ready to take off, but wait for me. Rory gives me a wide grin. It's sarcastic and shitty.

I glare, hating Dash just a little for screwing with the system. My system was perfect. My plan was perfect. I went in first to get a clue of how to add myself into her life and memory. Once I saw the cells and the other girls, I knew I could be one of them. I had a plan. *Damned Dash!*

I hurry to the chopper, keeping my head low, and jump into the back. Rory grins. "Thought you needed a little rest. How'd ya get past Angie? Did they debrief you yet?"

I roll my eyes. "Angie's still dealing with the aftermath. The girl died on the table. She has to clean that up and do the paperwork. I'll e-mail my report as we fly and they can debrief me later." I drag my phone out and start drafting an e-mail as we fly to the airport to board our private jet.

"How was it? What are we looking for? Did you see anything?"

"I'll know the house when we get to the road. He made the mistake of taking her there once in the light of day." I cringe, hearing his voice. My transfer to the military criminal and terrorist profiling section can't come quick enough.

I have always liked being his partner, and I always imagined I'd be sad to see either of us go. I have always liked Rory and his magical accent. Now, I can't wait for this file to be closed. It's going to take me a while to get past the whole thing. It's the reason I always take Dash in as the bad guy—I can look past anything he says or does or any evil he commits. I love him. It's also the reason I never take strangers or people like Rory into a mind run—I can't forgive everything they do in there. There is no love between us, and I don't have feelings that are stronger than the mind run. Not for him.

The flight from DC to Washington is long enough to finish a detailed report and e-mail the higher-ups about my situation. I don't tell them that Rory and Dash ruined the run, but I do mention that the original recording malfunctioned, and the new ones weren't adequate.

We land in Washington and run to the next chopper, the one that will take us to Granger Mountain.

"What's he like, our boy?" Rory asks as he buckles in and pulls on his headset.

I shake my head, sending the last of the details. "Not a clue. Dash and you screwing with my recording messed the entire thing up."

He winces. "Right, sorry about that. He was a bit miffed when he saw how many times good old Dr. Derek Russo appeared in your scenarios. Don't suppose you can blame the old chap for being a bit worried. You've pretty much made him the worst monster a man can be, over and over. I think he supposed you might be into things he wasn't completely comfortable with."

I lift my middle finger, refusing to tell him why I chose Dash to be my Mr. X in every scenario. That is going to remain a private matter if my life depends on it.

I press "send" just as the helicopter pilot gives me a look. "We have local uniforms on the ground, speeding to Granger Mountain as we speak. They should be about ten minutes behind us."

I nod, putting my phone away and ignoring the texts I'm getting from the guy responsible for the fact I don't know who our perp is.

Rory looks worried when the helicopter lowers over the highway, weaving around at the base of a mountain. "You sure you're all right? You look pissed."

I shake my head. "No, I'm not all right. And yes, I am pissed."

He nods. "Excellent. Hopefully our guy is there then, so you can take out some rage on him!"

I give him my grimmest smile. "Let's pray for that." The feeling of the ropes around her wrist, and the blood dripping down her arms, still haunts me. I plan on killing this guy a couple of different ways.

As we pass several mountains, I tingle with anxiety of recognition when I see the crashed truck at the base of the hill by the ravine. "We're on the right path. There's the truck." I point and let my eyes trail up the road. The pilot lowers as much as he can and follows it exactly.

We fly by several beautiful homes, all truly stunning and like nothing I have ever been in. Not in my real mind anyway. Riding other people's minds has afforded me houses and lifestyles like I could never even imagine. It's also put me in hell like I have never imagined either. I'll take my mediocre lifestyle and my shallow problems over this shit any day.

As we climb, my insides tighten.

I see the house that was four houses down, the one she hid behind. My mouth dries and my heart rate increases as we pass the third house. Then the second one. As we round the corner, I point. "This is it." I point to the place with the garage next to it. It's exactly as she recalled.

The chopper lowers with the three military personnel dropping out, guns and eyes at the ready. They start to storm the house, kicking the door in and clearing before we come out. But I don't wait. I grab a gun from the racks and jump down too, running past the house and into the garage. Rory follows me. His footsteps don't make me worried; he's my partner. He has my back. Even if he is still sort of the creepy man of my dreams and nightmares.

And this is why I choose Dash.

He can be the man of my nightmares, but in the end it doesn't stay. Not like with Rory. I've always incorporated Rory. Just never as the bad guy.

I grab the door handle of the barn, my whole journey inside of her mind flashing before my eyes. The word *barn* is even hers. In my mind I use the word *garage*.

The door's locked, so I nudge it with my shoulder.

"Wait!" One of the soldiers comes barreling out of the house, kicking the front door off its hinges and brandishing his gun as he clears past the snowmobiles and ATVs. He creeps about, listening and making hand signals I haven't seen in a while. I walk straight for the hatch, pressing the button on the wall that matches the one below. As it lifts the soldier gives me a look. "Oh, wow."

I nod. "It's bad down there, so let's not be hasty. Clear every closet. I don't know the entirety of the floor plan, but it's mostly cells."

Rory gives me a dubious stare. "Cells?"

I lift a hand, shaking my head. "You are gonna barf when you read that report." He has a serious issue with women who are tortured and raped.

"Great." He nods, following the soldier down the stairs into the dark. I go last, my skin crawling and my stomach aching.

As I get halfway down the stairs the soldier cries, "One dead in a cell so far." I know whom he means, and I am sorry for the girl whose life I took on. She is perhaps the bravest person I have ever seen, even if she was long dead after I saw her.

The whole place reeks of death and human waste. I had never noticed the smell, inside of Ashley's mind. The smell was nothing compared to the other horrors, I suppose.

But to us it's almost unbearable. We cover our faces as we clear the areas, kicking in cells.

Rory opens a door, but I stop him. "That's just the bedroom and bathroom where he played out his fantasies with them. It's not a cell. The injured women are in the cells here—we need to help them."

He gives me another awkward look, but closes the door. I know he just doesn't want to go farther in. He doesn't want to see the girls. But he doesn't realize I'm trying to help him; seeing the room where they were assaulted isn't going to be better for him. Sexual assault is his kryptonite. For all his joking, he's not a fan of the scenes where it's going on.

A soldier comes in behind me, gun up. I nod at the room. "You go clear up there, and we'll check it after."

"Clear. We got another deceased," one soldier cries out.

The other soldier responds, sounding a little upset, "Yeah, and another here!"

Rory gives me a look, one that suggests he might get sick. "Looks like he was ready for us."

"Open the doors!" I hurry to the rooms where the voices had become almost like friends. A soldier comes, smashing the door open. The redhead lies on the floor, staring up at us. Her eyes have glazed over, and I know she hasn't been dead long. Her thick, ropey hair is strewn about the floor around her, like a newly deceased Rapunzel.

Each room is the same. When I reach the room with the girl whose life I took, Jane, I drop to my knees. Her name isn't Jane in the real world. I pretended I was her in Ashley's mind, making Ashley see this brave young woman as me so she would trust me even more. The girl is cold as ice and her skin is gray, and I can tell she's been dead for days. The rigor is gone.

I cup her hand in mine, and for a moment I feel like we might have been sisters, even if it was just for a second.

"They're all dead, and it's clear," Rory says blankly.

"He left them, just like he knew we would find them," I mutter. "He didn't even dispose of them—bury them."

Rory places a hand on my shoulder. "I gotta go back up. I can't do this. You were right."

I would have smiled had it been any normal case, maybe even made fun of him for his weak stomach. But this time I understand. It's the fucking sickest thing we have yet to encounter. The other perps we have come across murdered after they tortured or raped, but these girls have been years in the process of slow and painful destruction. To find each one dead is a blow I wasn't prepared for. We never released any information about finding the girl on the shores of the river. He shouldn't have known she survived.

I don't get a chance to digest what we have found. Forensics and the local uniforms arrive, and my instincts kick in, take over.

We catalogue, we ID, we photograph everything, and we spend twenty-four straight hours living in their world. It isn't even scratching the surface, but it is getting rid of the bodies, bagging and tagging so the morgue can start their work.

At the end of it all I am standing in the kitchen, admiring the view as the sun begins to set, just as I did when Ashley was here. I remember the view, but I had seen it from her eyes.

"You all right?"

I look at Rory as he walks into the house, and shake my head.

"I wish we'd found even one alive. I can't believe he poisoned them all."

"Apart from the one with the stab wounds in her back. She definitely didn't get poisoned, right?"

That makes me lower my gaze. "No. She died a few days before the others. She was the reason our girl got out. Ashley escaped because that girl saved her."

His right eye twitches. "I can't talk about this in here, Jane. I don't mean to flake on you, but this place—it's freaking me out. Can we talk about it away from here where it'll be more of a file and less of a reality? Those girls, their life here—I can't." He shakes his head and turns, waving a hand. "I'll take spies and terrorism and hostages any day of the week over this shit. Let's get the hell out of here. They have an address on the owner. We're going to Seattle to check him out."

I walk behind him, feeling the same vibe he is. I just want to be away from this.

12. LITTLE ORPHAN JANEY

The ring on my finger feels like it weighs a ton.

"Hey, did you talk to Rory today?"

I shake my head at Dash, not really into the conversation. There's a pit in the bottom of my stomach. I stare out the window, finding horses in the clouds. I can't help but wonder what Ashley or Bethany found in the clouds.

"I did. He says the address turned out to be another fiasco. The owner of the Granger Mountain home died in a tragic car accident two years ago. The mountain getaway and his place in the city are under contest, with several relatives warring over it all. It belonged to him and his wife. She died of cancer five years ago. They had a son and daughter and an adopted daughter." Dash wrinkles his nose, tapping his fingers along the steering wheel. "Anyway, the biological son and daughter tried to screw the adopted daughter out of everything. Got the dad to sign everything over to them and leave the adopted girl out completely." He shakes his head. "She was adopted when she was three years old. She's been their little sister for thirty-something years, and they still tried to screw her over. I can't even imagine people like that existing." His voice fades off as he drives into a suburb that I'm starting to get scared his parents live in. Perfect homes for perfect families made of perfect people.

I twist the ring on my finger and nod, half listening.

"I guess we all know worse people exist, don't we?" He gives me a look when we pause at a stop sign. "You okay?"

I look behind us, checking for other cars since he's sitting at the sign. We have hardly seen any cars since we got into the suburbs. "I will be when we solve it. You know how I like to mull over details until we get it right? Are you going to go?" I ask.

"Not until you tell me you're going to be with it and not obsessed with the case."

I lean in, feeling myself stuck in the mind ride and the facts and the missing information. This distracted zombie act is one reason he hates that I do this job. I place the softest of kisses on his lips, resting there for a breath. "I can forget about it for the Thanksgiving weekend of doom you have planned for me. So long as you tell me you don't live in this bullshit neighborhood with the perfect families everywhere?"

He winces. "I don't live here." He's been acting funny too, and with him I know it's not the case. He kisses back, smiling against my lips. "Stop being scared to meet my mother. She's way less frightening than any of the files you've worked. She's easy—bring her a drink and compliment her hair and jewelry, she'll love you forever."

I smile back, loving that he thinks his mom is scaring me, instead of my brain being stuck on a file that's unsolved. He pulls back, stroking my cheek with his finger and staring into my eyes. For the first time I'm actually glad I didn't take him with me to that place. I'm glad he completely screwed up and made Rory the bad guy. If I only see Rory a couple of times a year, no biggie. But seeing Dash every day might get hard if I imagine him doing those things to Ashley.

He leans in, kissing my forehead. "Thank you for doing this. You have no idea how excited she'll be—they'll be." I smile wide, loving the funny look on his face. He's as worried about his family as I am, but he's lying to himself about it. Bringing home an orphan to Virginia is a bad idea; 'round here people need family to prove who they are. He's lucky I love him. Who am I kidding? I'm lucky he loves me. Being with him smooths over the rough edges and plugs the holes and softens the gaps. I am an actual person with him.

My whole body fills with a warm glow until he winces as he pulls away from the stop sign finally and says, "But there are a couple of things we need to discuss, about my family."

I cock an eyebrow. "We are almost there, aren't we? You saved telling me stuff until we got here?"

He takes a deep breath, making a turn onto another street. "It's not so bad, just little things like they are richer than I might have mentioned, and we have to sleep in separate rooms. Or she'll think you're easy."

"I am easy," I mutter through bared teeth.

He laughs like he doesn't believe it, but I don't have the same regard for sex many other girls do. I don't see the rules and boundaries they do. His other words flit about my brain. "Richer than you might have mentioned?" I can't believe this is happening.

"Right." He laughs again, weakly and sort of like a girl might. A nervous girl. A nervous schoolgirl. "Just a bit. Like the top of the food chain in a country-club family."

"So they are crazy rich and we have to sleep apart? But we're engaged." I lift the huge ring weighing my finger down. Of course it's huge; he's probably used a fucking trust fund to pay for the fucking thing. Fuck. I need to stop cussing so much! Shit!

"But we are not *married*. There would be a scandal for my poor mother if anyone ever knew that we shared a bed. There would be talk of the vengeful slut from the North who befouled my poor mother's house. And of course she would have to let them slander you, out of respect for me. Trust me, this is not where you draw attention to the fact you're a Yankee."

"You just said befouled? You're getting weird. And you Southerners do realize we're all American, right?" Friggin' Southerners with their War of Northern Aggression bullshit. I am suddenly terrified of this woman.

"You're licking your nose again." He smiles, nodding at me like this whole thing is nothing. "Stop being nervous. This is why I never warned you; you'd be half mad by now if I had. You'll be fine, just try not to flash your Gene Simmons tongue at my parents. Licking one's nose is a bit circus freak for them, especially with the eyes being different colored. All you need is to flutter them the way you do and lick your nose, and my mother will pass out."

"I'll remember that." I sigh. I want to say he's a circus freak, but I don't. I know what I am and what he is. At least I thought I knew what he was.

He reaches for me, holding my hand. "We just can't share a bed. It's no big deal. And you should know they have some quirks, just not licking noses or different-colored eyes. I can't even explain it, you just have to see it."

Quirks? Licking my nose is a quirk? It's a nervous habit. I sit back in my seat and send a quick text to one of the secretaries Rory and I use to ensure we have everything we need.

He turns out of the snooty-looking area, making my breathing easier as he heads along a long and winding road. I start to relax until I realize he has driven to an area with estates and houses so big I can't breathe again. They look like the White House.

"Do they own a hotel?" I ask, actually scared of the answer. His laugh does nothing to soothe me.

My insides tighten, and I send a text to Angie demanding to know why she didn't warn me of this.

How could you send me to the South and not tell me his parents are ESTATE RICH? You suck!

Her reply appears quickly.

You know I love you, but there was no warning you. It's big, like hotel big. Expect a huge group of people to greet you too, like forty. Use your best manners and act like a demure orphan, the sweet and demure orphan I know is in there!

I choke. Demure? Shit!

"You okay?" He sounds worried.

I nod and shrug in a jerky movement and look out the side window until my phone buzzes again.

Forget them, remember you're a killer with uncanny instincts and ex-military and exceptionally badass! Just keep looking around the room, figuring out ways to kill them.

That text makes me smile, so I look like an idiot when we drive up to a gate with boys peeping over the ledge. Not real boys, mind you, but cast-iron boys, naked cast-iron boys. The weird smile stays on my face, frozen, as I try to understand the naked peeping boys.

As the gates open, my heart starts to skip beats, like it's seizing.

The long drive up to the house is ridiculous—old-movie-that-Angie-has-made-me-watch ridiculous. Hedges are carved like we are at a children's zoo or some crap. They aren't the weirdest part either. No, a hedge shaped like an animal is crazy, but the massive fountain is worse. It has three naked boys frolicking in the water, like they're splashing, only they're made of cast iron like the other boys.

The pool, oddly enough, is out front and long and thin; not what you'd expect for a house of such grandeur. At the very end of the long driveway is another cast-iron sculpture of two boys, naked boys, playing leapfrog. I cough a little to avoid the questions threatening to leave my lips about his parents' obsession with naked boys. It's something I have seen only in Europe and usually at overly fancy places with stodgy and annoying people who think too much of their own opinions and self-worth.

At the end of the weird and pervy driveway is a house that puts all houses, and most Italian castles, to shame. It's Elizabethan in style if I'm not mistaken, which I know only because I have actually taken the tours, and it has turrets, real ones.

No, the house I cannot prepare for.

It looks like it might still have slaves and a cotton plantation out back, but it's the castle edition of plantation house tours.

The front steps form a half oval with staircases on either side, in case you prefer to leave from the left instead of the right. The kind you would imagine a woman in one of those huge old-fashioned dresses going down, like *Cinderella*, the Disney cartoon.

I immediately start sweating. He reaches over. "See, I knew you'd like it." The stupid smile is still plastered in shock to my face from the cheeky spy comment, so he thinks I love it.

When he parks, a man comes out to the car. Dash jumps out, offering the man a hug. He's older, clearly Dash's father, with gray hair and a white mustache. He's in a suit, which makes me uncomfortable, but if I lived here I would wear a suit every day too. Why not?

"Jane, this is Nichols, our driver and valet."

I don't understand what that means. I have seen thirty-two countries and fought in a war, and I still don't know what a valet does. I assume he means valet parking, as in he has a man who is paid a salary to park cars. How did I not know this was a job possibility?

The man bows to me, making me sweat more. "Miss Jane, it is lovely to finally meet you."

He's English, of course. Why wouldn't he be?

"Jane." Dash mutters my name. It means I'm not doing the right thing. He and Angie always say, *Jane, the correct response is to blah blah blah*, when I am not making the right choice or action or saying the right thing.

"It's so nice to meet you, sir." I step out as he gets the door and offer him my hand. He gives Dash a strange look and smiles wide like he knows a secret I don't.

Dash blushes. Clearly I didn't have the right response.

"Young Master Benjamin has spoken very highly of you, miss."

He said *master*? Did he, or did I mishear because of the accent?

Dash slides an arm behind my back, leading me to the large front steps. "Oh, Nichols, you old charmer." I notice there is a difference in Dash's tone and accent. He speaks differently here. There's an affect in his words he doesn't have in the North.

He leads me up the stairs, leaving our bags in the car. I glance back, and the poor old man is lifting them from the trunk. I pull from Dash's arm but am whisked back in. "You will let the poor man do his job, Jane. He'll think you think he can't do it."

I snarl under my breath and pull my cell phone from my pocket, sending the message I had typed out to Nancy, the secretary whom I consider my favorite. "Mr. Nichols, can you leave my bags, please? I'm staying at the inn in Middleton, actually."

"You mean Middleburg, miss? Am I to understand you have made prior arrangements?" He asks like he might chuckle.

Dash's hand tightens on my waist, making me nearly jump, but I breathe through it. I will not let him see me cry because he may or may not have lied about his entire fucking childhood. When he said *country-club rich*, he knew I thought he meant I might have to drink a martini and smile when they told weird stories about their trips abroad. I might have to wear argyle. He lied. When he said *affluent* he meant *blue blood*. When he said *hoity-toity* he meant something I don't think I have a measurement for.

I am fuming, which is almost refreshing since my brain desperately wants to solve the murder and vicious torture of eleven women.

But that's cool, we can hang here and they can all laugh and wear sweaters and make me drinks I don't like.

"Will the young lady be staying here, sir?" poor Nichols asks softly.

"Oh, you've arrived!" someone says from the top of the stairs.

My head snaps back from the driver to a blonde woman more intimidating than I have ever seen. "Staying here? Of course you both will be. Right, darling, please come in." She's also English, so I don't know if she's his mother or another form of modern-day slavery.

"She'll be staying here," Dash says calmly to the serf and then turns his head to the woman in front of us. "Mother!"

His mother is British? Does that make him British?

I feel like that's something people in a relationship would have talked about by now. How could he not tell me he's British? My brain whispers that it might be one of those *I don't share so he doesn't share* things. Not to mention, I don't really ask. I wish I had now.

I wish she just carried a knife or a gun so I could treat her appropriately, like a threat. But she doesn't. She has a slightly sharp canine like Dash and is so beautiful I don't know whether to kiss her or ask for the person who does her makeup for my next spy assignment when I leave the mind running behind.

She grabs my shoulders, squeezing slightly, and pretends to kiss my cheek. I gulp, actually out loud, and freeze as she brushes our cheeks, acting like she's kissing, but instead saying the word *kiss* as she does it. She's so tall I feel like a dwarf next to her and Dash both.

It's confusing and overwhelming, but she isn't alone.

There's a man who looks like he might be an actor. He's tanned and golden like Dash, tall and broad like Dash, but he's wearing a double-breasted suit. He smiles, and a dimple puckers in his right cheek. His eyes are dazzling blue, and his teeth are so white I press my lips together, looking like I have to pee instead of smiling. My coffee-stained teeth will make him wince; I feel like we both know that at this point. He grabs his son and shakes his hand, awkward also.

The mother has the very same green eyes as Dash—ones that reveal too much. Her disapproval or surprise in me is obvious. I didn't expect his parents to be as old as I suspect they are. But even with her age, she is handsome. Pretty but older in a way that you would use the word *handsome*. And agile. She moves with such grace and manners, making everything I do feel robotic.

My phone vibrates, causing me to glance down at it. It's another text from Angie. You are a superspy! It makes me smile, a real smile, and is followed by a nervous laugh. That lifts the lips of his parents when they look at me.

"You are so much more—well, more than we expected." His mother gushes and looks at Dash. "You never told us she was Asian." She leans in, speaking louder. "Is English your first language?" Her eyes narrow. "Oh, how charming. Your eyes are different colors. Is that a contact? Like a fad you young people are doing?"

I give him a look. He knows what it means but laughs it off a little nervously. "Jane's family is Irish and Scottish. Not Asian, Mother. And her eyes are naturally that way."

"Right, of course they are. It's a birth defect. My cousin had it. Died early." Dash's father gives me an appraising stare. "You do look quite Asian for an Irish girl." His father is English as well and possibly a bigger asshole than his mom. So that makes me excited. Not only do they hate the Irish, they loathe the Scottish, and they think I'm Asian. Adding to all of that the fact I have a birth defect, which may or may not kill me early on. I just smile, forcing silence.

Dash grips my arm. His eyes are worried, intensely worried. Nichols strolls past us with my bags. I quickly skirt the parents as they turn their focus to their son and start the millions of questions. I walk with Nichols. "Sir, I need my bags."

He turns, shaking his head so subtly I nearly miss it.

I nod, reaching for them. His eyes dart to the family, but I insist and snatch my bag. "I have a reservation." He winces as I say it.

"Jane, dearest, you must stay here." She tries to force the issue.

I suspect Dash's mother is a special woman, and I will end up feeling a special fondness for her, but to avoid that specialness getting out of hand or becoming something negative, I turn and shake my head. "I am so sorry, but I was raised Catholic by some very stringent nuns, and they would never have heard of me staying in a gentleman's home when we are unwed." I feel like an idiot, but I don't want to talk like the heathen I am while trying to convince them I have some fucking boundaries . . .

His mother's jaw drops. "Catholic?" I can nearly hear her dying inside. It's point one for Jane, and I am not giving it up. Not even when his green eyes turn to me, flashing disappointment. I could stab him in the eye for the lies he's told to get me here.

I carry my bag back to the car. "I was just coming in to say hello and then getting Das—Benjamin to take me to my hotel— inn. It's an inn."

His mother nods her head in my direction. "We have a guesthouse for just these sorts of situations. Now surely nuns wouldn't shun you, such a devout Catholic girl, for staying in a guesthouse? The rooms are quite sizable and you will find the general splendor of the guest house more to your liking, I believe."

I open my mouth and snap my jaw shut. A point for Mrs. Dash.

Nichols snatches my bag back and hustles inside before I attempt to do his job again.

Dash grabs my hand and pulls me along, all the while still chatting with his father about something to do with golf.

His mother loops her arm in mine, placing a perfectly manicured hand on my arm. "Benjamin did mention that you were orphaned during a terrible car accident when you were a young girl. How tragic."

The sweating starts again. I don't understand why she's touching me. I don't touch people I don't know, ever. It's weird to go sharing yourself so easily.

She leans in, her words turning to a full whisper: "We are grateful to be able to offer you our family as a replacement for your own. We only hope we are able to help you fit in." She pats my arm and walks gracefully inside, floating as if steered by the giant carrot in her ass. "I have laid out some dresses for you, something more suitable for tonight."

I want to stab Dash, but I remind myself repeatedly that he isn't at fault. It doesn't work because, in my mind, he is completely at fault. He lied. He lied and he knows it.

But meeting them confirms exactly why he lied.

I never would have come.

A girl in a maid's uniform, and not the naughty Halloween kind, slinks up next to me and curtseys. Dash's mother nods at the girl. "Evangeline will show you to your room."

"Please, come with me." The maid holds a soft hand out for me, guiding me in another direction. I sigh the moment we are out of range of their prying eyes.

"Tell me you aren't as stuffy as they are."

She gives me a coy grin. "I try not to be, but they prefer we all have the same set of manners, opinions, and habits."

"Can you not curtsey and act stuffy when it's just us?"

She nods. "If that is what you wish." She winks animatedly, giving the exact opposite effect a wink is meant to. Instead of it feeling like she is joking, I feel like she is laughing at me. But she does seem to relax a bit when she speaks again. "They just stopped making the staff line up on the stairs in formation when they arrived home. Apparently they still have to do it in Europe, but here in Virginia everyone finds it antiquated, so they have told us we no longer have to."

Good God. "Where are you from?" I ask, glancing around the vast hallways and huge rooms as my stomach balls into knots I am certain will never heal.

She pauses, giving me a look. "What do you mean? Here, of course."

I roll my eyes as she leads me to a set of doors. "You were bred in captivity?"

She lifts a brow. "No, Canada, actually. I'm from the East Coast, but I have worked here for five years. Since I turned eighteen." She opens the back doors to a terrace that takes my breath away. It's ridiculous, like the house. We walk under a long pergola next to a huge pool with a water slide and a hot tub. I stop. "What's with the two pools? Is one heated?"

She pauses too. "I don't understand what you mean."

"The pool out front and this one—is the one out front the cold pool? Like in Mexico?"

She giggles, as if she were ten years old. "No, it's part of the garden, part of the fountain. That's not a swimming pool out front. This is the only pool."

I don't even say the things floating around in my mind, and change the subject. "How big is the house?"

"Twenty-four thousand square feet for the main house, a thousand square feet for the pool house, and two thousand square feet in the guesthouse." She holds a hand out to the small house that's actually a regular-sized house in the real world. We walk beneath purple flowers and vines growing on the top of the pergola. They smell like lilacs but aren't bushes. I've never seen them this way. It really is beautiful. Even if it's more of a retreat than a personal home.

When we get inside of the guesthouse I sigh. It's cozy and large, a perfect space. The small kitchen is a bar, really, and the sitting area has a huge fireplace and three oversized sofas. There are windows all around the house, letting in tons of natural light.

"There are three bedrooms, all with en suites, for you to choose from." She bows slightly, like she forgot but remembered last minute. "I hope you will be comfortable and let me know if you require anything at all."

I smile and watch her walk away. Dash passes her, looking spicy, so I quickly close the door and head for the bedrooms. He bursts through the door, instantly shouting in a lowered but not less angry tone, "Jane!"

I close the door to a bedroom and pause there, hoping he will just give up and go back to his kind in the house that's the size of an urban high school.

But he doesn't.

He rushes through this door as well, just as I'm pretending to admire the general splendor of the oversized rooms. And looking for things to knock him out with so I can make my escape.

"This is the guesthouse for people with children. It's not suitable for my fiancée." His face is red and weird.

I back up slowly, lifting a finger. "You lied! You are a liar! Mr. Perfect Doctor is a liar! Who knew?" It isn't even strong enough or what I am feeling, but I don't know how to get it all out. I feel like I might explode, but if I do he might end up dead.

He slumps, and my Dash comes sailing back in. "You never would have come. And I desperately needed you to come. Why can't you see that? You aren't easy to introduce because you like your routine and you hate everyone."

"What! I don't hate everyone." *He's blaming me?* I fling my arms, suddenly angrier than I have ever been. He's blaming me, which infuriates me, but I am far more pissed because he's admitted to lying, which is petty since we both already knew he was. "You are an asshole! *You—*"

"Stop shouting, please."

I lean in, not shouting but my tone getting much sharper. "You lied. You said your family was country-club wealthy. This is something else. She mocked my eyes, and your dad said I might die early from it. And the whole Asian thing was weird. It was like being with Angie during one of her Klan moments. Here in Virginia, I actually believe there still are some Klan."

He starts to make a motion toward me but stops himself, maybe realizing where it will get him.

"Your mother hates me. She called me an orphan and told me she would help me fit in! Who even says that?" I stomp to my bed and lift the silk and fluffy gowns from the bed. "She left these here for me—*picked my clothes for me!* This one doesn't even have a back. Maybe I'll wear that one, and we can talk about my scars all night long." I am on the verge of tears.

He lifts his hands like he might choke me and walks toward me. He doesn't choke me but takes the dresses and tosses them into the pile of fluff and lace and silk. "Baby, she means well. I swear. They aren't racist. You do look a little ethnic in some lights, but I like that about you. You're beautiful. I love every scar and flaw on you. And your eyes make you look unique."

"No girl, even an emotionally disabled one like me, likes to be called *unique* or *flawed*! I'm a hobbit here! A little circus freak with the weird eyes and the birth defects and the scars. Your mom isn't even human. No older woman can walk in those shoes. Did you see her heels? They're four inches, and she's already probably five eight! She doesn't even need them."

"Nine, she's five foot nine, but it doesn't matter. I love you. I love that you're short and sort of different from anyone else I've ever dated. I did leave here, Jane, you will recall. I don't live the way they do; I don't need it. I never did."

"You sound like them too! You sound weird here. You said befouled before and now you're all," I mimic him. " 'You will recall.' "

He wraps his huge hands around my face and kisses my cheek. "Stop! You are overreacting."

I pull back. "Really? After the circus freak comments and the birth defects and the 'oh, you must be Asian,' that's where you want to go right now—overreacting? That's the choice you're making here?"

"No." He thinks for a second. He looks scared, and not because I'm a sniper. He's never seen me flip out about things that are not work related. He's never seen me act like a girl. I've never really seen it either, but I can't stop. "Where is my super-cool unemotional fiancée who never gets worked up or fazed by anything? You never have the right response, I always have to remind you how to be or when to hug. Now you're emotional and crazy? When old you returns, let her know I miss her."

He's teasing me but he doesn't realize I'm actually hurt. I'm actually feeling the pain I am trying to share with him. "She is never coming back! This spastic mess your family has made me, that you have made me, is sticking around forever." I try joking back with him, hating that my heart is showing.

He laughs like I don't mean it, but I do. I vow silently never to be cool around him again. He strokes my cheek again and kisses me softly. "I adore you, Jane. I love you, but there is so much more to it, and I don't know how to explain it. They are my family; I see them once a year. I put in the visit, and that's that. You are my life. I am marrying you because you are my everything."

A cheesy grin finds its way to my lips as my eyes lower and a soft blush creeps along my cheeks.

He smiles wider, and the green eyes dazzle me like my very own snake charmer. "There she is. I knew you'd come back."

I lean in, resting my head on his chest. "I wanted to be me, genuinely, not just Jane who can survive every situation. Does that make sense?"

He kisses the top of my head. "Of course."

"Is there anything I should know going forward from here, beyond, obviously, the fact that you grew up in a ten-million-dollar home?" I ask as he tenses, making me pull back and look up into his eyes. He hesitates, but I sigh. "At this point, you might as well just say it, whatever it is. We have far surpassed the level of shit I can take in a night, so whatever is left, just do it. Lay it on me."

"There is the small matter of your job. I told them you are a scientist at the research facility I work at. We met at work. You are incredibly smart, and we are incredibly in love. I proposed in France at the bridge with the keys you are so fond of. You're not quite as Catholic as you would have my parents believe. You hold a PhD in molecular biology but will quit working when we marry."

"Are you high? You went for molecular bio instead of psycho-analyzing like I do? I'm a criminal profiler. It's a job—a real one. It's respectable. If you wanted you could have told them about the years as an assassin and spy. I do have a title in the military if you were desperate. I am Master Sergeant Spears in the real world. Is that not respectable enough? If not you could have said I was a shop girl. Anything is better than *molecular biology*! I don't know my ass from a molecule."

He chuckles softly. "Deep breaths! Don't get upset again." He looks back at the window behind him, where his parents' house is in perfect view. "They won't even talk about your job, Jane. Women in society don't hold jobs after they marry. They partake in tax deductions like charities and such. They raise kids and maintain the home."

"'Maintain the home'?" I don't even want to get started on kids. In my mind that conversation ended when he perused my file illegally. I roll my eyes. "Let me guess, you have our house already picked out for us, and it's just down the road?"

"No. I never come here. My houses aren't near here." He swallows hard.

"Did you just say houses?" I pinch the bridge of my nose. "It doesn't matter. I just can't believe you say I am bad for keeping things to myself. You picked out a house without me? You picked out a mansion, didn't you? And you clearly have others. You said houses." When he doesn't answer I open my eyes and glare. "How big is our home, Dash?" I can't help but say his name like it tastes bad. "Did you buy it already?" I don't actually like the ranting psycho I have become. I sound like a real girl.

He swallows hard. "Actually, that is the funny part." He looks nervous and glances back at the house. "I know I've been staying with you at your place—"

"Our place."

He nods and laughs nervously. "Right, of course. Our place. But I have actually got a house, well, several, which is why I said houses. Real estate is an excellent investment. And while I own a few, there is one that is my main house. It isn't close enough to DC, so I never really go there, and the staff—"

"You *do* own houses? Hous*es*?" I push back, fighting back bile. "Oh my God! Stop." The panic is building inside of me again. "We can talk about it another time. I don't need to know this shit for this mission. We are pushing this to need-to-know, that's it. I don't need to know you own houses with staff and expect me to go to these houses and keep them up for you."

"Mission?"

I nod, taking a deep breath and looking around the room for possible weapons again. It's surprisingly diverting. "Yes, this is a mission. I am a doctor named Jane Spears, and you are my mark." I snarl at him. "Let's see if you can live through the entire night."

I walk past him as he clears his throat. "We have to get ready for dinner."

I glance down at my jeans and sweater. "I am ready."

He shakes his head. "It's a five-star affair, Jane. You may not wear pants unless they are designer and made from silk or wool."

I sigh. "I don't own anything that will work for a fancy dinner, Dash. I brought my regular clothes. T-shirts and jeans, sweaters, and a hoodie in case we were going to be going anywhere that required me to be warm. And those dresses will make me hate myself for agreeing to endure this bullshit and pretending to be good enough for your family."

He clenches his jaw, clearly done talking about it all, and walks to the front of the house, down the long hallway, and grabs a bag I didn't pack. It isn't mine. And yet, somehow Nichols has snuck in here and planted it on me. He must be part spy and part servant.

"I packed a bag for you." He saunters back down the hall, dropping the bag at the entry of the room. The fight has been sucked out of him. "So get dressed. I'll ask Evangeline to come back and ensure you look appropriate, and I will see you at dinner in an hour."

"An hour? Who needs an hour to get ready?" I wrinkle my nose when he laughs. "I hate you."

"I hope you can forgive me for all of this. And I really hope you see that it is they who are not good enough for you and that this is obligation on our part and not who we are." He looks completely gutted, totally wounded. I know he doesn't realize Angie and I say we hate each other jokingly twice a day. Granted, she says it more than I do, but she jokes more. Whereas I think it a lot.

My heart sort of breaks, and not because of him but because of me when he turns to walk away. So I say, "I don't think I'll ever forgive you, but I will use it to get my way in everything we ever do."

He glances back, smiling wide when he realizes that I'm kidding. "Sold." He turns and leaves the room, leaving me with the fancy piece of luggage that says Gucci on the small tag at the top. I have a terrible feeling it cost more than my townhouse.

13. BARONS AND DUKES AND SENATORS, OH MY!

I don't recognize myself.

Not because I am crawling around in the mind of another person either.

It is entirely because Evangeline has done my makeup. There was a whole bag of it from a store called Sephora. This is something I have endured with Angie a time or two, only Evangeline is some kind of wizard with the contents of the bag.

I recognized the blush, the face powder, the liquid liner, and the mascara. The rest has been something else altogether. Little containers of blues and grays that look like paste but dry with a shimmer over my eyes, and tubes of gloss that swell your lips for you, like instant plastic surgery.

I lean in, mystified at where my pores went and why my brows look so different. I don't look like I might be just a little ethnic, not even a touch. I look like Barbie's dark-haired friend. I turn to the side, marveling at it all.

She nods, stepping back and smiling. "You look lovely. Lady Townshend will have no complaints."

I pause. "Lady? She makes you call her that?" I have never in my life met a woman who was given the title *lady* without being someone of importance. And the two I have met both remind me a lot of his mother.

Evangeline doesn't seem to understand, but then smiles widely. "He never told you?"

I'm excited we have gotten past the curtseying and nonsense, but the comical look on her face makes my insides twist. "Told me what, exactly?"

"Oh lord, he is already in hot water for asking you to marry him, I can't believe he hasn't told you. They're gentry, something Americans would consider royalty. His father is a cousin to the queen of England. Sir George Townshend is a baronet. He's been retired for some time from politics and Her Majesty's Privy Council and the courts. We travel back to England in the summer and spend winters here in Virginia or in southern France."

"Oh, dear God." I plop into the rattan chair next to me, completely mystified at his keeping such a remarkable piece of information to himself. I feel like a frog who's been placed in a pot to boil and only now do I realize the water is burning me, when it's too late to get out. I can't believe he let me believe he was a simple and sweet doctor. I knew he was out of my league, but I didn't know we were different species.

I can't swallow. My mouth is dry yet welling with spit, and my throat is knotted with my stomach. I look back at the reflection and start to laugh. "So his last name isn't Dash? His name isn't Benjamin Dash?"

He walks into the room, forcing a curtsey from her. She flees from the room quickly, as if scared of the pussycat before her. She doesn't realize it's me who's the dangerous one. Especially when cornered.

"I am sorry. I had intended to tell you on the way over." He pauses for a second, as if just seeing this shitty thing he has done to me. "Dashiell is my middle name."

I laugh harder. "Dashiell is not a name. Dash is a last name."

He shakes his head. "I swear to you, Dashiell is my middle name. Benjamin Edward Dashiell Townshend is my full name."

"You are lying. That's a terrible middle name. No one would do that to their child."

He sighs, reaching for his pocket and pulling his wallet out. He offers the driver's license I have never seen, something I should have checked. Jesus, it says Dashiell. I choke a little bit. "It's a lovely name."

"It's my mother's maiden name, which is why I have it as my middle name." He drops to his knees, making us nearly the same height. "It all means nothing. I am not the eldest; I will never take the title of sir from my father. His baronetcy will pass to my eldest brother, Henry, who is heir apparent. This isn't my life. I left it a long time ago."

"Have you seen a purple scarf or a black-and-white cat?" I ask, starting to look around. "I think I'm being fucked with. I think I'm actually in a mind run. Oh God, I'm in a coma. I was in that girl and she died, and I'm stuck in here?"

"No, this is very real." He shakes his head, gripping my cheeks and forcing my face to turn and see him. "This doesn't change who we are. You are you, and I am me. If I could tell the truth about who you are, how you're a profiler and mind reader who used to be a top-secret spy for the UN, I would. If I could tell them who we really are, I would. But we are both sworn to secrecy on the matter, so I lie about being doctors together in a research facility."

I squeeze my eyes shut. "First rule in lying and spying, Dash, is that you pick a lie close to the truth. So close, you believe it too." I open my eyes, licking my lips and nodding. "Okay, so your parents are not American. They're some sort of gentry, and you are not the heir apparent, 'cause that's apparently a thing. Who knew? Anything else?"

He shakes his head. "I don't think so."

"You ever hear the phrase, 'Is the juice worth the squeeze?'"
He nods slowly.

"I'm starting to wonder that very question."

"If I am worth it?" He looks genuinely hurt.

"Not you, just love in general." He doesn't realize I have never loved a single person in my entire life except him. I don't recall loving my family, not properly. I never truly loved the nuns or the other children. We knew what we all were. But Dash and Binx, I love with all my heart.

He kisses me softly so as not to smear whatever the fuck is all over my face. "None of this reality is ours. If you only knew how many baronets there are—it's not a special term. It means that during the 1600s one of my relatives bought his way into the courts to help the king at the time, James the First. It's no different than being mayor or senator or a judge."

"I don't care. I care that they think I am way fucking smarter than I am in a subject I know nothing about. I care that they think I'm somehow lesser because I don't have any family. I care that they clearly had a path for you in life and you're using me to stray from it. And I wonder if you ever really loved me at all!"

"Don't say that." He clenches his jaw. "I strayed a long time ago. I went to Eton, as was expected. But I never chose politics as my father did. Or as my brother did. I chose to be me, a man of science. I joined the UN out of university and never looked back." His hands shake a tiny bit, and I can tell now that he fights to not have an accent in everything. He actually tries to sound American. "I need you to understand why I kept this from you. I was preventing you from giving up on me and us. It's so easy for you to walk away unscathed, but I have nothing if we aren't together."

I sigh, fully aware of the weight of it all. The rational creature I am is slowly stamping out the fires built by the silly girl in me. "I know. You're completely right, I never would have come. I would have hit you up with some sleeping pills and phoned to cancel for us. I probably would have said you'd come down with something. I *never* would have come here. And I might have never given us a chance." I redirect all the fight in me. "I have been trained to lie for a living. Now I hunt and solve for a job. I can handle three days of this bullshit. I killed the head of state in Algeria without getting caught when I was twenty-two—I can do this too." I nod, take a deep breath, and roll my shoulders. "Let's do this."

He sighs, as if I have told him the greatest news in the world. "I knew once you processed it you'd see how minor this all is. How it isn't us and doesn't actually involve us."

"No." I lift a finger into his face as he stands. "No. I am never going to admit this is small. In my world this is some Cinderella-bullshit fairy tale that never comes true for kids like me. This is the crap that movies and books try to sell orphans, or abused and neglected kids. I was one of the few who knew that this shit was never happening for me. Now you've come along with your fancy titles, billion-dollar house and snooty parents, and an heir apparent, thank you very much, and fucked up my reality." I snarl a little at the end. "I already have issues with reality. And here we have you hiding an entire life behind my back and hiding an accent. And God knows what else. My trust in you has diminished to almost nothing."

"I will do everything in my power to earn it back, Jane. Love you."

"I hate you right now."

He winces, giving me a worried look. "You sure you can do this, then? I will make excuses for you if we need to leave."

"No, absolutely not. We aren't running away like cowards. But your parents won't ever know I am struggling with every moment here and every lie you have told me. I refuse to let them see me squirm. If being an orphan has one perk, that's it. I know how to be invisible and how to blend in." And with that I turn and leave the room, leaving him stressing.

"Fucking king of the world!" I mutter and send a text to Angie.

Come and find me if this goes badly. I'll send a 911 and then you send a helicopter. I'll make something up to get out.

She is instantly typing:

It's not that bad. His family is gentry. The house is worth Rhode Island and there are slaves everywhere. His dad has a title in England.

She sends a smiley face and adds more.

They always do. That's just like saying he's a senator here in the US. You're fine. Dash isn't one of them, trust me. I have met his family. NOT MY CUP OF TEA!

I groan and slide my phone into the clutch Evangeline forced upon me. I had assumed it was fake gems, but now I think it might be covered in diamonds. At least I can hock it and get a flight out if that's the case.

Dash hurries, wrapping an arm around me and kissing the side of my head. "You'll be fine."

I nod. "I know I will be, but you should be worried about you."

He laughs like I don't mean it, but I do. I really might do a little harm before the night is through.

As we cross the grounds I can't help but marvel again at the beautiful pergola with the lights revealing the climbing lilacs. It smells like summer in the South and makes me forget where we are. When he opens the door to the dazzling house I remember instantly. But I'm not scared. I have lived bigger lies than this for worse people.

His mother greets us as we walk in. She has a glass of champagne and enough jewelry to cast shadows with her sparkle. She offers us both a kiss-kiss hug-hug, something I still don't understand and don't appreciate. Being touched is high on the totem pole of things I dislike. Especially from strangers.

"You look marvelous, Jane. Less exhausted and far more refreshed. I take it you found everything to be to your satisfaction?"

"I did, thank you. The guesthouse is—amazing. A whole family could live in there." I force myself to use words I think are safe. Instead of "oh my God it's super nice" or "wicked" or "completely wasteful and disturbing, and why aren't you adopting ten children from the orphanage?"

She beams, blinking slowly. I don't know how to respond so I go for the thing he mentioned earlier. "Your necklace is stunning. Very eye-catching."

She looks down at it. "Oh, this old thing? Thank you, dear." She offers her arm to her son. "Drinks are being served as the guests arrive."

He pales but doesn't even bat an eyelash. "Excellent. Jane would love a drink, I'm sure." He looks back at me.

I force a smile. "Jane would love a drink."

He chuckles and moseys off to the man with the tray. He brings white wine, as if he doesn't know me at all, and actually has the balls to hand me the slim glass. I notice everyone has white wine or champagne.

I narrow my gaze, accepting his challenge at drinking something I hate, and take a sip. It's not the worst and it's certainly not the best, but it works to give me something to do with my hands. Fidgeting is so unprofessional.

His father struts over, one hand in his dinner jacket and the other holding a glass of champagne. "How do you like Virginia, Jane?"

I nod. "It's very lovely. I have been here a few times for work."

"Yes, that's right. You're a medical scientist with our dear boy here."

I smile wide again, not committing to the lie. These people might actually be my family one day, and I will not utter the lie to them. If he wants to be that person, it's his choice.

"How do you like your work?"

"Love it! I am actually in the middle of something very important as we speak." I sip and nod. "Very engaging." What else do you call a serial rapist-torturer who kidnaps and stores his victims and forces them to play along?

"Fascinating." He says it like he means exactly the opposite. He turns and smiles at his son. "And you, my boy, how is it you are getting on so well with so many distractions in your life?"

Dash is the master of his emotions. He tilts his head to the side subtly and smiles. "I am enjoying the work still, Father. The UN is a wonderful opportunity for someone with empathy and compassion for their fellow man. Jane is actually part of something quite remarkable. The program she is in uses modern science to solve crimes." That's about as far as we can ever take the explanation, so my back straightens when he says that.

His father gasps. "Like one of those charming nighttime shows with the DNA analysis and what have you? Are you that type of scientist?"

"Molecular." I laugh to stop myself from saying the wrong thing. "I am involved in something similar to Dash. The details are obviously restricted."

Dash frowns, but I don't care. He's an idiot for bringing me into this bullshit and an even bigger idiot for making my cover smarter than I am.

"Yes, of course," Dash's father replies. "That's the sort of job that involves processing the grime and filth of society. You must spend immense amounts of time with the rugged classes, up close and personal. How brave you must be." He says it like he might be talking about something quaint and charming, instead of saying things like *classes.*

His wife concurs, "That is very admirable in a woman. When will you leave, before or after the wedding?"

I grip my glass, praying to the God of all that is patient and good. "I don't know." That is the truth. I don't know. "I start a new position with the American military shortly before the wedding. Still with the UN, though."

She coughs a little on her drink. "Before the wedding?"

I nod, giving Dash a look. His eyes tell me I should not have said that. I know I shouldn't have, but I panicked.

"Oh, we had assumed you intended to remain here for the planning and then come with us to England for the final preparations."

It's my turn to gulp. "England?"

Dash drains the entire contents of his glass before forcing a smile. "I hadn't spoken to Jane about the church yet."

His mother's eyes narrow as she turns and faces her son. "Well, what better time than the present?" She walks to her husband's arm and strolls back to the other room just as a man and woman arrive.

My secretive fiancé's eyes land on the people with a miserable look. "Jesus, help us." He grabs another drink and slams it. It's clear he's having the worse night, which I predicted and he laughed off. What did he think would happen, bringing me here?

I follow his desperate stare to a blonde with a beautiful face and a stunning cocktail dress. She looks like a model or a celebrity. In fact, everyone in the room does. I honestly want to know who their plastic surgeon is. I hold myself upright as Dash walks to the woman, holding out a hand. She slips hers in his and allows him to kiss the back of it. He rests his lips there for a moment. Much more than I would have expected, and I don't even have manners.

My entire body bursts into a sweat.

"Jane, I would love for you to meet Melody Astor. She's an old friend from school."

Of course her name is Melody, and of course she's an old friend. From the way her blue eyes rest on his and the way her hand naturally fits in his, it is obvious they were once far more than friends. His face is flushed, and he looks like he might burst.

But he doesn't get a chance; many more people start to enter the grand foyer. Melody comes to my side, smiling like she knows all my secrets. "It is so lovely to finally meet you, Jane Spears."

I smile back. "Yes, I am so sorry I don't know who you are. I mean, I know the last name. Everyone knows the last name."

She waves her hand. "Oh, please, distant relatives. My family is from England, not America." She says it like we are all dirty.

"Cool." I honestly don't have another word for it.

"Ben and I go back a long way." Her cheeks flush as she stares at him, clearly reliving something fantastic.

Ben?

His mother points my way as she chats with someone. The woman standing next to her eyes me appraisingly. She doesn't look super impressed with what she sees. They lean into each other and continue talking, even though I can completely see them and am aware they are judging me.

Melody turns and smiles again. "So, when will you start having babies? Directly after the wedding, like Will and Kate?"

I shrug, not caring about Will and Kate and certainly not wanting to tell her we will never have kids.

"His mother is certain you are already with child and that is why the wedding is on."

I give her a look. "We aren't planning to get married until the spring. I would be due by then if I were pregnant now." I say it more harshly than I had intended, earning a wide-eyed look from her.

She laughs, placing a hand on my shoulder, recovering quickly from the shock of my tone. "Oh, of course you would. How silly of me. I suppose they are just very anxious to have grandchildren. It isn't as if Henry is in any hurry to settle down." Her eyes lower.

It's then that I answer my own question: is the juice worth the squeeze? It is not. This family is batshit crazy, and I am on the verge of tears, mostly because I know it won't ever work. As much as he pretends they aren't his life, I can see they are.

I don't need to be with him to love him. I loved him for years before we ever got together, and I will continue to love him throughout the life he is so obviously meant to have with this blonde who wants to rub that in my face.

I pull out my phone, sending my 911 request.

It won't even look weird leaving by helicopter here. I imagine each of the guests have several.

The house gets busier, but Angie doesn't answer my message. I don't even get a "delivered" receipt. She's turned her phone off, knowing I would need rescuing? Dick move.

Melody introduces me as Ben's charming girlfriend, obviously ignoring the ring on my finger. The one everyone's eyes land on.

I meet a senator, a doctor, a lawyer, a judge, a lady with a ring on every finger like she's wearing all her jewelry at once. I meet women with such obvious plastic surgery I fight not to stare, and men who constantly stare at my nearly flat chest in disappointment. Melody, of course, has beautiful breasts—the validity of them is in question at least in my mind.

The white wine starts to give me a headache, something that happens every single time. Something that Dash knew when he gave me the glass. I dump it into a plant as I walk past, desperate to find my escape out on the terrace again, with the lilacs and the moon, which has just risen.

I slump into a seat, a very fine seat for patio furniture, and stare at the cast-iron statue of the boys frolicking in the garden.

"Are you hiding?" The voice is Dash's but then it's not. I glance up to see the face and eyes of Dash but just a little different. I don't know what to make of it.

"Yes," I answer honestly.

"I'm Henry, Ben's older brother." *His very English brother with a very English accent.*

"I'm Jane, Dash's—er—friend from above the Mason–Dixon line." I should have said girlfriend but I didn't. The word felt wrong, less so than fiancée, but still wrong.

"Of course you are." He chuckles and sits in the chair next to me. "Dash—I haven't heard that since Eton. He always loved that name." He gives me a sly grin. "I assume he likes you more than a friend might if he lets you call him that. Only his best friends ever called him Dash."

I exhale my laugh. "Well, I think he loves the idea of being his own man, and I suspect I help him with that."

"He has always enjoyed rebelling against the fold." Henry nods, sipping his glass of red wine.

I scowl. "How did you get a glass of red?"

"I poured it. Sir George insists we drink white or champagne before dinner, and red with it. He's a stickler for tradition. This is my version of rebellion." He takes a huge gulp and passes me the glass. I take a drink from the other side of the glass.

"How badly was he broken when Melody dumped him?"

Henry chuckles just the way Dash does. "Oh, he told you about that, did he?"

I shake my head. "Not a word on it, ever."

"So she told you then?"

I shake my head again.

"How do you know?"

I shrug. "I get paid to read people."

His eyes narrow. "Liar! That can't be a real profession."

I sigh and stare back out into the garden. "It is."

"It must be hard to read people." I can tell he's mocking me, challenging me.

"It's easy once you figure it out. Take your family, for instance: Your father is reckless, and he's never been good at doing what he's told. But he can't be caught doing them, so he does a lot of bad things on the sly. I assume he has mistresses and scandals, but they're buried deep—not because he's smart, though, but because he knows how to work the system. His whole family is made up of cheating men." The words hurt on the way out as I realize Dash is one of them. "Your mother knows about it all. She's smarter than your father is, far smarter. She wasn't as wealthy as he was growing up. She's more rigid than he is because she had to learn the rules and doesn't want any of her poverty or lack of breeding accidentally showing."

I turn and look at him. "You are like your father in the desire to be a free spirit, but at the same time you are smarter than he is. You have never allowed them to stifle you so you have no need to rebel the way he does. You joke of rebelling, but you don't do it. You just live according to the rules that matter, the ones people talk about. The rest you ignore and love the fact it creates a slight bad-boy air about you." I turn back to the garden with a smirk when he looks shocked. "And then there is the ever-fair Melody, who dumped Dash because you and she were having an affair, which is why your brother doesn't really like you. She loved Dash, with all her cold heart, but you are the heir so she broke up with him, in hopes you would love her back. But that's not your style. The sad part is that your mother invited her here in hopes of her and Dash reconnecting so he would break it off with me, not knowing how much it would hurt Dash to actually see the first girl who broke his heart. And ironically, she forced you to come in hopes that you and Dash would mend fences, but obviously with seeing Melody here that isn't going to happen. The wound is now fresh in Dash's heart, even with me here." I pause, turning and looking at him again. "But that's not the only problem with you two, is it? Everything that's legacy in your family is going to go to you, and Dash resents that a little, I think, even if he doesn't want to admit it to himself. He doesn't think you are worthy of any of it. He sees the real you."

His jaw drops. "Blimey!" He takes his drink back and finishes it. "You are good at whatever it is they pay you for. I hope they pay well."

"Not really." I shake my head. "But sitting back and watching will always get you further than talking. People say the things they want themselves to believe. They are saying it aloud to convince themselves only. Their actions are who they are."

"Well, Jane Spears, I hate to say it, but I think my baby brother has bitten off more than he can chew."

I sigh, knowing it isn't true; it's quite the opposite, in fact. "Being good at parlor tricks doesn't make you desirable, Henry. It just makes you good at guessing the next move out of everyone else in the room."

His eyes dazzle in the moonlight. "The answer I want, Jane Spears, is what your next move will be."

I nod to the right. "A quick getaway if I'm lucky, between courses."

He winks. "We can get away now if you like."

I laugh right in his face. "Not a chance."

His smile fades away, and I think he feels sorry for me. "You love him, don't you?"

"My entire heart and soul, though unable to be much more than pathetic, are his." I say it so matter-of-factly I feel sorry for me too. I don't even think I meant to say it aloud, but the night has gotten the best of me.

"I will arrange a car out front for you. You can play at being Cinderella, and may leave when you wish. Tell no one, and slip out the office near the foyer. There is a door there for my father to smoke his cigars without the lady of the house *busting his chops*, as you Americans say."

"Thank you."

He nods. "Ben is an idiot to let you go, but I fear his bringing you here was his way of scaring you off. If he ends up with that ditz Melody I might have to just give him the title so I can run away with you."

I stand, completely uncomfortable with the forward way he is acting. "I don't run away, Henry. I either fit or I don't." Which is why I have one friend and one cat and nothing else. Because I never fit. I grew up in a house of people unlikely to fit. We rubbed off our awkward and discomfort all over each other. I walk back into the house to find the red wine and pour myself a glass.

When I see Dash and Melody talking to another couple I can't help but hate her for fitting him so perfectly. She's blonde and beautiful and perfect in every way. Together they're tall and flawless, no doubt a match in every way. She laughs, resting an arm on his forearm. He flinches; I see it before he relaxes and laughs too. I can see the discomfort on his face, and all I feel is hate for her. Not because he's mine but because she doesn't seem to care that she has injured him. She is so selfish that she doesn't see the agony she is causing. And his mother grinning from the other side of the room is just as clueless and cruel.

I force my eyes from them and head for the grand staircase in the foyer. I walk up the rounded staircase quickly, hurrying to the hall. "Evangeline?" I call out, searching each room. I can tell the right side of the stairs is where the guests sleep. Each room looks like a hotel, and the belongings are all in bags.

I turn to go to the left and Evangeline is there, smiling and breathless. "Are you all right?"

I shake my head. "I need your help. I need to find Dash— Benjamin's room."

She turns and walks back to the left wing of the house. She opens a door and waits as I hurry inside. I leave the ring on his pillow. My entire body aches, leaving it there.

My hand lifts, resting on the scar on my stomach, the one I

thought he understood. The one that means I can never have children. I am actually stunned at the entire situation. There is no other way to handle it.

I need to go home and hug my cat and pretend it was all a mind ride. It was all someone else's story. I never fell in love with a man so perfect that my broken heart doesn't stand a chance at mending. I will settle back into my plan—crazy cat lady. I will let it go the way I let everything else go.

I brush the tears from my eyes and walk back to Evangeline. "Does my makeup still look okay?"

She nods, giving me a smile. "You are beautiful. Even without the makeup."

I hug her. It's a desperate act for me; I don't hug and I don't hold and I don't touch. But I am all alone in the world at this very moment. I need my cat and my pasta from my dear sweet neighbor. I need my old life back. I pull back. "I'm so sorry, that was so inappropriate."

She shakes her head, sniffling a little. "I knew you were too good for them all when you walked in the door." She turns quickly and walks away, leaving me there to gather myself before I go back down into the pit of vipers.

As I get to the bottom of the stairs a glass of red wine meets my nose. Henry smiles as he hands it over. "I figured you needed this."

I take the glass, gulping it back too quickly. "Thanks." I reach over, stealing his wine while handing him the empty goblet. I'm nearly done swallowing Henry's drink when Dash makes his way to us. He smiles. "You have met my brother?"

Henry nudges him in the ribs. "Found her scaling the walls in the backyard."

I roll my eyes. "He found me checking out your parents' weird obsession with naked cast-iron boys. There must be twenty of them on the property."

"Wrought," Henry says.

"What?"

"Wrought iron. Cast iron would rust in the rain. They are wrought iron. And they are a common decoration for gardens. Like imps or fairies."

"Whatever. It's no less creepy with a different name."

Dash gives me a worried look. "You all right?"

I shrug. "Dandy."

Henry takes the empty glasses and turns. "I'll fetch more wine."

Dash takes my hand in his. "I'm sorry. I haven't been particularly attentive." His eyes get heavy with emotion. "But you know we only have to do this once. Then we're free for a whole year."

I scoff. "I can't do this right now."

"What's wrong?"

I walk past him, tearing my hand from his, and enter the office, the one with the door I will be leaving from. Dash follows me in. "Did Henry say something to bother you?"

"You honestly think your pompous playboy brother could upset my delicate nature?" I laugh with bitterness. "You don't think my years in the military might have rounded off those edges for me? He isn't the first player I have met in my life, Dash—sorry—Ben. And I suspect he won't be the last."

"What did he do?"

"Nothing. He got me a glass of red wine, and he listened to me complain about your ex-girlfriend. Because, apparently, your family has the magical ability to make me into a whiny and petty bitch. I do not like who I am here, and I will not be this girl."

He pauses. "What?" I can see the guilt all over his face.

"Oh, please. I know you and Melody were a thing. She cheated on you with your own brother in hopes of landing herself the heir of the family. I know she's money but not enough. She needs someone like your brother to make her the top of society. You were clearly crushed. And your conniving mother decided it might help us end our relationship a little sooner if Melody came back into your life to remind you of the good old days. If you can't see all that, then you are far less intelligent than I had given you credit for."

He looks like I've kicked him in the balls, but I don't let it end there. "You think I don't see the song and dance at this palace? I see it just fine. You lie about me because I'm not good enough. My years of military service aren't enough for your family. So I have to pretend to be a doctor. Well, fuck you, and fuck your family. Defending my country means more to me than either of your PhDs do. I know you're smarter than I am with books and science and all the other things people deem important, but I am smart enough to see you are happy with me. You and I are happy people. I didn't even know there was this other side to you, because I don't think this is who you are. This guy, I fucking hate this guy. And I know I can't ever be the girl you need me to be. I can't have kids; thanks for letting your mother rub her need for grandkids in my face. Benjamin Dashiell—stupidest name ever!" I turn and storm out the door, not even waiting for the entirety of my hateful words to hit. I'm in the car, speeding down the driveway, before I realize what I've said and done. And all without proof. The very thing I work to find in every case I work. I have assumed every bad thing about him.

But it isn't as if he denied any of it.

I curl up and let the driver whisk me away to the airport as I message for a flight to be booked in my name. I am so cliché I almost wish I'd left a shoe behind.

14. YOU FORGOT THAT YOU STILL LOVE ME

His fur smells exactly the way I remember it smelling. I curl around him, kissing his soft head. He's a ticking time bomb, and I'm going to be scratched any moment. But I don't care. I just need a hug from a safe person. When the microwave dings, letting me know that Mrs. Starling's pasta primavera is done, I kiss once more and jump up for my carb-filled feast. I love eating my feelings.

The doorbell rings as I touch the microwave. I sigh and walk to the door, assuming it'll be Angie and she'll want to share my dinner and listen to me go on and on like a regular girl about Dash and the fucking mess in the South.

I open the door, jumping back a bit when I see Dash holding my purse. "You forgot this."

"Keep the damn thing." I close the door in his face. It's been three days since I left him in Virginia, and if I get a say in the rest of the evening, I can wait another three days before I have to see him again.

Instead he opens the door with his own key and walks in. I turn away and grab my meal from the microwave and slump with it at the table.

"Jane, we have to talk. You actually left this on my pillow and came back to DC? You really broke off our engagement over my brother lying, and my mother conniving, and Melody being the money-grubbing bitch she was when I was in twelfth grade? I was head boy at school, all because I was a Townshend. And she wanted the title of being my girlfriend. Then when we broke up, I discovered she and my brother had been sleeping together for a long time. He saw how ridiculous she was then, and he sees it now. She wants him to marry her. And she is under the misapprehension that catching my eye and making me like her again might get her back in with my brother since he always wants what I have. Like having everything else isn't enough."

I clap my hands slowly. "Bravo. That's the meanest I have ever heard you be."

"Oh, screw off, Jane. I'm not a simpleton, and I'm not some polite ass everyone can take advantage of. It just took me a bit longer than you to see their scheme. But you naturally go in skeptical, so what do you expect? Of course you're going to find the worst in them, you were looking for it."

"It's self-preservation." I take a steamy bite, burning my lips a little. "I don't actually care about your family at all. That was a fiasco, and the fact you led me down there under false pretenses and let me be humiliated makes me pissed at you, not them."

He sits across from me, taking my plate and my fork and getting himself a bite of cheesy pasta. "You care. You and I love each other."

I shake my head. "You fed me to the wolves. I never would have done that to you. You made up so many lies I honestly doubted my being in my own body. I thought for sure I was mind riding. No one's life is that silly."

He passes me back the plate. "Mine was. My life was as silly as you saw. It's all fake. Like you said, a dance." He reaches his hand across, covering mine. "You are the real part."

I blink a hot tear down my cheek, hating that I'm crying in front of him, but there is one insult I have to admit feeling the burn from. "I can't have babies, Dash. I thought you knew that."

"I do know that." He nods. "I read your file."

"Then why did you let her tell people we are going to have kids? That's a lie."

He shakes his head. "It's not a lie. One day, we will have kids. We will just have to get a surrogate to carry them for us. Your eggs are probably fine, and my sperm is fine. I have tested it. We can *make* a baby."

I scowl. "The fact you're so obsessed with this makes me feel like I'm not the right girl for you. Have you considered that I don't want children? I don't know the first thing about having a baby."

He sighs, covering his eyes for a second. "Yes, I'm obsessed with making you and me a family. If we are the only two people in the family, I will live, quite happily. It's you that's the crucial part, Jane. I need *you* to be happy." He slides the ring across the table and cocks an eyebrow. "Put it back on, for the love of God, and stop messing with my heart."

I almost fight him on it, but it's actually the sweetest sentence two emotionally disabled people have ever gotten out of a relationship, and it far surpasses his proposal. I cover the ring with my hand and sigh. "You set me up to fail and then spent the entire time flirting with your old girlfriend."

He closes his eyes and breathes out heavily. "I didn't. I swear. I spoke to her for a second to be polite and then not again. She happened to be with a few of the people I was talking with. It's my obligation to greet everyone and spend a few moments with them."

"You kissed her hand and she touched your arm."

"I kissed the hand of every woman there; it's the polite thing to do. I suppose you missed all the others, no doubt under the pernicious governing of my troublemaking brother." He sounds English and flustered, and I hate that he looks so adorable when he's worked up. I rarely see it.

I scoff, pretending to be unfazed by his cuteness. "I don't know what that means. Don't go all Smarty McSmarter on me. Using big words isn't going to change the fact that your mother was cruel to me, and you let the whole thing happen. I'm not so dumb that I didn't see right through your jackass brother. Bringing me wine like a knight in shining Armani."

He laughs, and I have the feeling the fight is over. My sails are windless and my insides are jelly, mostly because he's giving me one of those gooey stares with his gray-green eyes, and his lips are toying with a grin. "I love you, Jane. Right now, I don't care if we ever see them all again, but if we do, my mother owes you an apology. My brother already got what he deserved."

I scowl. "I don't even want to know." I can guess by the state of his right hand. The knuckles are bruised, and one is even split.

"You have to see how crazy you make me. You see how much I love you?"

I shake my head slowly. "You can't choose me over your family. That's horrible, and I wouldn't ever be that girl who would ask you to."

"You don't have to ask. If they can't accept you, then they don't accept me either."

It stings to actually hear the words that they don't accept me. I knew it, but seeing that he knows it too is much worse, as if he finally sees my worth.

He reaches across, lifting my hand and picking the ring up. "I want to marry you, Jane. I want to be your husband and be your family and show you that people can rely on each other. If either of us made any mistakes this weekend, it was me trying to squeeze you into the mold my family has set for me and my life. I should have just told them you are a badass ex-military savage who can kill people with her hairclip and takes no nonsense from anyone." He slides the ring on my finger. "I am so sorry for trying to make you fit in their world, instead of just letting you be you."

I nod, realizing saying anything would be petty, and I don't like it when I get my petty on. So I smile and leave the ring on, even if it feels like it's burning through my flesh and weighs twenty pounds.

"Now, the one thing I have to ask is that you consider marrying me in the family church. I understand you are Catholic, and we're C of E, and that's a serious request to mull over, but please just think on it. I'm not going to force you. I'm not going to lie about anything else. I've had my fair share of it and hated every moment. It felt like we were skating on thin ice at every turn."

I agree. "Fine. I'll think about it. But I need intel on this church, location, who else has been married there, and what kind of service would be expected."

He laughs, and I can tell the fight is definitely over. He stands up, scooping me up into his arms, and carries me to our bed.

He places my head softly on the pillow on his side and closes the door, not before Binxy squeezes through and runs for the closet. Dash turns the lights off and flicks on the small light in the corner before walking to the edge of the bed, plucking my slippers from my feet, and tossing them in the corner where he throws my pants after taking them off.

I fight the images in my brain, the ones linked to Rory. The ones that sting a little bit everywhere still. I need Dash to make me forget them.

He kisses up my calves and thighs, spreading me open to him. He licks once, roughly, between my legs, and inserts his middle finger. My lips part, and a breath escapes like it's fleeing.

He slides the finger in and out slowly, lubricating and teasing. His thumb begins rubbing my clit in a slow circular motion. I can't watch any longer as my head falls backs and a gasp escapes my lips.

"Touch your breasts, show them to me." His voice is smooth.

Without even hesitating I drag my T-shirt up my torso and chest, letting my breasts sit in the open air. I cup them, squeezing and rolling the nipples the way he likes as he increases the thrusting finger inside of me.

The sound of his belt and pants fills the air as he releases his cock and pulls his pants and underwear down. I don't need to see it to know what he's doing.

His punishing penetration makes my eyes roll into the back of my head as each thrust jolts my ass and pussy with pleasure. Where he's landing when he pushes his finger in hits all the right nerve endings.

I squeeze my nipples, lifting my butt a bit to meet his rhythmic finger-fucking. He rolls me over, not letting me finish, and climbs between my thighs, spreading them wide and lifting my ass back to meet his ready and eager erection.

He rubs the head on my slit twice before pushing all the way in with a jerk. He pulls me to him with one hand and inserts the thumb of his other hand into my ass very slowly.

I moan, as he keeps his thumb planted deeply in my ass and punishes my pussy with his cock. The sound of him entering me is a mixture of the lubricant I have made and the gasping groans coming from us both. Mine is high-pitched and on the cusp as I near orgasm. His is deep and throaty, a grunt that mixes with a growl every time he is deep in me.

He pulls me back roughly, meeting my awaiting orgasm with his pulsating cock. Just as he feels me lose control of myself, he removes his thumb from my ass and slams my pussy as hard as he can. It's rough and angry in a few ways, but exactly what we both want. He owns my body, we agree on that fact silently as I orgasm all over him and he fills me with everything he has.

He collapses on top of me, kissing the side of my face and muttering, "Admit you missed me."

I shake my head. "Never."

He laughs like he knows I don't mean it. He knows me better than anyone.

15. BEDTIME STORIES

The text is a surprise. Mostly because it's not my file anymore and I am awaiting my final assessment and debriefing on it. I rode the mind, the girl died. My team and I should be off it, and yet Angie is asking me back in. I realize I haven't properly debriefed because the site has taken up everyone's energy, but she isn't ever my contact for debriefing.

I send her a message saying I'll meet her at the office, and run to the door.

"You leaving?" Dash asks from the kitchen, where he's holding a plate filled with cake. "I was going to feed you this in the bath and think of varying ways to call you beautiful in other languages."

I pause, wincing. "As tempting as that cake looks, I never want to sit in a bath and listen to you gush. I'll cut my wrists with my leg-shaving razor if you attempt it. And yes, I am leaving. I have to go back in."

"Why?"

"I don't actually know, maybe because the case has some loose ends they want to see if I can answer. Everyone is busy with the giant scene we have uncovered, and the higher-ups might just want the debriefing done."

He wrinkles his nose, but I lift a hand. "It's stuff I already know the answer to. I don't have to go searching. As far as I understand, it's routine in unsolved cases. You and Angie just aren't part of this usually, you're the mind-run team and doctors for the vic. I don't know why she is the one asking me in to debrief, but it's something I normally go through afterward. The difference with this one is that we haven't ever crossed the bridge where I can't solve the file with the mind run. This is new territory. But finding a den of dead women hasn't ever happened before either. The whole thing is a brand-new situation."

"When do you report in with the new profiling job?"

I wince, realizing I haven't yet explained the job offer to him. I haven't even had a chance to look at the details of the job. "I don't know much, just that the first year of the job is in Manhattan." That was the part I was not looking forward to discussing with him. Relocating when you're a couple is not easy.

"Manhattan? My job is here; why would you agree to a job in another city?" He slumps, immediately looking annoyed. "When were we going to talk about this?"

I grin like a jackass. "I'll leave you that to mull over while I go and help solve those eleven murders. You don't have to decide now. You can think on it."

"Have fun." He lifts his middle finger in the air and then looks at it like he's surprised to see it. I blow a kiss and walk out the door muttering obscenities and wishing I'd just taken the piece of cake.

On the drive over to the office I process; I can't stop processing. My brain won't stop sorting the details. We have lived in DC for a long time. Manhattan sounds appealing, but it's no life for a couple talking about surrogates and marriage and old, crappy English churches. Manhattan is more single-friendly and fun-loving with amazing takeout. However, Manhattan has never been a place I have wanted to live, even when I was young and into takeout, and fun-loving at times.

The job felt like the right choice when I was offered it, after I did the mind run with Samantha Barnes. I accepted before I knew all the details. I just knew it was the one way I could do another mind run for Ashley Potter without a fight with Dash. He has always said seven was the limit for any mind runner. We take on small parts of the person we enter, and seven was the number all the doctors felt was low enough that enough of the mind runner would be left behind to ensure the person remained sane.

But now, knowing it's in Manhattan, I don't know if I can do it. Maybe when I was younger.

Who am I kidding? I have never been fun-loving, and I have never liked Manhattan.

I've done UN security detail, and the UN headquarters creep me out. The whole *international soil* bothers me. What happens there stays there. I've seen it a lot. American rules do not apply, and I happen to like our rules regarding rape and women's rights. A whole year there is unappealing. Especially when I have a job I like.

Granted, I won't be able to do any more mind runs, I have clearly done too many already, but maybe I can help the new people who are set to take it on. I could even go back into active duty as far as tracking goes. Profiling terrorists for the military and living in Manhattan sounds about as much fun as having my teeth pulled out.

When I get to the building downtown, Angie gives me a warm hug. "How are ya?"

"Tired and annoyed."

She lifts my finger. "And still engaged, I see. Dr. Dash did his magic, did he?"

I sneer. "You know how adorable he is when he begs."

"The most adorable. It's unbearable." She laughs. "What's the plan with the new job?"

"Not sure. The details have started rolling in since this job is nearing its end. They want me to move to Manhattan, and Dash is here in DC, and my life is going to be poo."

She wrinkles her nose. "The UN is a rather interesting spot."

"Worst job ever, and Manhattan. I'm not a New York kind of girl. I don't do high heels and brunch and gluten-free and the next new thing that's hot for seven seconds."

"Stop, ya love brunch, and we both know it." She laughs again and points at the sheet of paper in her hands. "Anyway, we have the backstory on the girl, Ashley Potter. I need to cross-reference what ya know with what we know. We apparently have some blanks that need to be filled in. I haven't ever done this before, so bear with me, eh?"

"It's easy. We can be casual; the details can be fixed up to sound smart later when they transcribe the whole thing. Start the recorder." I cross the room to the huge desk and sit, getting comfy so I can start sifting through my brain. "This is Special Agent Jane Spears and Dr. Angela O'Conner doing the detailed report on the mind run for one Ashley Potter. As far as the details of the mind run are concerned she has given many of the details of her kidnapping, capture, confinement, escape, recapture, and attempted murder. Ashley Potter arrived at nursing school in Seattle from her hometown, Tanner, Washington, in the late summer, starting freshman year in 2014. Her mother smuggled in a cat, a ginger tabby named Angel. Her first roommate, a girl I did not ascertain the name of, but I am certain the report has her named, was a complete ass about the cat. They fought for a week or so, resulting in a girl named Stephanie Banks, or Steph, as Ashley knew her, proposing the great roommate switch. Steph was actually an assy bigot—that's not a technical name but it is what Ashley called her—who our girl Ashley rarely hung out with. It was believed the old roommates were lesbians. I don't recall their names, but Steph hated them. Flipped out when she discovered her roommate was a lesbian. Again, they are named in the file done by the patrol officers."

"In the report ya e-mailed me ya used names from previous files."

"Yeah, Michelle and Leona." I nod, not opening my eyes. "The scenery in Ashley's mind was moving fast, and I needed some anchors. I used Michelle and Leona because they reminded me of who I was and that I wasn't Ashley. Anyway, the other roommates moved into the room together, and Ashley ended up in a room with Stephanie and the cat. Finally Stephanie wears her down and gets Ashley out on the town with her. Both get completely trashed off their ass. Our guy, Mr. X, met Ashley that night. He brought her back to his place, under the guise of being friends with her roomie, but the roomie wasn't there. She apparently left the bar with a professor friend of our guy's from another college and ended up leaving school permanently."

"Ya think it's possible Stephanie was murdered to create a back-story for Mr. X? If Steph were gone Ashley wouldn't have known that Mr. X wasn't a friend of hers. He could claim a friendship with Stephanie, and she wasn't around to verify the truth or lies."

I nod. "I would assume as much. We should be dragging the harbor for the girl. We know he likes drowning them. He put Ashley into a river, after all." I sigh, trying to find my place in my thoughts again. "Anyway, Ashley ends up dating this guy, Mr. X, and no one knows him. He uses the whole *I'm a teacher, we can't be seen together.* After many dates and what I would consider a serious amount of self-control on Mr. X's part, he takes her to the cabin on the mountain. This is where things shift for me. I felt like this was abnormal behavior for him, from a profiler's standpoint. I think our guy liked her and didn't want to hurt her. I think he wanted it to go somewhere, and I think he liked having her there and her not knowing about the girls under the garage."

"Jesus!"

"Right! It's a power thing, though, huh. He has her there, swooning over him, but really he has a harem under the stairs." I shake my head, reliving that little bit of weirdness. "But our guy isn't a normal guy, he's *American Psycho* mixed with Norman Bates. He's crazy, so he can't even have normal sex with her. The date goes from sort of awesome to quite revealing about his personality. He has some kinky, weird masturbating-dominator action."

"Is that the clinical name for it? I have noticed ya use a lot of technical terms in this."

"We aren't here for my winning conversation, Angie. The transcribers fix it for me, adding the technical words on the report." I lift a middle finger, but maintain my focus. "Anyway, I believe Mr. X makes the decision to kill Ashley over Christmas, but she still has a spot in his heart. I think at first he honestly tried to figure out a way to fix things with her, stalking her and watching her, wishing he hadn't revealed his kinky weirdo within. She sees him stalking her once, and they have real sex in the Jeep, and he panics like a weirdo. Of course then he realizes his insanity is obvious and he can't do normal, so he breaks things off, driving away like a nut. I think he looked back at his reaction, knew it wasn't sane, knew she had to be thinking 'what the fuck' about it. And while I believe he started the whole thing wanting to keep her safe, I would say the voices got to be too much. The paranoia of what she must think of him got to be too much. He connected his craziness to the missing girls, so he assumed she might also. That's when he ended up taking her the night she got drunk with the old roommates, the lesbians, from school."

I can hear her writing. "Is there anything else ya can see in the beginning before the abduction that might help us nail down who he is?"

I shake my head. "Dash and Rory fucking around with the recording—so Dash wouldn't have hurt feelings—messed with Mr.

X. It rotated between Dash as the bad guy at the beginning, and Rory being my brother, to Rory being the bad guy. Even little things found their way in there—his accent and love of Ireland. Idiots. Leave that in there too; let them get in shit for it."

She sighs. She's clearly as pleased as I am.

"Mr. X's ability to cook and his gentlemanly behavior was all Derek; I don't think that happened. I think he tried, but he was mediocre at best."

She flips and shuffles papers. "Okay, and post-abduction?"

I roll my head a little, taking a deep breath. Something dawns on me, and I crack an eyelid. "Why are you doing this?"

She shakes her head, rolling her eyes. "The little stunt with messing with ya meant Rory isn't allowed to be part of this debriefing, and the people who turn this whole fecked-up mess into a file are still managing the site. I suspect they will be at that site for at least six months. They found another set of caves being dug out. Mr. X was midconstruction on more cells. He was a greedy fucker, if ya ask me."

"Let's get back to it; I want this over." I gulp, closing my eyes again. "So Ashley wakes in the cell, she's scared, and from what I could tell there was a drug in her system. I suspect drugs were part of the food or water all along. The water bottles never cracked like they were brand new; the lids were always opened prior to being put in the minibar. The food would have been enriched, to help with vitamins and nutrients. Loads of vitamin D and all the Bs to stop them from dying down there."

"To prevent them getting sick down there with no sunlight."

"Right. But it's a guess." I shrug. "She wakes, panics, and then settles. It's too easy a transition in the beginning. She has no fight in her, and it didn't feel natural. Her friendship with the girl next to her, Bethany, was what saved her in the long run."

"Bethany Jones, the girl who died saving Ashley. She was twenty-four, an orphan, and a college student at University of Portland. She was an only child, and the only person who ever looked for her was her caseworker from her days in the system. She was a lot like ya, actually."

I open my eyes. "What?"

She nods. "Looked similar; parents died when she was young, in a house fire. Dad tied Mom up and lit the place up. No siblings. Bethany was at Grandma's when it happened. Grandma died two years later, putting Bethany in the foster system at the tender age of seven."

"No one would have missed her?"

She shakes her head, biting her lip. "The girls in the cellar were all fairly similar. Girls who had just spoken about traveling Europe or cut themselves off from their family."

"That's what was so different from them and Ashley, then? She did feel different in that hole. She seemed to be a bit of a rule breaker compared to the other girls."

She nods again. "Ashley Potter was close to her brother, who is older and at school in Portland. His name is Jason, but ya named him Simon and made him a twin?"

I smile weakly. "He was an unknown to me in her mind, so I made him known. I have to make certain I remain in control in her mind so I don't get lost."

She wriggles her lips. "From how it looks in the reports and facts we have found, Ashley really was the odd man out in the cells. The other girls were hardly missed. Considered runaways and part of the stats until Miss Ashley went missing. Then dust started getting kicked up. The uniforms and FBI started to notice there's a pattern in all the other missing girls. That's how we got involved."

"Okay, back to it." I settle back in and close my eyes. "Bethany and Ashley became friends, often holding each other through the tiny gap in the corner of their walls. They sat and picked at the wall, flushing the pieces in toilet paper. The girls were each other's rocks. At one point I would have to assume Bethany knew what she had to do. I couldn't enter Bethany's mind, so I don't know if it was a plan, but it seemed like one. As one of the original girls down there, Bethany didn't get a lot of time with Mr. X. So she waited for him to come to her, and when he finally did, she attacked, and tossed the key to Ashley. Ashley escaped, freeing one of the girls along the way, Lacey perhaps."

"Lacey Kavinsky. Aged twenty-six, been missing the longest," Angie adds. "Why did you pretend to be Bethany if you were in Ashley's mind?" She asks with her eyes on her notes.

"Because I needed to get Ashley's trust. She trusted no one in her life the way she did Bethany. She loved her like a sister. So I made her think I was Bethany. I needed her to try to show me more. And Dash and Rory screwing around with things meant I had to think fast." I shake my head. "So Ashley frees Lacey and runs above, blazing a trail for the other girls. But somehow Mr. X manages to convince Lacey to unlock his door. He then goes after Ashley. She hides out in the woods, in shock I think that Bethany has died, and the girls down below never even tried to escape. But they aren't as strong as Ashley is. They are all broken down, maybe even before Mr. X came along. Ashley runs to a cabin, sitting behind it, sort of defeated, I think. She's so tired and lost. She needs to figure out a plan, but the drugs in her system have her blurry a bit. Hazy in the brain so to speak. She hears a car, thinks it's him, returning to the cabin. So she gets up and runs through the woods, heading for the cabins on the lower part of the road. She finds an unlocked truck with keys in the visor, and drives it down the hill. But Mr. X is waiting down there for her. It clearly wasn't him who came up the hill. He rams the truck, causes an accident. Hits her over the head and takes her back." This is the part I can't take. I cringe.

"I think we know what happens next. I don't think we need to rehash the room. Is she awake when she goes into the water?" Angie sounds disturbed.

I nod, swallowing my bile. "Yes, she had been knocked out in the room of torture, but woke—" I heave, and everything inside of me threatens to come back up. "She woke from the cold water as it rushed over her. Her eyes opened, and she saw him, Mr. X. He was there, rinsing the blood from his hands. She managed to get her face above water and gasp some air in. It went black, her vision went black, as she washed down the shore. I don't think he even came close to expecting her to make it."

Angie's voice sounds shaken. "That river is known for being particularly violent. A few years ago a girl went missing from up there, and her car was parked near the river. So the police attached a tracker to a dead bear along the shore, tossed the bear's carcass in the river, and tracked its movements. They lost the bloody bear in the rapids. They had hoped the bear would lead them to the girl, but they lost the bear too. So technically Ashley shouldn't have made it."

I shrug. "Mild winter. All it did was rain this year, not a lot of snow. Rapids might have been less, giving poor Ashley a chance. Something he clearly never expected."

"This really was the worst of the worst, eh?" She taps a finger against her lips. "I wonder if that river is where the others are? Girls like Steph who would have gotten in the way of his story or planning? Or girls who didn't fit into the cellar lifestyle. People like him have been proven to habitually dump bodies the same way."

I nod. "Look at Samantha Barnes and her father."

"Aye." Angie runs her fingers down the page. "And how strange that all the other girls are all dead when we got there."

"It is strange."

She wrinkles her nose. "Almost as if he somehow knew we had found Ashley, even though no one leaked the information of a girl being found to the press."

"Yeah, that's true."

"And there's the DNA. The forensics said that the girls have DNA all over the damned place—fecking blood and all. That room was all about the vaginal fluids, and they have apparently found fluids from seven other girls too. But as far as he was concerned . . . I wonder if the way he knows Ashley survived the river is the same way he knows how to clean a scene. Maybe we need to think about the possibility that he killed off all the girls and cleaned his DNA off the scene because he's a uniform or a Fed?"

It hits me right in the guts. She's completely right. "Seriously! You are probably dead on. And had it not been for the fact uniforms found her and the FBI came in instantly to take over the scene, he might have been able to kill her off in the hospital. But the moment the FBI took over, no one was going into the room without security. So even if he was a uniform he didn't stand a chance." I shake my head.

She turns off the recorder and nods. "That is all a strange coincidence."

"Where is the file going now?"

"We're stuck with it. None of us have been taken off. I have heard nada about transfers to the next thing. It seems to me until they have some answers, this is our gig for now. At least you won't be going to Manhattan for a while."

I glance around, wanting a subject change from Manhattan desperately. "Well, then I guess we should see if any of the other information triggers anything in my mind or makes sense to us. Have you seen the rest of the intel on the guy who owned the cabin? The one who was dead a couple of years ago?"

She winces. "That's another nearly dead end. Whoever our Mr. X is, he's a smart asshole. The family who own the cabin are useless for us at this point, as far as I can see." She lifts a huge folder off the desk and slides it my way. "Interesting reading, to say the least. The owners are about as scummy as it gets." She cocks an eyebrow.

"Great." I drag the folder to me and open it. The first page is a picture of the cabin. I flip past it, shivering with memories.

"So why don't ya want the military gig now?" she asks as she scans the page. "There must be something behind you taking it and now looking ready to back out."

I shrug but don't answer, pretending to be looking at something.

"No, ya have to tell me."

I don't lift my gaze from the photos of the garage and the cabin as I scan. "I don't think I ever really wanted it. I said yes because it was what Dash wanted and I knew that; he wants us to be two office workers who start at nine and are off at five. He wants normal. But I'm not sure I do." Something catches my eye. I narrow my gaze, staring at the bedroom photos. The bed that was there, the one Mr. X cuffed Ashley to when he masturbated on her, is different. I remember the frame being metal and the headboard being scratched up from the cuffs. This one isn't metal. "Did we shoot all the bedrooms?" I flip through the pictures, but none of the rooms have the railings I'm looking for. "Where's the metal bed?"

She gives me a look. "What metal bed? Don't think we aren't going to finish this conversation, but what metal bed?"

"The black frame with the scratch marks. It was a queen-sized bed in one of the rooms."

She glances over the desk at the photos and scowls. "I don't recall a metal bed."

"One of those bed frames is brand fucking new." The time frame is off in my head.

"Brand new last spring when he took her?"

I shake my head. "I—she never saw the bed again. So it was bought sometime between last winter when she was on it and this fall when she escaped." I pause. "If I had to guess I would say he brought the bed and replaced it when he knew he was going to bring her there. He had to clean up the things in his place she had touched. She slept on that bed, she clung to it with her wrists handcuffed there. She was on that bed. She was sitting on the couch, but a thorough vacuuming would remove the evidence. She ate from the dishes, but everything goes in the dishwasher. So he replaced the bed with that one." I point at the wooden bed with the dark stain. "It's that room. I recognize the view from that room and the curtains."

She whistles. "Ya might possibly be redeeming yourself with this one."

I open my mouth to defend our work, but this whole mind run has been a cock-up from the start. Acid stirs in my stomach when I look at the bed. "Don't tell anyone what we found. The way he cleaned up the house and fixed everything and killed the girls with poison makes me wonder if we somehow have a leak with the police department."

She frowns, furrowing her barely-there ginger brows. "All right, but just so ya know, I am not going door to door with ya on this shite. I'm a doctor, not an investigator."

I roll my eyes. "I'll go by myself."

"Ya think that's a good idea?"

"I do. The fewer people involved, the less likely it is to get fucked up again."

I need to stop cussing so much.

16. SEE A MAN ABOUT A BED

"The Coal Arched bed frame is here." The man points at it, giving me a weird look. I follow him across Barrel & Barn at the University Village Shopping Center. I never come to places like this, ever, but if by some random unluckiness I do, I always try to look homeless. Pressure sales are not my thing, and coming in here like you might have ten dollars to your name is a bad idea. Barrel & Barn is one of those stores where you look at things that will make your house so much homier until you happen upon the price tag. Then you vomit and buy whatever you need off Craigslist like sensible people.

"Why are you so dressed down?" Dash leans in, probably wondering why we are bed shopping since he had demanded we buy a new one when he moved in with me. His diva ways really should have revealed his blue blood sooner.

I sip my latte and smile. "They harass you less if they know you're poor."

"Dear God, why didn't you say something? I would have changed. Are they going to harass me?"

"Yeah, most likely." I nod at the pretty salesgirl in the corner. "Especially her."

"Great!" He grimaces but I ignore it and drag him over to the bed, away from the pretty girl. We round the corner, and I stop dead in my tracks; it's exactly the bed.

"What is this? I don't even understand why we had to come back to Seattle, let alone here. Honestly, why are we at Barrel & Barn? This store is so—"

"Expensive?"

His eyes narrow. "Uhhh, yeah. Okay."

"You were going to put it down for being a place where peasants like me shop, weren't you?"

He opens his mouth and then snaps it shut.

"I wouldn't shop here, just so you're aware."

He nods. "Well, good, the furniture is subpar and would likely need repairs or replacement—" He pauses. "Wait, why wouldn't you shop here?"

I blink, stunned at his snobbery. "Not even trying to keep that shit locked up anymore, huh?" I point at the two-thousand-dollar price tag next to him on a small round dining-room table. "Because that's more than one of my paychecks."

He blinks staring at it. "Are you being serious?"

I stare at him deadpan. "You want to go joint account with me so we can both laugh when I get paid?"

"You mean you'll finally agree to let me buy you things?"

"No, and since I met your parents, extra no."

He laughs like I'm kidding, but I'm not.

An older salesman strolls over to us, but he looks through me at Dash. "We have some lovely end tables that just came in from Africa—rubberwood, and very charming." I don't know what that has to do with anything, so I make an attempt to ignore them both and stare at the bed that's been haunting my dreams.

"Oh, I don't need any end tables, thanks."

"They are exactly the right size for any room in the house, no matter the living room or recreation-room size. They will fit, I guarantee it."

Dash cocks an eyebrow. "You guarantee they'd fit in any room? That's a boastful recommendation."

I roll my eyes and leave them there to haggle out whether we are buying new end tables for our townhouse in DC. Dash of course is wearing high-end clothing and very expensive shoes, making him a direct target for the sales people. He says he wears expensive shoes for the support, but I think he just can't bring himself to wear some poor-people shoes. He won't dress down, at all. I always thought it was cute before, the way he looked so put together. But now I see it's bred into him. When I bought Toms in the summer, just some canvas boat shoes for bumming around in, he nearly stroked. I thought I was spending a ridiculous amount on shoes. He couldn't believe I would wear canvas shoes and tried to convince me to buy some sensible Italian shoes at eight hundred dollars a pair. It's like dating a college girl with a shoe fetish.

The thought flits about in my head as I walk to the bed where I once saw an actual college girl handcuffed. It's identical, and up close it's creepy. The feel of the cold metal makes my skin burn.

I don't even know how to be near it without losing my mind. I swallow hard and turn back, sending a text to Angie.

Barrel & Barn, University Village Shopping Center, has the bed in stock. I bet it was purchased from here. I'll get some videos for surveillance if I can and purchase dates for the bed. But I need you to make it rain with creds! Send in the bigwigs to force the hands of these hipster punks so they give me what I want. Get me the president of fucking Barrel & Barn if you have to.

I turn and leave Dash still bartering with the man who has now managed to get Dash over to the end tables. I can see the price tag from here. It's not pretty. Unfortunately, the pretty saleslady I pointed out, *young* pretty saleslady, has been sucked into the conversation with Dash and the other salesman now too. She's mostly giggling and toying with her hair like a nimrod. I almost hope he buys the damned tables and gets them on sale because she is lost in his dream-boat doctor crap.

Lord knows I have been lost in it too, from day one. Dreamy and funny and sexy. Best kind of doctor. If we played fetish or role-playing games I'd never let him change from being the doctor, but we don't.

I turn away, leaving the three of them to argue rubberwood and furniture buying.

I'm not here for that anyway.

I am seeking out the most important looking person in the store. I snigger when I find him, noting he is of course a hipster. In an urban store like this one the lead salesman behind the counter always will be.

His probably fake eye glasses, skinny jeans, and sweater with a plaid shirt beneath make me suspect he is going to be fun to speak with.

I stroll over, watching him with a steady gaze as he looks up from his binder, giving me a snooty smile. He patronizes before I've even opened my mouth. "The salespeople are over there. I'm sure when they're done, one of them will help you."

"No, I think you are the one I need to speak to." I smile, with a little patronization of my own, and continue to walk toward him.

He sighs, aggravated by my very existence. But he has no idea what I have been through, how much sighing and patronizing I can take without it wounding my delicate self. He pushes his glasses up and tilts his head. "If this is a complaint, you'll have to wait for the manager to be in."

I shake my head, stopping when I get to the desk. "I'm Special Agent Spears, and I need to ask you a few questions."

His jaw drops. "I think I need—"

"Identification, sure, why not." I pull my wallet out and flash the badge I almost *never* show anyone. It's not even real, technically. It's government issue, but I am not entirely FBI. I'm not entirely one thing or another, but I have some form of credentials for every single country in the free world.

He swallows hard. "Th-there must be some sort of mistake. You must be in the wrong store."

I stare at him blankly. "You think I make mistakes?" I glance at his nametag. "Mark?"

He shakes his head, and I can see just how nervous he is.

"I need to know every single sale you have had, whether in store or an online purchase where the person picks it up here or even has it delivered somewhere, for that bed. The Coal Arched bed frame. Queen-size only. And your surveillance footage for the days when one was bought." It took me three hours to find the stupid bed. I used Google Image search until my head was spinning, but now we know exactly the bed it was. The uniqueness of the frame saved me from spending the rest of my life searching.

Mark's shoulders slump, and I can see he's going to try the old "pawn it off on someone else" or ask me to come back later to pick it up. I smile wider as the phone next to him rings. I know it's Angie coming through with credentials. I know she's made some kind of magic happen.

"Excuse me." He instantly perks up, lifting a finger and answering. "Barrel & Barn, Mark speaking." His face drops, his cheeks flushing. "Oh, hello, sir. Of course." He swallows hard, nodding, as if that will help, and then not speaking for several moments. The phone clicks loudly, and with a shaking hand he puts it back on the counter.

I sigh, looking back at Dash and the sales team. He has them all laughing and smiling. It makes me want to stroll over there like the little rain cloud I am. The girl's face will be precious when she realizes that hot and charming man is dating this little hobo in a hoodie and ripped jeans.

When I look back Mark winces. "So do you have particular dates?"

"I do." I nod. "Who was that on the phone?"

"One of the Ottos from Hamburg, Germany. The owners of Barrel & Barn. He said the vice president of the United States had called him personally and said I am to—to oblige you in everything."

"Sounds about right." I lean in a little. "Dates are November 2014 through to let's say November 2015. One year exactly. And I need you to be fast, very fast. By the time that guy buys whatever crap they're selling him, I need to be ready to walk out of the store. Oh, and give him the store discount so he thinks he's getting a deal. It'll kill him if he doesn't get one after all that charming he's doing." I turn and stalk back to the mini party midfloor. When I glance back, Mark is scurrying like a little weasel.

As I approach, the girl's brows draw close. She cocks one of the perfectly manicured things and eyes me up. I nudge Dash like we are buddies, not wanting to kill his sale. "So, rubberwood."

"African rubberwood." He corrects me and then frowns. "Don't you think it looks a little damaged here on the corner?"

I purse my lips and shake my head. "I think that is the thing they do to make it look that way. Like it's old already, but it's new."

The salesguy claps his hands together victoriously. "It is, indeed, distressed to appear antiqued."

Dash looks disheartened. "They distress perfectly good furniture as a fad?"

The guy's face falls.

"It's all the rage," I comment dryly, glancing back again to check on Mark and the scurrying.

"She is absolutely correct. It is all the rage. And we only have five of the tables. They would be the only set in Seattle."

"Unless you order online."

The guy's love for me wanes. "Right." His lips move like he might try a different tactic, but I look over at Dash and shrug. "Just get them. You can have them delivered to the house. I'm sure if you buy all five they'll give you a deal because five is such a randomly odd number. They don't want one table just chilling here." I am completely joking since we live on the other side of the country.

But my version of joking is always lost on people.

Dash's eyes light up, and the guy's fill with worry. He glances at his boss, the ass manager at the counter. "I'm sure we can work something out."

The sales team scatters as Dash turns and pulls me into his embrace. I stiffen, not loving the PDA at all. I don't mind an arm around my shoulder, but wrapped around my waist is a whole other thing. "You are a smart girl."

I roll my eyes. "So I know how to get things on sale. It's not an admirable trait. It's a necessity because I am poor. You may not be, but I am." I tilt my head, trying to pull back even more. "Wait, if your brother is getting everything, does that mean you're poor too and have to live on wages?"

He shakes his head. "No. That's not how that works at all." He smiles. "I can't believe I got a discounted price. My father and mother would be appalled that I negotiated a price on warehouse furniture, but I did it."

"Yes, you stooped pretty low." I manage to step back, but his hands are huge and strong, forcing me to stay.

"I feel a rush from it. It was exciting." He presses his lips to mine, ignoring the lack of enthusiasm I'm flashing. He kisses, oblivious to my not kissing back, and pulls back. "Let's go arrange for shipping them."

"You realize you have no longer gotten them on sale and the store in DC could have sold you the same tables, right? Now you've paid some insane amount of money for them. You should just back out. They can't make you buy them."

He wraps a hand around my mouth. "Shhhhhh."

When we get to the counter, poor Mark is sweating. I've clearly asked him to do the hardest thing since inventing the telephone. His eyes dart at Dash, no doubt assuming he's a mark or a spy or a Fed too, but not sure which. But then Dash speaks: "I would like to buy the tables at a discounted price because of the odd number." The salesguy rounds the corner and slaps down the tags and gets Dash to start filling out the forms for delivery.

Mark continues whatever he's doing for me as the guy and Dash finish the sale.

Everyone's face drops, including mine, when he says England. The cost of the tables isn't even half the cost of the shipping, but Dash doesn't bat an eyelash at spending that much. I'm ready to stab Dash, but I don't, mostly because I need Mark to focus on the paperwork and not on the spurts of Dash's blood getting on the store's merchandise.

The pretty salesgirl continues eyeballing Dash and then stink-eyeballing me. I ignore it. I'm actually excited to leave so Mark can tell them what was going on. I can imagine just the way he'll do it, flailing his arms and exaggerating the whole thing. He seems the type—enthusiastic.

Mark slips me a bag of thumb drives and paperwork as Dash completes the paperwork for the shipping. Mark winks on the sly, only not on the sly. I offer an awkward wave and walk out. "Why are you shipping that to England?"

Dash shrugs. "We don't have Barrel & Barn in England; it'll be a novelty there. Besides, it suits a lodge we have in the north for hunting. The wood is similar to the mounting my great-grandfather had done in Africa. I'm almost curious if that was rubberwood he used. So I'm sending it home, and we shall see."

I don't know what to say, beyond maybe make a face. Mounting things from Africa certainly means animals, often rare animals. The sort that are endangered.

He offers up a look like he's annoyed with me. "Not that any of that nonsense matters. From the look of things back there I have to assume he hit on you. Did he?"

"What?"

"He winked, I saw him."

I roll my eyes. "Yeah, guys are hitting on me in front of you, 'cause they know they stand a chance at getting me out from under your fat thumb."

He grins. "You like my fat thumbs."

I walk faster to escape his version of a dirty joke as he chuckles to himself like an old pervert. I don't know how to respond to dirty jokes about stuff we have actually done.

17. FREQUENT FLYER MILES

I don't understand why in the gods ya had to go all the way back to Seattle to do that. Isn't Dash getting a wee bit suspicious about the file that doesn't seem to be ending? Does he suspect you're avoiding the new job?" Angie asks, gazing over the pages I have brought back to DC. Meeting her at the office for nighttime chow and research hasn't ever happened before. We meet for random things, usually involving my health and welfare. Or things not work-related at all.

"No, he thinks this is routine. You and he are never part of the debriefing afterward, so I have been able to buy a bit of time with that. And whenever anyone from the team flies, we use one of the Fed jets, so it's no hassle. Or helicopters for short distances. It isn't like going through the airport."

She cocks an eyebrow. "Right, but you and Rory have never had a file unsolved before."

"I know. It's driving me insane. I don't know what to do. The Feds are on it, the locals are on it, everyone is on it, and it's going nowhere fast." I sigh, feeling a sickness wash over me every time I think of it. "We are searching high and low for connections to possible avenues we haven't searched yet." I lean on the desk and sip my tea.

She has an orange highlighter, and I have a yellow one. She marks down the bed purchases, since Mark was only able to print out the days where one sold, with all the other sales included. After spending three hours searching the Internet for the exact bed and then flying all the way to Seattle, this is nothing.

I highlight the customers who left an address to run in the system. I'm assuming we won't find Mr. X in the system, but weirder things have happened, directly to Angie and me.

"So, on a scale of one to ten, how bad was Thanksgiving?"

I scoff. "Forty."

She laughs. "They were that evil to ya?"

"Hands down, Dash's family are the most evil people I have ever met. I mean aside from this job and criminals, but then again I never spent enough time with them to know what they were truly capable of."

She stops laughing. "You'd know right away if you were sitting next to evil, true evil! You're very good at judging people. I'm shite. One drink and I love everyone."

"Except the English and all the Irish, apart from Rory, and none of the Germans, and—"

"All right, all right, ya sassy wee thing. I don't hate all of them; just more often than not they are assholes. And don't be fooled, I do hate Rory. Who ya kidding on that one? The man's a savage. And when he kisses, he spits too much. Got a glandular thing. You have to rein him in or you'll drown."

I wrinkle my nose. "Oh gross, too much!" I shake my head, still scanning the page. "No. I don't think I'm that good a judge of character. And even if I were, everyone has a preconceived notion of people they know through someone else, which changes everything. You would not know in a case like that."

"Enlighten me, O wise one," she snarks and leaves another orange mark on the page.

"Firstly, you go into something like meeting a person's family with preconceived notions. These people raised Dash, how bad could they be? They're upper class and clean, so you assume they aren't half bad. We can't even fight it; as a people we find it hard to find attractive people guilty. Secondly, your preconceived notions are usually confirmed in your first few minutes of meeting them, when they're on their best behavior. You've already given them several chances, and they have behaved in the way they have, so you automatically make a judgment. It's called a first impression, and we absolutely do it. So that means that later on, when they fuck up, we make excuses for their behavior, instead of seeing them for what they are. Thirdly, the moment someone is family or friend or friend of a friend, we offer them more of a chance. We don't want to hurt the person we love, and we offer the offender an olive branch out of the kindness of our hearts."

She rolls her eyes. "All but you, ya mean."

I shrug. "I've had the unfortunate opportunity to see that most people are awful, and watching a person make excuse after excuse for their loved one's terrible behavior is hard, but you learn a lot by seeing it. I don't trust people because I have to, not normally. I trust them because they earn it, and there are not many who have. But it's always someone I least expect to trust."

She scoffs. "I have yet to see ya make a bad call as far as a man went, friend went, or suspect went. You even nail it when it's a vic and the rest of us believe, but you're not sure. It's 'cause you're so quiet and creepy, sitting there taking it all in."

"Well, it'll happen the other way one day, and you'll see. No one is a perfect judge of character."

"Dogs are." She looks up at me and sighs. "But to make fun of and try to ruin the happiness of an orphan who has made her way in the world? They really are special people."

I lift my cup of tea and she lifts hers, and we clink glasses before returning to our work.

She passes out an hour later, and I want to too, but I have to keep going, scanning through the videos on the thumb drives Mark gave me. Angie doesn't have the show in her head that I do. I have to solve this. It's never happened before.

My eyes are closing and the clock strikes three when I finish cross-referencing all the people who bought the beds with the information left in the system. My phone vibrates with a message from Dash—Miss you, come home! Binx is making me pet him. He's worried.

I roll my eyes and plug the next thumb drive into my laptop and fast-forward to the time of the purchase. Each person resolves themselves in my mind when I can cross-check them in the system, check their social media, and scratch them from the list.

In my head I know it's likely I'm looking for law enforcement or a spouse of an officer. Or I'm looking for someone who works with the City of Seattle and has access to inside information. When I come across a banker who's five feet tall and chubby, I don't even bother with the social media.

There were seventy-nine of those beds sold in the time frame I have. I believe the bed was purchased in January or February, when he knew he was going to abduct or kill her. He's made himself vulnerable then.

The majority of the purchases were made by women; I eliminate them immediately. I might not have seen Mr. X, but I know he was handsome enough to land a bunch of college girls, and he wasn't a she.

My eyes grow heavy, so I get up to make another coffee. From the kitchen I am still sort of watching the video as I fill the water reservoir in the coffee machine. I am yawning and stretching when I swear a section of the video glitches. I hurry over, rewinding and watching as a man wearing a baseball cap and sunglasses comes up to the counter. He points as he talks, waving his hands back to where the beds are. He's white, tall, broad, and fit, and that's about all I can see. All shit I knew before we started this.

He turns his face toward the camera, and it glitches as he makes eye contact—well, as his sunglasses do. There's a halo for half a second, and then the whole picture goes black. If it were in color I suspect it might be red.

The coffee finishes brewing as I rewind it again.

"What the bloody hell is going on?" Angie lifts her face, sputtering and moaning. "I wasn't asleep. I was resting my eyes." She rubs her eyes and lays her face back down on Rory's desk.

I grab the coffee and hurry back to the picture. I rewind and watch three more times, but there's nothing. He's wearing a generic pair of pants and a hoodie. He looks like a criminal if you ask me, but I know that's the first choice cops go for when they disguise themselves.

I sit back and watch him walk. Of course he's familiar to me, I've spent months in my head with him. I watch it over and over, knowing it's him. He knows about the cameras; he knows about using a laser pointer against a camera.

He doesn't go anywhere else in the store, and he pays with cash. I scan his order of the bed and mattress, raising my eyebrows when I see the purchase was shipped to the fucking townhouse in downtown Seattle. The one the old man owned—the dead old man, who also owned the cabin where the girls were tortured.

Damn!

Someone is using that house still. I close up the computer, remove the thumb drives, and put the papers in my bag, before waking Angie with a nudge. She gets up from Rory's desk and stumbles out of the office and down the corridor with me guiding her. I will have to go back to Seattle in the morning. And I'm making Angie come along.

I nod at the guards as we leave and head for the car parked out front. She falls asleep in the car, while I plot.

18. SURPRISE

I chew my licorice, watching the house. My cell phone rings again, another angry call from Dash. How do I explain I know what's going on, that even though I'm not supposed to be doing the job, I can't let it go? All it does is confirm his hatred for my work. It proves he's right and that I can't separate from a file.

I text Angie: Cover for me if Dash calls, huh?

Her response is immediate.

I would if a huge and spicy doctor wasn't sitting here eyeballing my every move from our little apartment here in Seattle . . .

I wince. "I'll tell him where I am, don't bother," I type. But that isn't as easy as texting Angie. I watch the house, a brownstone townhouse in an older but wealthy downtown area in Seattle. I can't believe he flew here. It's my eighth flight to Seattle in three weeks. Thank God for our plane. Everything is easy and at my disposal, so stalking this house from my rental car is simple. Far simpler than explaining to my fiancé why I can't let go.

I text the address I am at and the color of my rental car.

We need to talk!

His message makes my insides clench but not enough to stop me from texting: Be astute, please!

I scowl at the word *astute*, not confident I am correct in what it means. I had meant to write *cautious* but my crappy spelling got it autocorrected to *astute*. I send one more message: And by that I mean careful to not be seen!

Thank you, Jane, I am completely aware of what ASTUTE means!

I slump, dropping the phone on the console, and sit back to watch the house again.

The passenger door opens far faster than it should, but he has hate driving him on when he sits in the seat next to me. I can tell by the way he's breathing. "Hello, love!"

I jump when Rory gets in. "You scared the piss out of me! Why are you here too? Did they fly you down? Did we find something?"

"Too?" He grins widely. "I think the question is what in the bloody hell are you doing here? The cops over there watching the house phoned you in. I was already here, never made it back to DC yet. I was meant to go home a couple of days ago, but the boss man wanted me to ensure everyone is being wrangled and none of the uniforms or Feds are going to leak any information." He chuckles and sits back. "So what has made you and Angie circle back here? Angie never told me she was coming back."

"Nothing. Women's intuition is all. We decided to take a quick trip and see if a couple of stupid leads turned out to be anything." I scowl at him, not sure he hasn't blabbed to the police. He always gets chatty with them, whereas I stay behind. He does seem to learn more from them, but I feel like the relationship is reciprocated. Someone leaked that the girl was found; someone let him kill all those other girls. And I can't rule out Rory. He might have let it slip by accident.

"Women's intuition?" He wrinkles his nose. "I think it's something more. I think you found something and you aren't sharing it." His eyes flash a little hurt. "Ya know Angie doesn't keep secrets from me."

To crack the awkward shell we seem to be encased in, I mutter clumsily, "Yeah, me either. She never told me you were staying behind. In fact, no one mentioned it. Did you volunteer?"

"Wow, that woman doesn't check her messages. If I had feelings they'd be bloody hurt." He turns, scowling, and it's in that moment something feels off.

I laugh, but it's weird, uncomfortable. He pauses, no longer smiling. His face slowly drops. "You all right, Jane?"

I nod slowly, but my vision starts to fill with a thousand images, each one slowly progressing into something worse. His face, his laugh, his smile, his snarl. The way his teeth gnash when he speaks with a sneer. I swallow hard.

"What is wrong, Princess?" he asks, lifting a hand and dragging it down my cheek. Everything inside of me screams but I sit frozen; a small piece of me is still the girl he tormented. I feel everything she felt, every moment of horror and agony.

It takes approximately seven seconds for me to completely realize he is Mr. X. Mr. X is him. Every piece of the puzzle slips into place.

"How?" The word falls from my lips, my eyes flood with tears, and my brain points out all of the clues that are now so obvious. "I know you tricked Dash into changing the recording when you recognized who Ashley Potter was. You must have panicked when you realized she was alive. That she had survived the river. This is why you got Dash to confuse me by introducing you as the bad guy so you could make a cover for yourself. I see now how you knew we were coming and killed all those girls, and how you used all of your skills to avoid detection. I guess I only have to ask you one thing, Rory. How could you? Being who we are, and seeing what we see, how could you?" I press a button on my phone, something he doesn't see me do as I pick it up from the console.

"How could I? How could I not? Each one of them was mine." His eyes lose the Irish charm and roguish flair. Instead, the dark-blue seems to blacken as he tilts his head forward, casting a shadow over his eyes. His smile becomes menacing as evil—the pure evil in his heart—takes over. His eyebrows even arch differently. He is sick, which I can see. "You can't be surprised, Jane. Not after everything. You were attracted to me in there, in Ashley's mind. You wanted me. You moaned and writhed while you were in there like I have never seen you do. Angie, that twat, was jealous that you got to have me as your Dr. Russo, Derek the sex machine. You're the only mind runner I've ever seen who uses sex in someone's head." He twirls a strand of my hair that's escaped my ponytail. "You want a dark and scary man to hate-fuck, to conquer you." His eyes light up. "You like it in there, don't you? You've gotten addicted to riding their minds and feeling their pain. In there you're a real girl. Having family and friends and a life that's real, beyond this bullshit lot you've been handed. That wanker Dash never deserved you. He sees the light, but I see you, Princess, I see you for who you are. I know you want love in all the wrong places."

He grips the side of my face, pulling me into him. His lips bubble over with spit, but before he can attempt to kiss me the door is opened and he's thrown from the car. "What in the hell are you doing?" Dash grabs him but shouts at me. The conversation with Angie over his drooling problem mixes with the spit-filled kisses he gave Ashley. The whole world feels like it crumbles, but I manage to point as my hand shakes and my eyes dart. "It's—it's him."

Dash sees the look on my face and spins, but he's no match for Rory. Dash swings, and Rory punches him twice, knocking him to the ground, and breaks into a sprint.

I get out, running after him, before I've even given it much thought. I point at the police in the car across from us. *"Get them to help us!"*

Dash scrambles across the road for the cop car as I kick my legs into high gear.

I'm not like Rory. I'm not crazy. He runs through the traffic once we get onto Queen Anne Avenue from the side street we were on. He slides over the hoods of moving cars and dashes into traffic like a madman, almost as if he's toying with me. He wants me to come and get him. I stop running, sending a quick video message and calling a number much more powerful than 911.

"It's Agent Spears, 549621, go for code."

The phone makes a dial tone just before a man picks up—not just any man, the vice president of the country. "Agent Spears?" he asks softly.

"Mr. Vice President, this is Agent Jane Spears. My partner, Rory Guthrie, is the perp on the Granger Mountain homicides. I don't know how, but he has just gone rogue on me, admitting to it all. I have sent the recording I made as he spoke in the car."

"Are you fucking kidding me?" The man loses the composure he has maintained through previous crises. Ones I would have lost mine in. The video starts playing. Rory confessing to it all fills the background as the vice president's breath increases. "This is a situation, Spears. He's a fully trained op."

"Yes, sir. He's gone black. He's running across Queen Anne Avenue in Seattle, heading east toward the Lake Union houses." I pause. "He's wearing a black jacket and dark-blue jeans. I can't get to him from here. You have to send out cars."

"Mother of God."

"Sir, I have everything to take him down, but I need you to send a guard to the house, the townhouse we are watching. There is already one car on-scene, but I suspect the police squad car is full of dead cops. He ran past them without even batting an eyelash. I suspect there are dead people in the house also. I will need as much backup as possible to finish this safely."

"I will dispatch as many as I can. You get on the local radios and tell the boys in blue what's what. They are our best chance right now to mobilize. Seattle has SWAT. I'll take care of that." He sighs into the phone. "Get your ass back to that townhouse and find me some goddamned answers, agent!" He hangs up the phone, and I watch as Rory becomes a small black dot and then is gone.

I want to chase him. My instincts tell me to chase him. But something whispers to me that he is setting me up. And he knows me nearly as well as Angie and Dash do.

"They're dead, Jane. Both—dead." Dash catches up to me, his voice wavering from the exertion of running. When I look back I wince; his nose is clearly broken. He points. "You know how, right?"

I nod and walk over, lifting my hands to his cheeks. Hot tears stream from my eyes as I line up my thumbs along his nose and press my fingers into his cheeks. "One, two—" I shove his nose before saying *three* to trick him into relaxing. The bones snap back into place, and blood instantly starts gushing. He grunts like he wants to scream but keeps it together for me. He lifts his shirt to catch the blood, but his eyes wander to the road. "Where is he? How the hell did this happen?"

"Gone. Not sure." My voice cracks. "What will Angie say?" I shake my head. She is as dear to me as family.

"I believe I would die inside if I found out it was you who was responsible for so much horror."

I nod, hating where this will take our team at work. Hating that one of ours has betrayed us. But I don't have time to worry about it. My body reacts, as it has been taught to. Tears stream down my cheeks as I sniffle and drag my bleeding fiancé back to the townhouse. Another squad car is there already.

"Stop!" One officer has his gun out already as the other is clearing the street and calling for more backup.

"I'm Agent Spears. I'm going for my badge. I am unarmed." I

lift my badge slowly to show the trembling man. He takes it, looking it over many times before putting his gun away. I nod at his radio. "May I?"

He nods. His eyes are filled with tears for his brothers on the force.

I click the radio on. "My name is Agent Jane Spears. You will not know who I am. I work intel. That is all you need to know. Two of your own have been shot in the Queen Anne area." I point back toward the park for the benefit of the men next to me. "The man you are chasing, the man who killed your friends here today and many others, is Irish, ex–Irish Intelligence. He's CIA trained, American military trained, and works with the UN for the FBI and Secret Service. His name is Rory Guthrie. His file is being faxed and e-mailed to every one of the police departments in the city and outskirts. It will be limited viewing, but you will have what you need. You will be supported by my unit, and you will assist us so that we can assist you. We want you to have your retribution, but we need to be smart about it. No more loss of life. This is one of ours who has done this; we want our retribution as well, but no vigilante efforts. We need teamwork. Your chiefs are being briefed as we speak. Ror—the killer has gone toward the Lake Union area. He's a dark-haired male in his midthirties with an olive complexion, dark-blue eyes, and an Irish accent, though he can speak without it. He was last seen wearing a dark jacket and dark-blue jeans. He is six foot two, two hundred and twenty pounds. SWAT is being called in. If you see him he should be considered armed and dangerous; he's a Caution Victor." I click the radio off, passing it back to the man, who is visibly shaken but is ready to do his job. "Thank you."

He steps back, and I can tell he's not sure what to do, so I tell him. "Please help my fiancé find some bandages." I hold a hand out to Dash, who looks shell-shocked. I dial Angie's number and start toward the house, stopping by the police car to ensure both men are dead—but no visible injuries are present. The air around us outside smells fine, but I have a bad feeling. Rory is smart and creative.

I wave my hand. "Don't go near the car. There could be gas inside, or poison." The three police who are near the car step back. "Call for hazmat suits and people to test the air."

One guy instantly talks on his radio as Angie answers the phone.

"Ya want to tell me why three FBI agents just showed up at the apartment and started taking all our stuff?"

I don't have a filter, especially not when I get to this place. "Rory is the one."

"What? What in the bloody—" She pauses before I can hear the change. "Oh God, of course he is, isn't he? What the bloody hell else would he be doing with a girl like me? He's been using me all along, hasn't he?"

I hate him. "You need to go somewhere safe. Let the FBI take you into custody to a lab. Start thinking about how it is him and how we missed things. All kinds of things."

"The bed, the bed frame with the cuts in the railings . . ." Her voice trails off. "I have to go." She hangs up.

We both have the same journey; we must backtrack our brains and every file and find where he's been and what he's used against us. Against our work.

I take the steps to the townhouse slowly, peering in the windows as I approach. There's no one here, but that doesn't mean he hasn't booby-trapped it for me. I glance at the house next door, where a small woman with white hair looks out her window, scrutinizing us and what we are doing.

I glance back at Dash and the police. "I'll get this lady. Evacuate the block until we know what's in that car and this townhouse. Think we need a bomb squad."

The police officer talking on the radio doesn't even question anything I say, he just calls it in.

Dash looks like he might argue, but he doesn't. He nods, blotting his face and turning to go to the other homes along the street. I go down the stairs and walk over to the lady's house, smiling at her and flashing my badge. She opens the door when I get to it. I nod. "My name is Jane. I need to ask you some questions. Do you have a backyard we can talk in?"

"It's very cold." Her voice is frail and squeaky; I like it.

"I know, but we need to be away from the front of the house."

She pulls a sweater from the old wooden stand at the front door. "Okay, Jane. My name is Esther." She shrugs it on and shuffles through the house.

When we get to the back door she opens it and walks to the brown grass. "It's so cold it feels like it might snow. It is Christmas next week, so that's likely, I suppose. Sometimes we get lucky with a few flakes at Christmas."

"Christmas and snow go hand in hand." I smile with awkwardness, pulling my phone from my pocket. "There is a man I am looking for." I lift the phone and scroll through the pictures until I find the one I am looking for. I point it at her.

She leans in. "Derek, the nephew of old Richard next door. He's a sweet boy."

I swallow hard. "I need to know everything you know about Derek."

She gives me a skeptical look from behind her hazel eyes and drawn-on eyebrows. "Why?"

"Because he's in danger. I think he's in trouble, and I need to help him. He's my partner, and someone has framed him for something terrible."

Her jaw drops. "He knew it was coming. He said it was only a matter of time before they came looking for him. He said he'd had some bad dealings with the wrong people. Boys his age make bad choices, though, ya know?"

I nod, completely confused as to whether she knew Rory/Derek or not.

"He was the executor of the will for old Richard, or Dick, as I always called him. Derek was his executor. Poor boy, those greedy kids of Dick's made him sign the one daughter out because she was adopted, so the house sits empty. It's very bad for the neighborhood, you know? That's how I met Derek; I wanted to know what was being done about the empty house. No one was mowing the lawn. It was terrible."

Simple things work her up, but she's earned that right. She looks a hundred if she's a day. I can't imagine how old Dick was if she's calling him old.

"So Derek said that he was gonna make sure it was taken care of. That boy was good to his word. He kept the lawn nice and made sure the lights were automatic so no one got any funny ideas. He's a very good boy."

If she only knew.

"He came over whenever he could and let me know what was happening. Those greedy kids of Dick's are in talks now to divide the whole thing—the cabins and house here in the city and properties in Canada."

I cock an eyebrow. "Canada?"

"Vancouver—Vancouver something. It will come to me."

"Do you know when the last time was he came to this house here?"

"Yesterday. He came by and told me he was having these problems. Said it was just a matter of time before things got bad for him, but that he would still make sure someone came and took care of the house. He told me not to go inside, no matter what. Something about a funny gas leak he was having someone look at next week."

I sigh. "What can you tell me about Dick?"

"Died in a car accident on his way up to Granger Mountain. He went there every weekend. Was an avid hiker and backcountry skier, I guess. And there's a bit of a backcountry lodge up there."

"Did his kids ski?"

She shakes her head. "Those kids hated their father, never wanted anything to do with him. Hated the mother before she died too. Always going away to college and living as far as they could. Selfish brats. When people get old they need some extra help, ya know?"

I offer her a warm smile. "I am going to get one of the police officers out front to take you to the hotel we are setting up for all the nice people here on the street. We are going to check that gas leak now."

"A hotel?" She looks like she might argue.

I walk her to the back gate, through to the alley. "The gas leak might be bad inside. We need to clean it up. The whole block is being evacuated."

"Oh, all right then."

"Is there anyone else inside?"

"No. Just me." She wraps her arms around herself. "I will need my purse, though. It's on the table at the front door. Would you be a dear and lock up when you grab it? The back door locks on its own."

I wince and turn, running back to the house. I snag her purse, lock her door, and run it out to the back. Quickly, before I reach her, I call Dash's cell. "Send a car to the back alley here. A lady needs a ride to the hotel where the people are being evacuated to."

"Okay, are you all right?"

"Yup." I hang up so I don't have to talk in front of her. I am far from okay. I have a terrible feeling about how Old Dick lived and died. The car is there within seconds. "Thank you, Esther, for talking to me."

"It's my pleasure, Jane. You take care, and when you find dear Derek, you let him know I said good luck." She climbs into the car and waves as they drive her away. I jog around the block, hurrying back to the front of the house where the cordoned-off area is.

Men in hazmat suits begin their slow walk to the car. They have tools to test the air quality, and mirrors to check the underside of the vehicle for explosives.

We all back up even more. Dash finds me in the crowd and wraps his arms around my shoulders and kisses the top of my head gingerly. "I just want this to be over."

"I can't believe this is happening," I mutter.

"Me either. I knew he was weird, but not like that. No way was he like that."

I nod, pulling my cell phone out and making another call. "I need to speak to the three kids who are fighting over the will over here at this house; guy's name is Richard. Rory is the executor of the will. Somehow he used the alias Derek and became the old man's nephew. How did we not notice Derek was the name of the nephew?"

The voice on the other side is an analyst named Antoine, a member of my team back home. "Lady Jane, what're the chances this is a mess-up and my best buddy isn't a homicidal pervert?"

"Don't be naive. Not everyone we love is a good person. Most are shit."

He chuckles into the phone. "I do adore you, Jane!" It's not affectionate. It's bitter, and he's basically using my own words to call me shit. "The son and daughter live at the same house. Address is just sent to your cell, but no one has seen hide nor hair of them for about a month. The adopted daughter lives out of town, close to a place called Tanner. Also sent that address; anything else?"

"Tanner? Stay close to the phone. This shit is unraveling faster than I can keep up, and I am down one partner."

"Yes, the one who always called in with funny jokes and had donuts couriered over to me."

"This is serious."

"Aye, aye, Captain." He hangs up as I glance at Dash. "The adopted daughter lives just outside of the town where Ashley Potter was from."

"Where was that again?"

"Tanner. You want me to take you to a hotel?"

It's obvious Dash doesn't know how to take this all in. He's slowly swelling from Rory's punches and looking more miserable by the second. He shakes his head. "No, that's okay."

I cup his face as the area we are in fills with onlookers. In my peripheral vision I catch a glimpse of the hazmat guys circling around the back of the car. "I love you, Dash. And I am so glad you came along when you did. I honestly didn't know what to say or do when I figured it out. I never would have suspected Rory. I was having a heart attack. You saved me."

He gets a big cheesy grin, but it doesn't last long. "Holy shit!" He grabs me and runs, dragging me along.

I don't have a chance to look back and see what it is. I'm thrown to the ground as the sound of a large explosion fills the air. From the ground I can see people rolling and falling, tripping and shoving as they scream with their mouths open wide. My ears ring so I can't hear the sounds well, but from what I can see all the people within two blocks are on the ground, in obvious pain and shock.

Around us buildings shake, and windows break and drop onto the sidewalk.

When I look back at the source of our situation, I can tell the car was clearly the bomb.

Thankfully we are all far enough away that no one seems to be in grave condition, but there's something about the white smoke billowing from the trunk that makes my skin crawl. "We need to keep running." I nod at the smoke filling the air.

Dash barely hears me in the screaming around us. I climb off him, knowing his instinct is going to be to help, and grab his hand. Without giving it another thought, I pull him to a safe distance, watching as the smoke seems to thicken, like a chemical reaction and not smoke from a bomb. I have a terrible feeling about what it might be.

I drag Dash a little farther as the police try to move everyone even farther back. There are no horribly wounded people because we cordoned off a large area, but everyone is shaken up. Car alarms up and down the block are filling the air with even more noise than the screaming people. But I ignore it all and continue to push Dash back. "That's possibly anhydrous ammonia."

He wrinkles his forehead. "What? Why—?" He shakes his head slowly. "Never mind. I suppose I know why."

I nod, gripping his hand and attempting to drag him away from it all, as I send Antoine a text telling him to call the City of Seattle about the cloud of gas that could kill if it is inhaled. He makes a weird face that suggests he might be throwing up.

"You aren't going to warn these people about the danger?" Dash asks, still holding me in one spot.

I shake my head. "We are running short on time. You think this is the only thing he has planned? He could be, and probably is, doing something far worse, and this is just a diversion."

"You have to think of the people. I legally have to think of the people. I'm a doctor."

"Fine, let's incite a little panic." I sigh and walk back toward it all, waving my hands and screaming like a maniac about the danger in front of us as everyone runs screaming away from it.

A policeman comes rushing over. "What is it?"

"Poisonous gas, likely the kind you drop dead from the moment you breathe it in. We need to evac the area and keep everyone away from this block. Empty the houses, all of it."

His eyes widen. "Jesus H. Christ, what in the hell?"

"He was a maniacal bastard, what can I say?" I turn and pull Dash along, hailing a cab when we get back to the main road. "Happy?"

He nods, but he doesn't look happy.

19. ALONG CAME A SPIDER

The house makes me tingle, but I make myself go inside it. I force the steps I don't want to take. Two FBI agents are with me. One is named Henrico, and the other is Stanley. They both look like they might toss up their lunches onto the floor at any moment. Neither handled the cells well.

No matter how hard I search the house and the rooms, I cannot find a single thing to link the old man to the thoughts I'm having, the suspicions I need confirmed.

"What are the odds we will catch him?"

"Who?"

"Guthrie, of course."

I shake my head. "Not great. He's very good at blending in and even better at fighting his way out." I walk the halls of the gutted cabin. Not a single wall has gone without a piece of drywall being cut away or smashed in. Like a teenagers' party has ruined an upper-class home.

I shake my head, crouching down and looking up at the hill. It hits me then. "Ski lodge?" Esther had mentioned a backcountry ski lodge.

"What?"

I turn, knowing it must be found. "The lady next door said Old Dick came up here every weekend. He was a real outdoorsman, loved the backcountry, and she said he went to an old ski lodge up this way."

Stanley lifts an eyebrow. "Worth a try."

Henrico points. "We saw one, other side of this peak here. There's a huge lodge in a bowl. I pointed it out to the pilot. It was stunning, but in the middle of nowhere."

We turn and run from the house for the chopper that's sitting there. The guards wave, looking like they might end their lives any moment due to boredom.

The pilot gets the helicopter going as we buckle in. My spidey senses start to go crazy—my stomach is roiling and my scalp tingling.

"What makes you so sure this lodge has anything going on?" Henrico asks. "It looked pretty swanky. One of those fly-in-only places."

I outline the thoughts I have been having for a couple of days. "The tunnels and caves and cells are too perfect. Those would require years of effort and money and dedication. Rory has none of those things. No, I suspect Old Dick was into something quite similar to what Rory is into. I believe Dick built the cabin and the garage and the cells, and Rory somehow stumbled upon it. He's been using the house for a couple of years, since the old man died."

"You think Guthrie killed the old man and took his house on purpose?"

I nod slowly.

"Wow, where the hell do ya meet your psycho soul mate? How do you even know some fucking crazy bastard has the same taste in evil as you?"

I shake my head, feeling like the answer is there somehow.

Stanley sighs, looking disturbed. "This whole thing has me wanting to move my kids to an isolated island. These people are everywhere."

He's right. Part of the reason I never spent a large amount of time mourning the loss of my womb, once I realized I had lost it, was that I never believed having children in the world we live in would be easy. I would never let them out of my sight.

We fly toward the mountain peak, hovering as we cross it, and Henrico gives directions to the pilot, reminding him of where it was. He lowers us, flying just above the treetops. My jaw drops when I see the lodge. It's beautiful and honestly in the middle of nowhere.

"How would they even get here?"

"Snowmobiles, or the same way we are," Stanley answers his partner flatly as we all stare at the distant lodge. "It looks more like a hotel than anything."

The pilot swings around the back and points. "Helipad," he shouts.

That makes my stomach turn. It is intended for people with money.

"What did the man who owned the cabin do for a living?"

I cover my ears and shout, "The guy's name was Dick Russell, or Richard Russell. He owned a dry cleaning business when he was young. It had been his father's. Somehow that dry cleaning business earned him enough money to invest in several start-ups. He was a cousin to one of the initial investors in Apple and a few other major companies. A man who clearly knew his investments. After he made his first fifty million, Dick retired, selling the dry cleaners and living off his investments, but learning the other side of being an investment broker. He ended up back in college at the age of fifty, got his master's, and went into banking. Died a very wealthy man at the tender age of seventy-five in a car accident. Hit and run. He'd been getting very senile in his older years, so the police assumed that contributed. His kids had managed to convince him to sign over all his fortune to them, leaving out the youngest, who was adopted as a small child. The fortune, including a few houses, has been stuck in litigation for the two years since the man died."

Henrico winces. "Wow, so they're all good people?"

I scoff. "All of them, apart from perhaps the adopted daughter. I don't know. I don't want to make that assumption until I meet the kids."

Stanley shakes his head. "What a nightmare."

I point at the lodge. "I suspect it isn't anything compared to this place."

Henrico gives me a dubious look. "You really expect this is going to be an open-and-shut case?"

I nod. "Again I don't want to make an assumption, but I will say I do expect this will be relatively enlightening." I make a quick call. "Ping my phone and tell me who owns this."

"Yes, Captain."

"It's Master Sergeant, if you want to get technical." I hang up and climb out after Henrico. We walk along the crusty snow, following footprints that have been here since the last snowfall. A little snow has filled them in, but not much, and they are crusty and frozen so I would have to assume they are days or weeks old. I would bet they belong to Rory, but I don't gamble much. However I would bet he's been here plenty.

We trek to the main door under a huge entryway made of beams and stones. It's grandeur like Dash's family would have, only maybe as a small winter cabin. I ring the bell, but nothing happens, no one comes.

"It looks closed for the season. Look, no tracks from snowmobiles or skis." Henrico points.

"This place is pretty swanky. I think we might need a warrant." Stanley knocks, listening with his ear against the door.

I press "redial" on my phone. "Get me a warrant to search the place too. It's cold; hurry up."

Antoine sighs. "It's owned by—oh God. I'm going to need to clear this with the man upstairs. The owner is someone we all know well." He puts me on hold.

I swallow hard, confused. I expected it would be Dick who owned it and it would be some sort of playhouse for him and maybe a couple of his rich, pervy friends.

Antoine comes back right away. "We have a warrant. It will expire in an hour. The owner will be notified by then, and his lawyers are better than ours, so expect it shut down."

"Shit!" I look at Henrico. "We have an hour before this place is crawling with private security."

Henrico shakes his head. "No, I don't think we have an hour. Look at the security system on this place. Looks pretty feisty." He points at the door and the globes of cameras mounted inside and out. There are fingerprint scanners mounted on the wall inside and out.

I squint and read the tiny label. "Minotaur Security. Antoine, what do we know about them?"

He sighs again. "That they set the house to explode if the triggers are messed with. You can't pick the locks. It's going to take a whole team of nerds to get you in there, and by then I suspect whatever you are looking for will be gone. Chances are you have triggered the system now just by landing and walking around."

"Fuck! What are you good for?"

He chuckles. "Oh, Jane, you know I am far better than a team of nerds. Give me two minutes." He hangs up on me.

My face is cold, my hands are frozen, and I suspect we are being recorded. I glance back at Stanley. "This is why I don't get cocky and assume shit."

He chuckles, rubbing his hands together. "Lucky you didn't then, huh?" He winks. "How is there even this level of security on a hill like this one?" Stanley looks around.

"Satellite system run on solar panels."

He gives me a dubious stare. "What if the weather turns to shit? Your system goes down?"

I shake my head. "This will have some storage for the power. Batteries that are charged for all the summer months, storing up for winter. They'll go a long time without sunlight."

"Man, I need that. My kids are killing us with the power bills." Henrico gives us both a grin. "Teenagers." He looks young to have teenagers. But I suspect he's just got a baby face. Guys like him—agents or military or secret service—make me comfortable. I can handle myself and conversation with people like this. We all think the same. And we all expect to have one another's back. It's comfortable silence because we are all listening.

The door clicks several times, making us back up from it. Then it opens, and Antoine's voice fills the air. "Jane, my dear, let me introduce you to the most advanced butler service in the world. Welcome to the Chateau Margolis."

"As in Arthur Margolis, Her Majesty's Principal Secretary of State for Energy and Climate Change?" I ask, completely baffled that a Brit would own the property.

His voice fills the air around us. "Indeed. You have forty-nine minutes."

Stanley doesn't look like he wants to go in, and Henrico gives me a subtle headshake. "If we lose our jobs—"

"You guys wait here. I'll be right back. If the security detail lands, distract them for me. I'll meet you at the chopper in forty-eight minutes." I turn and run into the beautiful chalet-style lodge. The main hall is a greeting area, lobby, and sitting room. There are large windows and expensive furnishings. The paintings on the wall are portraits of very important men. Some I recognize. Several of them the whole world would recognize.

I hurry down the hall, clearing bedrooms and steam rooms and corridors with finery in every corner. The main floor seems like guest quarters mostly. I run up the stairs to the top floor, where guest quarters continue but the rooms are all themed, with closets full of costumes to suit the bedrooms. My insides twist as each room gets a bit weirder. What starts with the circus, ancient Greece, and the Elizabethan age becomes a dungeon with cuffs and chains, a brothel, a harem, and a bare room with no windows.

My stomach sort of drops into my bowels as I turn and run for the stairs again.

"You have thirty minutes," Antoine says softly. I know he can see everything I can see.

"You're recording, right?" My voice cracks a bit.

"Yes." There is no snarky or cheeky tone, just the single word. We are both grossed out. The artwork on the third floor is more personal, more intense. Woman bent over a man's knee. Woman tied up in ropes. Woman performing sexual acts on many men at once. The drawings are done as if they are funny or comical, but I can see they are not.

At least I do not find them that way, and I suspect Antoine is less impressed.

I hurry downstairs, waving at the FBI agents at the front door as I pass. "So far not much!" I shout.

But downstairs is something different altogether.

Antoine doesn't seem to be with me now, and when I call to him he doesn't answer. I turn on my phone, recording with that. The basement appears to be made up of cells and giant washrooms that have a bathhouse feel to them. Large hot tubs and spa-like tables. But I get the feeling it is an area the guests don't visit. The finery is gone, the area sterile-looking, but that is all.

I flick on lights as I walk past rooms, wincing at the cells with old cots and stacks of clothes. One stack of short plaid skirts and another stack of turtleneck sweaters—all black. One stack is geisha-style dresses and one stack of togas. One stack of clothes is made up of nurses' uniforms, but they are the kind you don't actually work in. Another stack is French maid outfits, and the last one I look at is girls' soccer jerseys.

There is a flavor of every brand of sin a man could think of. Or a woman, I suppose.

I slink down the hall, away from the huge laundry room to a large wooden door. When I open it I see a small sauna inside. I close it and look at the size of the room, compared to the size it looks like it might be. I had expected a huge room, not a tiny little cupboard of a sauna.

I walk along the wall tapping my knuckles, rapping until I hear the hollow sound I want. There is a window next to me, so I look out to see a bit of an overhang on the wall outside. Whatever is behind this wall goes out farther than the rest of the walls. I turn and walk around the wall, but there is no way in from the inside. And when I glance out the window again it seems the wall would be covered mostly by snow by the end of the season. So a door might be unlikely.

I go back inside the sauna, but it appears sound. It doesn't look like there is a secret door. I touch everything along the walls and benches, and nothing moves.

I turn the camera onto myself. "Whatever is behind this wall is what we came here for."

I leave the sauna and run back to the stairs, listening for voices as I climb back toward the sunny main floor. My phone gets a text—RUN!

I want in that room; I need in that room. Whatever happens here, that room has the answers, but it isn't worth me dying. I slink up the stairs to see the guys having a pissing contest with men armed with machine guns. Instead of heading that way, I run for the back hallway, toward the ski and boot room.

"Unlock the back door, Antoine!" I say loud enough for him to hear. He doesn't respond. I get to the door, unsure if I should open it or if an alarm will go off. "The back door!"

"Got it!" he says with labored breathing as the locks click. I open it and run out into the snow. A second helicopter has landed next to ours. I circle around the house to the front door, giving the guys a look when I get there. "Are you the ones who are supposed to let us in?" I shiver and hug myself, trying to give off a damsel-in-distress air about me.

One of the guys narrows his gaze, lifting his machine gun toward me. "You are trespassing."

I shake my head, shivering some more. "No, we were told to wait here for someone to come and let us in. We have a warrant."

He grins. "Warrant's been killed. Get the fuck out of here before I end all of you."

I lift my hands in the air, not revealing the gun on my hip. "We'll be back with that warrant."

He scoffs. "Try it, bitch. We'll be waiting."

I want to punch him in the throat, but I don't. I let Henrico grab me by the arm and drag me to the chopper. When we get inside and the doors are closed, I sigh. "It's a brothel of sorts. Something is in that room on the far side. We need to get in there before they try to clean it out, now that they know we are aware of this place."

I make another call as we take off. "I need to go back, and I need you with me this time, Antoine."

Antoine sighs. "Why do you have so little faith in me? You think I was just sightseeing like you were? Where do you think I was when you were calling me from the back door?"

A grin spreads across my lips. "You fucking broke into that room?"

"Goddamned right I did."

It's my turn to sigh, just not the annoyed way he always does.

20. DINNER AND A MOVIE

I sit back with the footage and my Bluetooth in my ear so Antoine can talk me through it. "Okay, what am I seeing?"

"The first part of what I was able to do is tour the room. See that hatch above? It's the way in. One of those rooms you were in, it's got a hatch in the floor. I bet under a rug. These douche bags always go for the hatch under the rug. Keeping it old school."

"Stop nattering, I have to drive to Tanner in an hour. Let's focus."

"I miss Rory not being a creepy fuck. You're not nearly as fun."

"I also am not nearly as disturbed. And let's not forget it's Rory who made all this work for you and me."

"Right. I actually forgot that for a second." He moves the mouse on my laptop, having fully taken control of it, and clicks on a small box in the corner. "This is the bank; they have a video bank. I've been doing facial recognition on the footage for the three hours it took you to get to the computer." I catch the tone he's giving off loud and clear.

"The FBI has a lot of paperwork, and I had to check on Dash. The city needed me to fill out a bunch of forms explaining the massive gas leak one of us let off in their area. It isn't all play on my side of this on the Internet."

He chuckles. "You have it easy, trust me. I'm the sorry bastard watching the porn from slave hell. I might never have regular sex again after this."

My skin crawls as he starts a video and narrates. "It's seven hundred hours of footage. Games and sexcapades and sexathons. The girls are a bit of a story. So far I have found eleven missing girls in the lot. Three are Italian, two are Saudi, and one is Haitian. The other five are Canadian, believe it or not. All missing from the East Coast, suspected to have been moved by a gang out there that's notorious for human trafficking across the border. I can't even begin to tell you how fucking insane this is."

The footage clicks over to the rooms, the harem first. "So this is the horse game, I guess. It's some kind of kinky group thing." He sounds annoyed, but I think we are both a little scared.

In the video, girls are on all fours, with long, straight ponytails and bridles on their heads, and that is it. They prance, still on all fours, swinging their ponytails as several men strut about the room. One man drops to his knees, pulling his erection from his pants and mounting a girl with dark hair. He grips the reins and pumps wildly but only for a moment. He then gets up and struts again, erection to the wind, until choosing another girl, this time a blonde. He grabs onto the reins and bucks. Her face is turned toward the camera; she seems to be enjoying it. The other men do the same. "What the fuck?" The words slip from my lips.

"Right, that's about how I felt. This is the gentle shit. It starts to shift here. This little chestnut goes on for an hour."

I don't know what to add to that.

He clicks the mouse, and the movie switches to the room with ancient Greece as the decor. A woman in a toga and a wreath made of ivy walks about in a figure eight. She plays a small instrument.

A fat old man in a cloth diaper sits as two girls in nothing but long necklaces and crowns fan him with huge palm leaves. Another girl feeds him grapes by hanging them over his face. Nothing sexual appears to be happening until the camera scans about the room, revealing two men and one woman. One is pumping into her face, then ejaculating on her face, as the other man thrusts wildly behind her. These men appear to be slaves like the woman. They finish with her and go and bow before the fat guy.

"So, I'm going to go because this sort of feels like we are watching porn together, and I don't know how I feel about that."

I have forgotten he is there on the phone. "Right. Okay, so I'll call from Tanner." I hang up the phone and sit there watching as the big fat guy gets up, pulling a long dick from his diaper, and gets behind one of the men. I close the laptop, hating where that was going and how I feel about it all.

"Human trafficking, not porn. Human trafficking, not porn," I mutter, cringing. I remind myself of the cages and open the laptop again. The footage starts back up immediately. I click, and it switches to another room where the brothel is. It's got several types of beds and lounging chairs and drapes hung all around. The girls look like hookers from the Old West, with garters and feathers in their hair. They wear lingerie and hold platters of food and drink. The men wear cowboy hats and chaps. One man smiles, laughing and stroking the head of the woman sucking him off.

I pause and zoom in on his face. My phone rings instantly.

"Firstly, there's a donkey in the circus room—do not watch that video. Secondly, we have a problem with the facial recognition."

I wonder if he knows the person I am looking at.

"I have six senators, three princes, five bishops, a cardinal, twelve actors, several Supreme Court judges, and the list is just growing. This is insane. We can't even take this to anyone."

"Is the vice president on here?"

"No. Not that I've seen." Antoine sounds weird.

"What?" I ask, scared of the answer.

He sighs. "The president is."

"No wonder the security is so high." I shake my head. "There's no way the vice president sent us there with FBI agents and knew about the footage or about the place."

"Unless he wants us to think that."

I nod. "Which is why I asked if his name was on there."

"I feel like we have bitten off more than we can chew."

A chuckle escapes my lips, but it's almost a sob. "I know we have. You know what I'm staring at right now?"

"Yeah."

I narrow my gaze, running my hands through my hair. "You know who that is?"

"I do. Took me a minute to realize who it *wasn't,* though. That scared me."

"Then you know what that means?"

"I do."

I purse my lips. "I hate this fucking case." I hang up the phone and sigh, not even sure what to do but thankfully unable to do anything because I have to go to Tanner and find the kid of the deceased and creepy Dick Russell.

My phone rings. "Hey!" I answer Dash and close the screen on my laptop.

"When are we heading back to DC?"

I look down at the closed computer screen. "We are not heading back. I am fully assigned to this case until it is solved. I'm working with the FBI, and I won't be done till it's done."

"Ang and I are headed back now, then. She's a mess. And even worse, we have been reassigned. They've closed us down. This has hit international shit lists."

I wince. "Of course she is, and of course it has." I haven't been there for her at all, and the week doesn't look like it's going to improve much.

"No, you don't understand. The bed in the damned apartment she has been staying in is the black metal bed. She never even noticed it before. But the pieces are falling into place. They are all coming together for her. He painted it, but the paint wasn't made for metal beds and has started chipping away. Forensics came, and of course the handprints are still there. Rory and Ashley's handprints are on the bed, like a filthy souvenir. He never wiped it down. The mattress is the same one. He let the FBI use it as a safe-house bed, knowing full well girls had been raped and tormented on it."

My stomach clenches. "Oh God."

"Yeah, so I'm taking her home. She's being reassigned to a section with lab work only, no patients to supervise. She'll get to spend some quiet time on her own. I am being sent to DC, reassigned also."

"Okay, well, wow. I'm headed to Tanner to speak to the daughter, the adopted one. Then I will be doing some analysis of my own."

He's quiet for a moment. "I don't know how you do this, how you've spent your life doing this. Seeing this type of hell every day. Going to war and being an agent, I just—I have so much more respect for you, Jane Spears. More than ever." He sounds affected or emotional. "I love you so much." It's not that every other I love you hasn't been sincere, but this one is the most sincere.

I glance down at the huge rock on my hand and smile. He's my forever. "I love you too." I hang up and sigh, completely unsure of what to do about who I saw on the computer and how I will tell him about it. I turn the movie back on and watch the scene from the circus, not because I want to but because I need to. I need to be as disgusted as I can for what I have to do.

The trip to Tanner takes an hour and a half longer than I expect because of traffic. It's bananas. Henrico comes, but Stanley stays behind to keep an eye on the son and daughter of Old Dick.

We finally pull into the driveway of a small home and sit there for a second. "So, your dad has a billion dollars, and yet you live in a middle-of-the-road home?" Henrico gives me a look.

"Yeah, weird." We get out and walk up to the house. I knock loudly. A small woman with fuzzy blonde hair and a wide smile answers the door. "Hi, can I help you?"

"We are looking for Amanda Russell." I pull my badge so she doesn't slam the door in my face.

She nods but her eyes don't leave the badge. "I'm Amanda." She opens the door wide for us. There are kids' toys on the floor, and the TV is blaring. It's like a normal home for any middle-to-lower class family. "Come on in; ignore the mess. The kids are home for Christmas break now."

I had forgotten about Christmas. It dawns on me that I have to go to the South for Christmas with the in-laws.

Henrico gives me a look. "I'll wait out here. Keep an eye out."

I nod and close the door. "My name is Jane. I'm with the FBI." I hold up my badge for her. It's never had as much use as it has on this file.

"How can I help you?" Her face is no longer friendly and sweet.

"We found your father's cabin and the cells below."

Her eyes dart to the right. She winces and nods. "You'd better sit down." She sits too, looking at the kids I didn't even see on the couch against the wall. "You guys go clean up that basement, now." Her tone is nervous, but I think they take it as angry. They scramble without making much fuss. When they're gone she turns back to me. "Now you listen here, I've worked long and hard to forget about all that. I don't need some media bullshit and scandal involving me or my kids."

"That won't ever happen."

"Good. Because that man is not my family."

My stomach drops. "So you were never one of the kids to him?"

She shakes her head. "I was never anything but a burden to her, something he wanted and she didn't. They didn't need to adopt; they had two kids. But he wanted—" She pauses. "Like I said, I have moved on. But I want my share. I have earned it." Her voice shakes a little.

"Yes, you have." I look down, hating that I have to do this. "Did the other kids know, your brother and sister?"

She nods once.

"And the wife, your adoptive mother?"

She nods again, less sharply. "It started when I was fifteen. I never understood why he wanted to adopt me until my fifteenth birthday. He took me to the cabin for my birthday. We skied and snowmobiled, and for the first time he was nice to me." Her eyes glaze over, and I am grateful she spares me the details.

"When did you leave the family? Your family?"

She sighs. "When I was seventeen, I ran away. I lived on the streets for a while, did some drugs. Then I met a priest who does an outreach program in Bellevue. He helped me. Got me off the streets, got me a job and some counseling. I met my husband and never looked back until that lawyer came. Roland Guthrie. He had a partner who wanted to take my case, wanted to help me get the money I was owed."

"Lawyer?"

She nods. "Yeah, he and his partner, Sven Kelpie, have made the case for me. They said I should have my third; I was legally adopted, and I was owed. Said it would take some time. All they wanted was the cabin. No commission, just the cabin and the land." She laughs bitterly, and I nearly wrinkle my nose.

"They must have known about the cabin."

She gives me a look, and I feel about one inch tall. "Everyone who is anyone knew about that lodge. You think you can have a fun lodge like that and not share it with all the successful important people in the world? Of course they knew, but if they wanted that nasty pit as their payment, I was fine with it. I just needed to win my share first. I earned it."

"Wait, so the will was never changed to take you out, you just were never in it?"

She nods again. "That's right. He could have sex with me and torment me, but he couldn't let me have my share of the money. I slept in a cell for a month once. Growing up, my bedroom was in the basement next to the boiler room."

"Of the house in Queen Anne?"

She shakes her head. "No, our main house was out on the water. It's not part of the will because it was gifted directly to my brother and sister before he died. The bullshit story about me being cut out was done by the media, leaked, but I don't know how. I can't imagine anyone who would benefit from such a move. All I know is there was no deathbed change to the will."

"What's the address on that house?"

She shakes her head but writes it down. "You are not going to like that house at all."

"Is it as bad as the cabin?"

She shakes her head. "Worse. The cabin was just to train the girls to work the lodge. They would suffer there, learning how to be women of the night, as he liked to call them. Then he would take them to the lodge, and they actually would be grateful. No more cells and starving and shitting in those nasty toilets. No more bugs and sickness. No more Old Dick teaching them how to be a woman."

I join her in a grimace. "Gross."

"Life at the lodge was so much better. Senators and princes and presidents and businessmen. Life there was easy, compared."

"Who ran it?"

"Dick. He was in charge of running it, delegated even. He had been given the job as part of a family heritage thing. He was like the head pimp, but he hired a woman to do the job of running the girls. It's all very sick."

"Have you ever been there?"

Her eyes tell me the answer before her lips. "Got to spend all of twelfth grade there. Took that month in a cell at the cabin to convince me the lodge was the better choice and that a few of the girls there could teach me far better than my schoolteacher. It was the reason I ran away at seventeen."

"Why's it closed down now?"

"I have no idea. I have remained detached from all of that." She shrugs. "I imagine since Dick died, it was harder to keep it running; with no firm hand. Or maybe they are waiting for all the snow up there to be good for skiing and not crusty. It gets crusty this time of year. It's a winter lodge, after all. Or maybe they just are taking a break so they don't get caught. There is no proof of any of it happening unless you go there. I know I couldn't prove any of it happened." She sounds detached from it as she speaks of it. It is exactly the way I would sound if it were me.

I don't have words for any of it. "This is all so much worse than I imagined. I am sorry for coming here and reminding you of everything."

"Don't be. I have lived my entire life with it and never speaking of it." She shakes her head. "I'm just glad you know about it. I'm guessing that means it will all be exposed for what it is. Modern-day slavery is just as real as the old kind. People just think 'cause a girl is smiling, she wants to play along. But there are things you can do to make yourself smile through anything." She slides the address over to me with a shaky hand, and a single tear splats onto her pale wooden table next to an old plate of noodles. She wipes her face and smiles. "Sorry. I didn't mean to get emotional."

"Don't be sorry." I lick my lips nervously, processing what to say. What do you say to someone who has had this as a life? "I will make them pay." It's all I have.

A smile crosses her lips. "Thank you." The horror she's witnessed still lives in her eyes. I can see it.

I get up and leave, taking the address with me. When we get back in the car Henrico gives me a look. "Why do I get the feeling this is about to go very badly for everyone but us?"

I nod and drive as fast as I can back to the city. "If you want to keep your job, you have a choice: look the other way and lie in the end, or get out of the car when we get back."

He laughs. "My mother always said I was the worst liar there was. I don't mind looking the other way, though."

"Okay."

21. HOUSE OF HORRORS

Henrico offers me another gun as he stashes his third one in his jacket.

Stanley passes me the shoe polish so we can all rub it over our faces and necks. I flex my hands when I pull on my gloves, giving the guys a signal, one I haven't used in a long time. It means it's time to move and no more speaking unless necessary.

We hurry away from the vehicle and run along the waterfront, jumping over a fence and down a sidewalk to the dock of the property next door. It's an estate, most likely owned by someone at Amazon, the nouveau riche in the Seattle area.

The three of us hurry along the grass and lapping waves as we get to the next yard, the one she gave the address for. The fence near the water is actually a massive rock wall. We jump it and hurry up the side yard, hugging the bricks and rocks but spread out. I get to a door in the basement and drop to my knees, picking the lock quickly.

I send the text then. Here!

Me too! He responds right away. Done!

Listening for any occupants, I turn the lock and slink inside. The light on the security system doesn't change at all. Once all three of us are inside, Stanley stays at the door to guard the entrance as Henrico and I slither through the house, making no noise.

The basement mostly is a series of rooms. I purposely find the boiler room so I can see Amanda's bedroom next to it. There are three locks on the door, all on the outside. I turn the locks slowly, opening it to find a cot and decorations fitting a girl's room.

They haven't even taken down the pictures she drew. I signal for Henrico to stay as I go inside. Her pictures break my heart. I have seen them before on the walls of kids who came from bad living situations. She draws sunshine and a garden and a sky, making it look like she had windows in the room. Each view is one from a window.

I turn, grimacing, when I see a bell above the door tied to a string. These people are monsters. She was a modern-day Cinderella. And then something much worse.

I slip from the room, closing the door and locking it again so we can clear the rest of the floor. There's a laundry room, a games room, and a utilities room. It isn't as exciting downstairs as it is up. We creep along the stairs, each watching wherever the other person's eyes aren't, covering all areas.

Henrico is the perfect partner, but I still don't trust him the way I should. We hardly know one another, and my previous partner whom I trusted with my life didn't turn out to be the man I thought him to be.

At the top of the stairs, we enter an enormous living room and kitchen–great room combination. It's so large there are three sitting areas and two fireplaces. The kitchen gleams with marble and excess. Henrico takes the right and I the left, ending up in a library off the dining room and circling back. He shakes his head and points at the round set of stairs in the middle of the massive entryway. I unlock the front door, just in case, and creep up the stairs after him. We have not made a sound nor heard one until we get to the top of the stairs. Then I pause, giving him an odd look. He wrinkles his nose, and I imagine we assume the same thing. I have to admit it never crossed my mind that this is what we would find.

But we do.

We clear all the rooms, including one with a wall of surveillance. I attach the remote access to the computers and cameras. Immediately Antoine goes to work.

There are several bedrooms on the top floor—five, to be exact. Each has its own en suite, again with marble and slate as the varying design features.

The lights are all chandeliers, and the walls all feature wainscoting and beautiful wallpaper. The whole house looks like it could be in a magazine.

Until we enter the last room, the one with the heavy breathing and grunting.

Then it pretty much goes to shit.

Henrico grimaces, turning his face away for a moment.

I continue in, feeling every part of me tingle with disgust and revulsion.

A man in his midforties holds a camcorder in his hands. He's filming as another man and woman have sex, but not a normal kind of sex. The man is older, maybe in his late sixties. He's tied down to the bed, spread-eagle. A soft and flabby woman in her forties, not a small woman and not a huge woman, lowers herself onto him, literally bouncing on his cock and balls. She is squatting over him, dropping her vagina in an awkward thrust. Somehow in the commotion and the large size of the room they do not notice us standing there with our mouths agape.

The woman has on a lacy bra, which about covers the clothing for all three of them. The man holding the camera is erect, completely, and naked, with his own penis going in and out of something very odd. I don't know what it is, but he's jerking off with it.

I have a terrible feeling it's a pocket pussy, something I saw once in a sex-toy collection.

Henrico leaves, not even able to keep a straight face. But I lean against the wall, still completely stunned at what we have found, until the man with the camera slips in behind the woman as she drops to her haunches and leans forward. I assume both men are inside of her, but I can't take the view any longer. No one should have to witness that.

We exit the front door, sending a message to Stanley to meet us at the car.

He's there before we are, giving us a look. "You find them?"

"Good God." Henrico shakes his head. "She was right, what is in this house is much worse than anywhere else."

He takes a minute, looking like he might take a knee. "So the two younger ones—" He gives Stanley a wide-eyed look. "And I am being generous with the *younger*." He spins back to me. "The younger ones are the brother and sister? Who the fuck was the old man getting raped?"

I shake my head as Stanley starts to giggle, as much as a man in his late thirties with a mustache and a slight belly can giggle. Which is surprisingly more than I imagined him capable of. "The brother and sister were raping an old dude?"

Henrico makes a face again. "And filming that shit, man!" He looks like he might cry. "I am never getting rid of that image. Never. I could turn to drugs and alcohol, and that shit is gonna still be there. I won't ever have normal sex again. I'm gonna cry and squeeze my eyes shut and pray it ends before my wife notices I'm sobbing."

Stanley laughs harder; even I laugh a little.

Henrico gets in the car, waving a hand at the house and then me. "It is the Sunday before Christmas, Jane! And that was unholy!" He spits before he slams the door, and it's Stanley's turn to take a knee. He's laughing so hard he can't breathe.

I roll my eyes. "Laugh it up—you're watching the video footage we got." I climb in too and cringe as the last few days make an attempt on my sanity.

"Look, Jane, I like you. But I gotta do Christmas morning in three days. I can't do that with old people jacking off in my head. Can we just take the week, gather our thoughts, and go from there?"

I look at Henrico and nod as I start the car. "Yeah, I don't think we are going to come up with anything groundbreaking until all the data is seen. We have protocol on the video footage that needs to be processed. You take what you need for the bureau, and I'll take everything else, and we will meet back up January 2 here. I'll send the location."

He scowls at Stanley in the headlights, still laughing and stumbling as he tries to get up from kneeling on the dirty street. "Look at this jackass!"

"I'm a little grateful it was what it was. When Amanda said it was worse than what we found in that lodge, worse than what was up that hill in that cellar, I was scared. I have to give it to her, visually, this was horrid. But kid porn still trumps this in my head."

"Yeah, that's part of the job I hate, the shit you can't unsee. Kid porn would have killed me inside, this just traumatized me. Not because they weren't attractive either, but because they're brother and sister. What is wrong with people?"

22. THE LONG WAY HOME

He's stunned, outright insanely silenced by my request. After a long pause Dash mutters, "You *want* to go to their house for Christmas?"

I want to say no and have a drink, but that's not an option. "Yes. I am getting the plane to stop in DC and pick you up on the way. Why don't you bring Angie with us? She won't want to stay in DC alone, not surrounded by the things she and Rory had."

He chuckles a little. "She burnt all his shit, so it's just hers and some ash. She went crazy too. She loaded it all up in that old T-roof Corvette he bought last year, and burned the whole car and bags of stuff. Then she jarred up the ash, said she saw it on a movie, and has the jars in a box on the back porch, getting snowed on as we speak. Scariest thing I have ever seen."

"Damn!"

"Oh, she is angry. She already agreed to spend Christmas with us so there should be a change of heart if it's at my mother's. Maybe my family will prove to be a distraction. I think she needs to see you anyway."

I nod. "We will be in DC in five hours, the pilot says."

"I can't wait to see you."

I close my eyes and sigh, savoring those words like they are food for my soul. "Me too."

I sit back in my chair and hang up the phone, then dial Antoine and put my headphones in. "Okay, lead me through this."

"Okay, well, thanks for the warning first of all. When you get an ass ton of sex tapes with old fat people in them, you could at least warn a guy. I was eating a big ol' plate of spaghetti my mom made, and then I was gagging and choking and throwing up. My mom comes running in, yells at me for watching porn, and takes my pasta away."

I chuckle, remembering the faces Henrico made. "It was bad, walking in on that. You don't even bother me with your First World problems. Stop taking your work home."

He scoffs. "The computer at work isn't as good as mine here. I built a new one, and it's amazing. Anyway, this hard drive is a hot mess. It's a million hours of old-people sex. They start, I'd say twenty years ago, so you know they loaded that shit up from CDs they made. Twenty years ago she was fatter too. These are not people who should be filming themselves naked."

"Anything with the parents?"

He scoffs again. "Oh, let me tell you. These people are frickin' weird. The mom and dad were bad people. I swear to God, these books don't add up either. I bet you they have done money laundering for the mob, which is how the dry cleaning made so much money. He went from nothing to a whole lot of something and fast. The whole financial situation is dodgy. And even better, Old Dick has weird videos of himself training girls in those cells. We won't go there. Then even more bizarre is the old movies on here—after they watch their porn or make it or whatever, they all settle in for Alfred Hitchcock. It's weird. The Google history is bad. Like 'how fast does lime dissolve a boy after he's been dead a week' bad. The amount of porn these people have searched is criminal. There are teenage boys who don't know about some of these sites."

"What about the will? The houses? How about some of the useful stuff?"

He chuckles. "Okay, so we have five bank accounts, all of which are bloated with cash. Three rental houses in Seattle alone."

"Get the locals to run well-being checks on those houses. They could be brothels in disguise."

"Oh God."

I massage my temples and close my eyes as we take off. "Right."

"There are two houses in Canada; coincidentally enough, one is on the East Coast. It doesn't look so hot either—a bad neighborhood in Halifax. And even worse, it's near the police department downtown. So if it *is* a brothel you know somebody's on the take, because there has been suspicious behavior there, like inquiries about prostitution. But it doesn't look like they have gone anywhere with it."

"Could be where the girls are coming from to supply the hookers-in-the-hills program."

"Sounds like an outreach program." He makes a fake coughing sound. "I found something else. In the will it states that the oceanfront house has been deeded to the children upon their mother's death, but the cabin in the woods is to be given to the Backcountry Brothers Society."

"Wow, they made a society?"

"Yeah. The Backcountry Brothers Society is a not-for-profit society that owns that entire mountain where the lodge and the slave cabin are. The property is eleven thousand acres and completely pie-shaped. It's narrow at the cabin and wide at the lodge. It's a property that's been attached to the cabin in the woods for fifty years—sold off and made to look like the man was setting up a private park. Signature is none other than the president of the United States in 1963. We won't mention names, because you should know that."

"Why the hell would the government sell him that land in the middle of nowhere?"

"It's hard to set up parks. They have to be approved, and inquiries have to be made. Then they have to be checked on. It leaves a paper trail."

I pause. "So sell the land and it's a private park?"

"Yeah, but the trick is to find a house to sell the land to, so that there is already a structure and you aren't getting approval for building permits and making more of a paper trail. So at the time, the only private residence up there belonged to one Mr. Francis Richard Russell. It was a shit shack back then."

"Oh my God. Attaching the land to the cabin totally makes sense. It was the closest structure up there, and the old man was clearly for sale, in his soul. It was an easy way to ensure the land was privatized, and no one had to know about it. The government wasn't giving it away—they sold it. No one is the wiser."

He coughs. "Yeah, and they sold an even eleven thousand acres for eleven thousand dollars. Old man Russell paid a dollar an acre, which even at that time was insane for land with no access. But if they were making a park with it no one would have batted an eyelid at this, unless they wanted to chuckle about the moron who bought land he couldn't even use."

My mind is blown. "So Old Dick's dad owned the cabin in the woods, which at the time was a shack, and the president and his cronies, who probably wanted to open a legal form of brothel slash resort, decided using the old man as a patsy was a good idea?"

"Yeah. But the old man wasn't a patsy. That explains where the money came from. That friggin' dry cleaners went from just making it to banking, fast. And get this—the fucking kids, the dirty, fat sex addicts, were the first ones to contest the will because of the nasty cabin in the woods. They contested because the land never went to them. It's worth a ton to the forestry companies, which is who it looks like the kids want to sell to. They even have a contract drawn up. It's dated two weeks after Daddy Dearest died. But then the will stated that the Backcountry men—or Backdoor, as we so fondly know them—got the cabin and the land."

"Holy shit. So then Rory comes along and wants the land to stay in the pervert's hands. He pretends to be a lawyer and an executor and gets the whole will tied up even more?"

Antoine sighs. "Even my brain is hurting from all this."

I scowl. "Why does Rory need to be the lawyer and the executor?"

"I bet he was pretending to be a lawyer to convince the adopted kid, Amanda, to sign the papers, and if she didn't then he would kill her or something nefarious. But if she does sign, Rory sweet-talks Amanda into going for the money and then earns her trust, which we all know he's good at. He then convinces her to go with the lawyer chosen by the horde of evil men. Rory probably told her he was the executor and was looking out for her best interests." Antoine gasps again. "Executors are the only people allowed on the property when buildings and plots of land are being contested. I always knew Rory was smart, but *dude*!"

"Oh my God, this is intense." I collapse my head into my arms. "And for the record, he's not that smart. This has him being the fall guy for the higher-ups written all over it. I bet you any money he was allowed up there and partied up there, and was convinced this was the right choice. But in the end, if shit goes south, he will be the fall guy."

He pauses. "Then why'd he take it to such a dark place if he's just a patsy?"

I sigh. "I don't know. I'm tired and my brain hurts. Send whatever the Feds need to charge the disgusting-piece-of-shit Russell family. I will call you tomorrow. We can rehash a little and see what else we come up with."

"Okay; night, Jane. I'm sorry about Rory." He sounds serious, which never happens.

I nod even though he can't see me. "Me too, Antoine. I know you guys were as close as we were."

"Yeah, we were. See ya, Jane." He hangs up as I realize the screen is still filled with people doing the nasty, and close the computer.

The plane rocks me like I am a baby, and eventually I fall asleep. My dreams absorb and re-present the past few days. It's uncomfortable and weird to have sex dreams that you can't admit to yourself you had. I end up feeling bothered by the visions when I wake.

I sit up to see we are just landing.

It's dark and I'm exhausted, but I can't help but be excited to see Angie and Dash. I fidget with the ring on my finger and wonder how she's doing with the truth we have all had to face. Rory was my partner, but outside of work I didn't see him nearly as much as Angie. He was someone I trusted, which is hard for me. Having him betray me hurts, but what he has done to Angie kills me.

When the jet finishes taxiing across the tarmac, the flight officer drops the door down, and Dash and Angie board instantly. I jump up, letting him wrap around me. He breathes me in, kissing the side of my head. When he lets go, I run at her, giving her the biggest hug I ever have.

She shakes her head, stifling tears and sadness. "I'm an idiot, Jane."

I lift her chin. "You are not an idiot. Not any more than the rest of us."

She sighs. "I am. I should have known. I slept beside him every night. I should have known."

I refuse to let her believe that. "No. You couldn't have known. He kept it so secret. He's a spy—he was taught how to lie perfectly."

She passes me a small crate and sits in her seat. I look down at the cloth crate to see a snarling Binx. "Binxy, why do you look so angry?"

"I gave him a cat sedative. He didn't relax, at all." Dash shakes his head, looking mystified at my savage cat's behavior.

I wince at Dash. "He doesn't relax with sedatives or tranquilizers. They make him anxious and stressed. They actually have the opposite effect."

"That explains why he started chewing at the bag. If he gets out, the pilot is going to kill us."

I grip Binx and hurry to my seat. He snarls and growls as I sit down and unzip the bag just enough for my hand to slip inside. I pet him as best I can before it's time to buckle up again.

Angie looks over at me, resting her hand on my leg. "I want the heavy version, Janey. No fucking about. Ya lay it on me."

My brow knits. "Angie, you don't want to know this."

"I have to know."

Dash nods. "I think we both have to know."

"Then I have to start at the beginning."

She nods and he grimaces but agrees.

As the plane takes off and my cat turns into a little savage, I slip my hand back inside and pet him softly and slowly, hoping to calm him down. "From what we have gathered thus far it seems the cabin used to be a small little shack on the hill. It was the only piece of property that was owned by any person for a hundred miles that had a structure on it. So the men who wanted to make a legal form of brothel—the men who were leading our country then—decided to let a man purchase eleven thousand acres of land for a dollar an acre. The acreage was meant to be a park, but a private one. Something no one could get into without his permission."

"Damn, that's a steal."

I shake my head at Angie. "No, back then the land was unreachable except for an old Forest Service road that led to a logging road. They put in a paved road later. It was about market price. We suspect old man Russell was given the money to buy the land, which he attached to the deed of his cabin, making it a large estate, technically. The lodge was built during those years, and men started having their erotic holidays. I imagine it started out as a bit more fun than it is now. I imagine most of the girls were regular hookers and not slaves stolen from their homes."

Dash winces. "Not unusual to have slaves in that time. It just was not televised all over the world every time it happened."

"Gross." I stroke Binx and continue. "The land was to be deeded back to the Backcountry Brothers Society when Old Dick's dad died. I assume he never deeded it to the society to begin with, because his son had grown quite fond of it and convinced his father not to. Or maybe he just wasn't certain the men who built the lodge would hold up to whatever bargain they struck. At any rate, the cabin in the woods was not deeded to the society until Old Dick died, but Dick's kids didn't know this. They probably don't know about the disgusting cabin at all. It would appear they made a deal with a logging company for the land when their father died, only to be surprised that they had not been given the cabin. They were the first to contest the will because the logging deal was huge money."

I pause, taking a long breath while contemplating how to tell the rest. "When I went to visit the neighbor next door to the town-house in the Queen Anne area, I discovered Rory was the executor of the will. He was named Derek and actually the nephew of Old Dick. Clearly, it was a lie fabricated to some end. We figured out that the only person able to go on a piece of property when it is being contested is the executor of the estate."

Dash nods, adding it up in his head faster than Angie does. She scowls. "So he was able to use the property but no one else was, even though it's not deeded to him?"

"Right, he can go and do checks on the place, though not use it. So while it was wrong to use the cabin, what he was doing there wouldn't have been noticed by anyone. He did regular checks and maintenance on the townhouse, however, like a good nephew."

She closes her eyes, absorbing or just shaken at the idea of it all.

"Then he pretended to be a lawyer and convinced the adopted sister, who by the way has served time at the lovely chateau and the cabin in the woods. She's a little different, but I think the most normal in the family. By far. Her name is Amanda." I cringe. "Rory tells Amanda his name is Roland Guthrie, a lawyer, who has a friend who would like to take her case and get her the share she is owed of the family fortune. The only fee they ask for is the cabin in the woods and all lands."

Dash's eyes widen. "Smart and evil. And seems to suggest Rory was not working alone in a lot of this. He was part of the society."

I nod. "Right. So that's something. He wasn't just a serial rapist and killer because—"

"Don't justify him to me."

I shake my head. "Sorry, I didn't actually have anything to add at the end of that anyway. He's a psycho."

"But not a lonely psycho. He's got connections and friends in the right places." Dash gives me a look. "How bad is the chateau?"

"Bad. It's got theme rooms and costumes and loads of orgies and fun, but the girls are broken at the cells first—the job that Rory seemed to be part of, in some sick way. I don't know how long they're meant to stay in the cells. It seemed to me they were there far longer than Old Dick used to keep them. One month is what Amanda, the adopted daughter, said."

Dash's eyes narrow. "So break them in, using the cell, and then take them to the chateau, which is nice, and then they'll be grateful and work hard?"

"Exactly."

Angie covers her face, sobbing. I hate that I have told her the story.

23. SLIPPERY WHEN WET

Back at the ranch in Virginia—or estate, as luck would have it—Dash's mother's eyes narrow. She lingers there in her hatred for a moment before she blinks and the look is gone. In its stead is a look of fake bliss, like she didn't just tell me off with her eyes. She hugs me, again with the touching. "We didn't expect you would be back so soon, Jane." She says it like she means well, but I feel like we both know otherwise.

I shrug and glance about the place. "Well, I had to rush off for work the last time. I felt bad."

Her eyes widen. "Work, was it?"

Dash wraps an arm around my shoulders. "Yes, Mother. Jane is part of a huge investigation right now."

Her eyes widen. "Not being charged?"

I laugh and sigh. "No." I think she's a touch disappointed for a second before she turns and hugs Angie with fervor. "Angela, how are you?"

"Och, ya know, dandy." She doesn't look dandy. She looks beat. She hugs his dad and follows her bags. "I'll just set myself up in the guesthouse then and find a bit of rest." I'm stunned at the comfort she has in his house. His parents even wave at her as she follows one of the maids I didn't meet last time.

Evangeline finds me with a smile and a nod. "If you wish to follow me, miss, I will see you to your room."

I smile and lean into Dash. "I would love to."

Dash shakes his head, holding me tightly. "Actually, Evangeline, if you want to put her things in my room, she will be with me tonight."

His mother's face turns red, but his father seems oblivious. He lifts his drink and tosses back a considerable amount. His mother looks at me. "What about the nuns?"

Dash squeezes. "She wrote to them and said she was denouncing the church to get married at our church and become Anglican."

His mother's eyes scowl, but she forces a smile across her lips. "Wonderful." She looks behind me. "Is that a cat?" Her voice cracks a bit. It's almost awesome.

Dash ignores her and continues talking. "And since we live together in DC, I figured, why pretend. We are both over the age when it matters anyway. Nichols, please bring the cat to the room. He needs to be fed and will require a washroom."

Dash's mother makes a sound I assume means she is displeased. But Dash doesn't care. He walks away from them, leading me after Evangeline.

When we get on the stairs I shove him slightly. "You shouldn't have done that. It was disrespectful." I glance back to see Nichols chuckling to himself.

"Well, she needs to lose sometimes too, Jane," Dash says like it was nothing.

"Not in her own house," I mutter. I can't believe I'm defending her.

"Especially in her own house." He kisses the side of my head, and when we get to his room I can tell Evangeline enjoyed the show as well. She gives me a smug grin when she curtseys, and leaves us alone in the huge room, as does Nichols. I wave and turn for Binx, letting him out of the carrying case. He dashes under the bed, and I know he'll come out on his own.

"You feeling sexy, milady?" Dash asks in a perfect English accent.

I shake my head. "Not so much. The amount of sex I have seen in the last week, I think I'm good for the whole year."

He rolls his eyes. "I'm pretty sure I can convince you." He squats and throws me over his shoulder. "For starters, I think you need a shower." He walks into the bathroom, lowering me as he turns the light on. The bathroom is remarkable. I didn't expect anything less, but I also didn't expect this. It's the size of a small apartment, with a large soaker tub, two sinks, a toilet, and bidet. On the far side there's another opening that's fully tiled. He strips me, not even being gentle. Then he smiles at me, and I forget the whole other world we live in. All I see are the dazzling eyes and wicked grin from my beautiful man. I lift his shirt off, letting my fingers drag along his chest and down his stomach. Every muscle feels hard and ready. I undo his pants and jerk them down, boxers and all. He's semi-hard, swelling more as the cool air of the room reaches him.

I start to walk toward the tub, but he takes my hand, kissing the back of it, and pulls me into the tiled room. It's like nothing I have ever seen. It's a shower room. The ceiling is a grate, and when he presses a button, it pours rain down upon us.

I tilt my head back, letting it wash over me as his body is suddenly pressed against mine and his mouth is grazing my lips. He doesn't stay long, kissing me on the lips. He's there one second and then gone again. When I open my eyes I see he has picked up the soap and a loofah, making lather. He massages my back and arms, my breasts and stomach, and finally he drops between my legs, spreading my thighs open to wash me. The rough loofah against my sensitive nipples was scratchy, but between my legs, each soft brush on my lips is a promise of so much more.

"Going natural?" he asks as he sits back, admiring the lack of grooming.

"Oh God. I forgot completely. I am so sorry."

He shakes his head. "I sort of fancy it, actually." He rinses me, massaging and smoothing over my entire body until I am soap free. Then he bends his face forward, using my small breasts as a little shield from the water, and licks softly between my lips. He spreads me, licking and touching so gently I almost don't recognize the lovemaking. That lasts but a second as he sits up, taking one of my nipples in his lips and inserting a finger into my doubly wet opening. I gasp as he works it slow and steady, getting me warmed up. I tilt my head back as the water pours over us and his teeth start to nibble at my tender flesh.

The gentle bites tug at my aroused buds, joining the thrusting finger to create something that stirs low in my belly. He stands abruptly, dragging his finger out and lifting me into the air. He carries us from the water to a spot in the shower room with jets. He lowers me facing the wall, pressing my face and hands into the wide stone tiles. He turns on a switch, and pulsating water finds its way between my legs. I cry out softly, jerking my breaths from my parted lips.

He stands behind me, pinning me with his hard body to the cool tiles and forcing my clit on the jet. His lips trail up and down my neck and back as his fingers roll both my nipples softly.

I lose the floor and the ceiling, adrift in the bliss and freedom of so many of my sensitive places being explored by hands and water and lips.

I reach around, sliding my fingers down his hard abs to his belly button. His cock greets me, standing tall and proud. I wrap around it, gripping and stroking with the water as my lube.

He squats, spreading my legs and pressing me into the wall. Pulsating water ravages my tender flesh, and he kisses along my lower back as his hands rub up and down my body. Just as I relax into the calm he has lulled me into, he spins me quickly, planting his lips on mine. We kiss as the water sprays my butt, making me jump. He looks back, smiling. "Not as amazing in the ass?"

I shake my head as he lifts me up into the air, pressing my back into the cool tiles. He lowers me onto his cock, letting me choose how quickly he enters me. But I don't rush it. I savor the feeling of him spreading me, and filling me up.

His fingers dig in, gripping with a slight tremor. I know he wants to take off. He wants the pounding and the brutal sex we both love. But I lower and rise slowly, lifting and falling on him. He fills me up, pulsating and twitching. A slow smile spreads across my lips. I sit on him, not moving at all, and pull back so I get a good view of the aggression inside of him that wants to release. It's the only time where he can't control what he's doing.

He growls, lowering his face over mine.

I lift my face to find his clenched jaw and soaked hair hanging in his face. I shake my head slowly, keeping his intense gaze as I lift and lower again.

"Let me fuck you."

I shake my head.

"Please?" He has never begged for real before.

I lift my hands, cupping his face, with his cock nearly splitting me, and kiss him with meaning and passion. He jerks like he might rut any moment, but he doesn't. He controls himself, or I control him. Either way he's calm on the surface.

"Lie down."

He wrinkles his nose but does it, lowering us with him still inside of me, but I can tell we are losing each other. He grips the jets, shaking his head. "I'm gonna slip, and then you're going to have to explain to my mom why I'm bleeding in the shower with a raging boner."

I roll my eyes. We never talk like this, never joke, during sex. He drops us down, lying back but losing our connection. I get into position better, lowering my breasts down into his face as I arch my back to get him back inside of me, slowly rising and falling again.

His legs flex and his hands try to drag, but I manage to get them to the water-covered floor. I lift slowly again, dropping back like I might start to rush it, but I don't. He grunts. "Jesus, Jane, you're killing me." He lifts, kissing me and pulling me down on his cock roughly again.

I get up quickly and stand under the water. "This is wasteful."

He cocks an eyebrow, giving me a look. "Are you fucking with me?"

I nod. "I am trying to see how angry I can actually make you."

He jumps up, but I run from the shower room into the bathroom and flee for the bed. I dive, soaking wet and giggling, into the sheets.

"You're dead!" He jumps into the bed, pinning me on my stomach and kissing my back. He laughs for the first time during sex. It isn't him who's different, it's me. I have never played with him before. I have never let him in like this.

But I see him suddenly, in a way I have never before.

He flips me on my side, entering me roughly and gripping my legs as he flings me on my back and arches it, lifting my lower half in the air by my hips and cheeks.

He thrusts, pushing me and pulling me back into him again to meet his thrust.

Something magical happens when he's inside of me, not magical-cock magical but heart-soaring magical. He pumps, filling the room with our sounds. My whole body tenses, and I come with him. We hang on to each other's skin, clinging and jerking as the explosion happens.

That's when the magic happens. He lies down on me like a sack of potatoes and exhales as I inhale, like we are making each other's air. He's squishing me, pretty much breaking a rib, but I don't feel the pain because I see *it*.

Nothing matters in this world but this guy. I see the point in it all. It's like the house fades away and there is nothing, just him and me and the stars.

There *is* something I would not live without. It's a person, not a cat like I always expected. Though I pretty much feel the same way about Binx.

But Dash is even something else. I will not live without him. I couldn't breathe if he wasn't the main thing in my life. He is my family. That hits me hard, in the chest.

I close my eyes and let him be bigger than everything in the world.

24. A GLASS OF REGRETS

Lady Jane Spears, how are we this evening?" Henry strolls into the room, giving me a smug smile and handing me a glass of red wine.

Angie waggles her brows and lifts her champagne. "I need a refill." She gets up and stumbles off.

"I think my mother and father are actually therapeutic for her. She is depressed in a way I haven't seen in another human being before. Pathetic, really."

I give Henry a look, knowing he's baiting me. But I don't take the bait. I bait back, and I am carrying some motherfucking bait. "Not even sad hookers or sex slaves, pardner?" I try to use a western accent like a cocky cowboy, but it fails.

"I think I'm lost." He looks confused.

"Yeah, wear that look for a night or two, and then maybe I'll let you know what I know." A terrible recovery, but it's what I have for the time being.

His jaw drops. "Kitty likes to scratch? Excellent. I just hope you like it rough."

I narrow my gaze, again not taking shit from him. "Oh, please,

I got the footage of how you like to swing. I'm not big on costumes and captive hookers—hard pass for me, thanks." I lift a finger. "When this shit hits state's evidence you need to hit the road.
England might not let you stay when they see how fond you are of
old leather chaps worn by every other guy ahead of you in the line."

His face pales. "I don't—I don't know what you're speaking of."

"Except you do, and if it gets out that a member of this family
was part of a huge, multinational sting, your father is going to dis-
own you. Remember when I told you that your dad was a bad boy,
but he was smart about where he dishonored his family?"

He swallows hard.

"You were not so smart, and there is a tech right now using face
recognition to track down every person who is part of the Backcountry
Brothers Society." I get up and storm from the room. I pull my phone
and send a text to Antoine.

I just warned Dash's brother. You need to set up shop somewhere
no one will ever find you. In case he calls this in and tries to get help
from the big boys in our op.

He sends an annoyed face meme and a reply.

You are so good with international secrecy.

I send him a text back.

You need to listen and stop acting like this isn't as serious as it is.
Follow your own advice and RUN!

I delete it as I walk to Dash. I hadn't intended to tell him, but I
am not worrying about my partner. One of the few people left that
I trust fully is possibly in danger.

Hands grab me hard by the wrist. Henry spins me. "How long
do I have?"

I shake my head, jerking my hand free. "A week."

He sighs, but I see something in his eyes I recognize from his
brother's. "You didn't have to warn me, and I suspect no one else is
getting this courtesy. So thank you." He pulls me in and hugs me.

I step out of his grip, pushing back. "I don't care about you. I care about the humiliation this would have brought your family—your brother."

He laughs. "Says the main source of our humiliation." He laughs again and walks off. He's actually laughing at me. I turn to find Dash in the crowd of guests that always seems to be here, but when I locate him he's standing next to an old man, chatting away. I wave, and he grins at me. I wonder if his parents know how lucky they are to have a son like him.

Angie stumbles over to me, linking her arm in mine. I hug her and pull her to the pergola, my favorite place on this whole estate.

When we get outside I lay her back on the expensive chaise and sit at her feet. I pull her shoes off.

She grins. "Wow, what is this? Touching, and she takes my shoes off? Who are you, and what have you done with my friend?"

I smile and place her shoes on the ground. "You ever feel yourself grow?"

She sighs and looks up at the lilacs and the stars. "I have felt that moment a few times. Once when my mother died. I felt her leave me, and I felt small for a minute." She grins through the watery eyes. "Okay, a month. But then one day I was okay. And I knew I would be okay. And I knew she loved me, no matter where she was. And it was okay that I didn't feel like I had a mother, because I did. She was just a star watching over me." She closes her eyes. "I am waiting for that moment to happen for me with Rory. Not because I think I can't live without him—I can. Not because I am heartbroken over his betrayal. But because I am honestly so disgusted that I was with a monster and didn't know. How could I be so blind, and support and love and care for a man who was that evil?" She gives me a hard stare. "I feel dirty in my soul, Jane. Dirty all the way into the fiber of who I am. To my very core. That's a type of filth you just don't wash off." She shudders. "He touched me with his monster hands and his monster lips and his monster soul." She just lets the tears fall down her ruddy cheeks and looks back at the stars. "What would my mom think?"

I reach over, wrapping myself around her. "I am so sorry, Ang." I hug her and hold her and offer up little bits of what's left of my soul.

Dash finds us, her sobbing and me just frozen and wishing all the good things in life on her. He reaches down and picks her up from my arms and carries her to the guesthouse where she demanded to sleep. Sitting on the chair and staring at the stars, I wait for him to come back.

The door opens, and Henry brings me another glass of wine. "Drink?"

I take it, assuming it's a peace offering. "Thanks."

He sits across from me. "I was invited once. I'm not a card-carrying member. The senator where we were staying invited me. He and his son and me and my friend." He looks down. "When I got there I understood it to be a regular brothel, just a regular-girl-who-was-paid-for-her-services sort of establishment."

I sigh, drinking the wine. "No."

He looks up. "I went the one time, enjoyed myself like any other man, and left happy. I gave all the girls a huge tip." He looks sincere, but I'm not an idiot. "I never went back. It's invite-only. Surely you can help me out. You don't want Dash to get in trouble, do you?"

The answer is obvious, and I have no intention of letting it slip from my lips. I drink my wine, shaking my head, certain he thinks he's manipulating me. "You had to know someone would know, eventually."

"No. That's the best part. Everyone was so cocky and arrogant, we never imagined anyone was filming. Everyone there had the same amount to lose."

That part is a bit weird; who would have installed the surveillance without anyone knowing?

I blink, realizing my lids are heavy suddenly. If I were a regular girl, I would think it was the wine and the exhaustion.

But being me means I know he has drugged my wine. I place the glass down slowly, using every bit of precision that I have, before standing and walking toward the guesthouse.

His hand lands on my wrist harshly, but I turn, swinging hard. I drop him with one punch.

"Jane!" Dash runs to me, catching me as I fall down.

"Henry drugged me. He was at the brothel in the mountains. I have him on video. He drugged me." I blink and pass out.

25. MERRY CHRISTMAS

Binx purring in my ear is the first thing I hear, but the pounding of my brain is the first thing I feel. I wince as something is pushed near my lips. "Take the painkillers. This type of drug has a harsh side effect," Dash whispers. I know it's him. I can tell by the rage in his whisper. He's angry. I am too.

I manage to get one eye open as I swallow the pill. The room is dark and quiet. "Where is he?"

"Gone. My parents threw him out. My father has disinherited him. It's bad, Jane. I barely got his confession on the type of drugs he used on you before my father nearly tried to kill him."

I wince. "I am so sorry, Dash. I should have told you, I just didn't know how."

His lips press against my face. "No, I'm sorry. My brother is a scumbag and a piece of shit, and he has no remorse for the terrible things he does. My parents are distraught. They had no idea."

My head hurts just imagining his mother distraught.

Binx snuggles against my face, rubbing Dash's face. "Oh God, my head, and the mess of explaining to your parents that they can't ever tell anyone what they know."

He kisses my forehead. "Don't think about it right now."

I don't. I close my eyes and let sleep take me again.

When I wake the pain is gone, but my neck is stiff. I open my eyes to find Binx and Dash sitting in the armchair in the corner, both fast asleep. The room is just light enough to see that.

I pull back the covers and grab my phone, sending a message to Antoine: You okay?

Yup, but your boys sent people to my known address.

I wince. Your mom's house?

He sends a selfie of him giving me a face.

No! My mom's house is safer than anywhere. You kidding?

Did you solve all our problems? Do we know who we can trust?

No. There's the VP, and that's about it.

I tap a finger against my head.

We need to find Rory. We need to know what they know. I could mind-run him and make him tell me.

He sends a worse photo of a scared face. No.

I hold my breath for a couple of minutes and then send the message I don't want to.

Send it to the world. The government is going to cover it up. Send it to the world. We will lose our jobs, but I don't care, do you? Those girls will never get the justice they deserve.

He sends a photo of him smiling with a thumbs-up. Best idea all week.

Merry Christmas, Antoine!

Merry Christmas, Jane!!!!

I put my phone away and wait for the scandal to hit the world. I know it won't take long. He's probably already made the report. Dash wakes, giving me a slow smile. "You're awake. You okay?"

"Yeah."

He sits up, lifting Binx, and comes to the bed. "You look worried."

I nod. "I am. Me and Antoine are about to get fired." I wince.

"I haven't not had a job since I was thirteen. I worked at this shitty chicken shack in our small town and the owner was this mean lady. She always called me useless and threw chicken at me." I grinned a little despite the fact I was terrified of what I had done. "The funny part was her name was Mrs. Beek. She had a chicken shack and her name was Beek." I laugh at my own joke but Dash doesn't smile. I cock an eyebrow. "You'll still love me jobless, right?"

He scoffs. "You are the golden girl of the entire world. What could you—" he pauses, no doubt coming to the conclusion of my worry and possible actions. "Shit, Jane, did you get Antoine to send the information out globally?"

I bite my lip, wishing I could say no. I have never leaked information before. Ever. "Yeah."

He closes his eyes, taking a deep breath. "So he's exposing them all? Every person who went there is about to become a public spectacle?"

"I couldn't let it get swept under the rug. I couldn't risk it." My insides hurt, but I have to ask even though I know the answer. "Did you go there?"

"No!" He offers up his answer and a wounded look. "Absolutely not. I never pay for sex; that's insane. Water and sex should both be free to everyone." He looks deeply into my eyes. "You realize what this means, right? You are done. No one will ever work with you again. I am for certain done. My career is over."

I hate that this is where he's going with it. "But they won't ever have their day in court. The government is going to do the national-security bullshit, and then it will vanish. It will be some urban legend. And all eleven of those dead girls will have died for nothing. My job is worth their lives. I couldn't risk it being swept away."

He nods, lifting my chin. "As is mine." He kisses me, and instantly my phone vibrates.

I glance at it, wincing as I answer. "Hello?"

"Going for code. Prepare," a man says slowly. He comes back a second later. "Agent Spears, is there a reason our entire case has just gone to every media outlet in the world with the precise list of who made it happen?" The vice president's voice is strong and harsh, even Christmas morning.

"No, sir."

"I think you are lying to me, Spears. I think you know why. I imagine it has something to do with the fact you have zero faith in the system and its ability to prosecute those guilty?"

I gulp. "Yes, sir."

"You have fucked this bad—really shit the bed on this one, but I suspect this was the option you were given. I don't suppose you regret anything?"

"Just not seeing Guthrie for the man he was."

He grunts a little. "Yeah, that is unfortunate. I suspect he will have very few friends now. Finding him might not be so hard after all."

My brow furrows. "Why?"

"Have you seen the media blitz, Spears?"

"No, sir." I point at the TV. Dash turns it on and scans channels until he comes upon one with Rory's face on it.

"Merry Christmas, Spears." The VP hangs up on me. I lower my phone, slack-jawed and shocked as Rory is named the whistle-blower of the biggest scandal in American history.

"Holy shit!" Dash snuggles in with me as Binx finds himself a new comfy spot to rest, oblivious of the outside world around him. "He's screwed. That organization has some of the most powerful men in the world in it, and Rory has just betrayed them all."

EPILOGUE

"So you'll be a lady then?" Angie is squealing she is so excited. I shove her a little. "No. I don't know. Dash's dad is still young. I don't think I have to think about this for a few years. I'm good. Just stop. Don't make that face." I point.

"What face?" She beams.

"That one, right there. The huge grin."

"What grin? Ya sassy little minx, I always knew being your friend meant I would go places. Like to see the queen."

I roll my eyes as we walk down the corridor of the building dedicated to finding out the truth behind the whole affair. "You hate the queen."

"Och, I don't hate the queen. I hate the monarchy. I love the queen. She's mighty feisty and acts like a lady, but ya know she'd kick ass when no one is looking." She opens the door for me with her scanner card. Mine isn't working yet.

Antoine grins at me from the booth where we have been sorting data. My phone vibrates. I flip it over, knowing damned well it's Dash and he's being cheeky. It's a selfie with an adorable black puppy, and it looks like it's sitting at my desk. "You have got to be kidding me," I mutter, not able to take my eyes off the picture.

I get up fast, hurrying to where I see the crowd surrounding my desk. I stop, scared, as Dash lifts a large pup into the air and gives me a sly grin.

"I got Binx a friend."

I cock an eyebrow. "Binx doesn't need friends. He has me. A cat's best friend is his mother."

"I got you a friend."

"A girl's best friend is her cat. You got *you* a friend."

Dash kisses the dog's little face. "I got me a friend. His name is Sirius, and he's a wolfhound. I think he'll look just like Sirius Black in dog form."

Antoine agrees, nodding excitedly. "It's true. I showed Dash the photo from Harry Potter, and we both think he's going to be identical." He stops talking when he sees my face.

I slap my hand over my eyes. "You got a dog? I don't even think I am allowed to have *Binx* in my building."

Dash hands the dog over to Angie, who starts squealing and hugging, and hurries to me. "I love these dogs. It's tradition for a man of importance to have one."

I roll my eyes. "You aren't even important, and we both know it. You're a biological analyst for an elite task force designated to root out the corruption in a sex-slave ring. Hardly noble."

His eyes are so green I can hardly take it. He's clearly happy. "But my dad is handing me everything, title and houses and inheritance. My brother, who has made the Internet list, by the way, is cut off. He's ruined."

"He's an idiot." A thought entered my head with the statement. "Does this mean eventually or now? Your father handing you everything?"

"Eventually. My father is still in excellent health, despite what my brother has done to our family." Dash winces. "I still feel like Henry got a raw deal. I actually remember him going to that senator's house. He should have just stayed home that weekend like Mother asked him to. I'm sure Henry was pressured."

I twirl the ring on my finger and fight the urge to tell him he always thinks the best of people. Instead I walk to the room where we have Rory on ice, our version of ice. "I still can't believe he turned himself in." I glance in at Rory lying on the bed, perfectly tranquil from the drug-induced coma he has been put into. One problem with being military is that we have no rights when it comes to justice.

"I can. What else was he going to do? He can try to plead out on some of the charges, but not the rape and murder of eleven women. Especially not after being seen at the lodge."

"Do you think he knew who made the footage?"

Dash folds his arms. "There is no way to know what he knew."

I sigh. "There's one way, but I don't think we have a trained person with enough experience to do it."

A man's voice behind me startles me with his gruff words. "There is one person I think who could do it."

I turn, saluting immediately. "Mr. Vice—Mr. President. To what do we owe the honor?"

He stares at Rory, narrowing his steely-blue gaze. "Just wanted to come down and personally ask you to solve this for me, Spears. I need to know it all. The data you have found is great. I feel confident we are headed in the right direction, but I need all the answers. The entire world is watching me on this one." His eyes dart to mine. "You know what you need to do."

I nod. "Yes, sir. I do."

He nods back. "Good to see you're still a soldier first, Master Sergeant. I will schedule it all. Dr. Dash, I know you will be eager to be a part of it all. And I know you'll take good care of our girl here."

Dash grits his teeth and nods once. "Yes, sir."

The president, the former vice president, turns and walks from the area.

I look at Dash and shake my head. "I didn't know, I swear."

He sighs. "I did. I knew he'd ask. I knew it. I was so hoping you'd be fired for being insubordinate."

"Mean! I'd lose my military pension if I got fired."

He cocks an eyebrow, not taking that skull-eating look from his eyes. "You don't need a pension now, Jane."

I ignore him as Angie comes strolling over with Sirius in her arms. "He wants you to go in?" Her face is pale, and her eyes are haunted, even with a puppy in her arms.

I nod, not sure how she can work here every day with him right there.

She smiles a little. "Well, you know what you have to do."

I turn back and look at Rory, my former partner, and sigh. I know exactly what I have to do.

DON'T MISS SOUL AND BLADE, THE THIRD AND FINAL
BOOK IN THE BLOOD AND BONE SERIES BY TARA BROWN.

WINTER 2015

ABOUT THE AUTHOR

 Tara Brown writes in a variety of genres. In addition to her futuristic Born Trilogy stories and her nine-part Devil's Roses fantasy series, she has also published a number of popular contemporary and paranormal romances, science fiction novels, thrillers, and romantic comedies. She enjoys writing dark and moody tales involving strong, often female, lead characters who are more prone to vanquishing evil than perpetrating it. She shares her home with her husband, two daughters, two cats, and a wolfhound.

Printed in Great Britain
by Amazon